MW01089496

The Hornet's Nest

Books By Sally Watson
by year of original publication

Highland Rebel 1954
Mistress Malapert 1955
To Build a Land 1957
Poor Felicity 1961
Witch of the Glens 1962
Lark 1962
Other Sandals 1966
The Hornet's Nest 1968
The Mukhtar's Children 1968
Jade 1969
Magic at Wychwood 1970
Linnet 1971

The Hornet's Nest

by Sally Watson

Image Cascade Publishing
www.ImageCascade.com

ORIGINAL COPYRIGHT © 1968
BY SALLY WATSON

All rights reserved. No part of this book may be reproduced in any form, except by a reviewer, without the permission of the publisher.

MANUFACTURED IN THE UNITED STATES
OF AMERICA

A hardcover edition of this book was originally published by New York: Holt, Rinehart and Winston, Inc. It is here reprinted by arrangement with Ms. Sally Watson.

First *Image Cascade Publishing* edition published 2002.

Library of Congress Cataloging in Publication Data
Watson, Sally, 1924-
The hornet's nest.

(Juvenile Girls)
Reprint. Originally published: New York: Holt, Rinehart and Winston, Inc., 1968.

ISBN 978-1-930009-66-0

To my oldest (in time, not years) and very very dear friends–in order of our meeting–James West, Anne Relph, and Geri West.

Acknowledgments

For my long-time fan-friends: Carla Kozak, Darice McMurrey, Donna Trifilo, Joy Canfield, and Michele Blake, who all conspired beautifully to make this reprint possible; and Caryn Cameron, who put me on a website, among other supportive things.

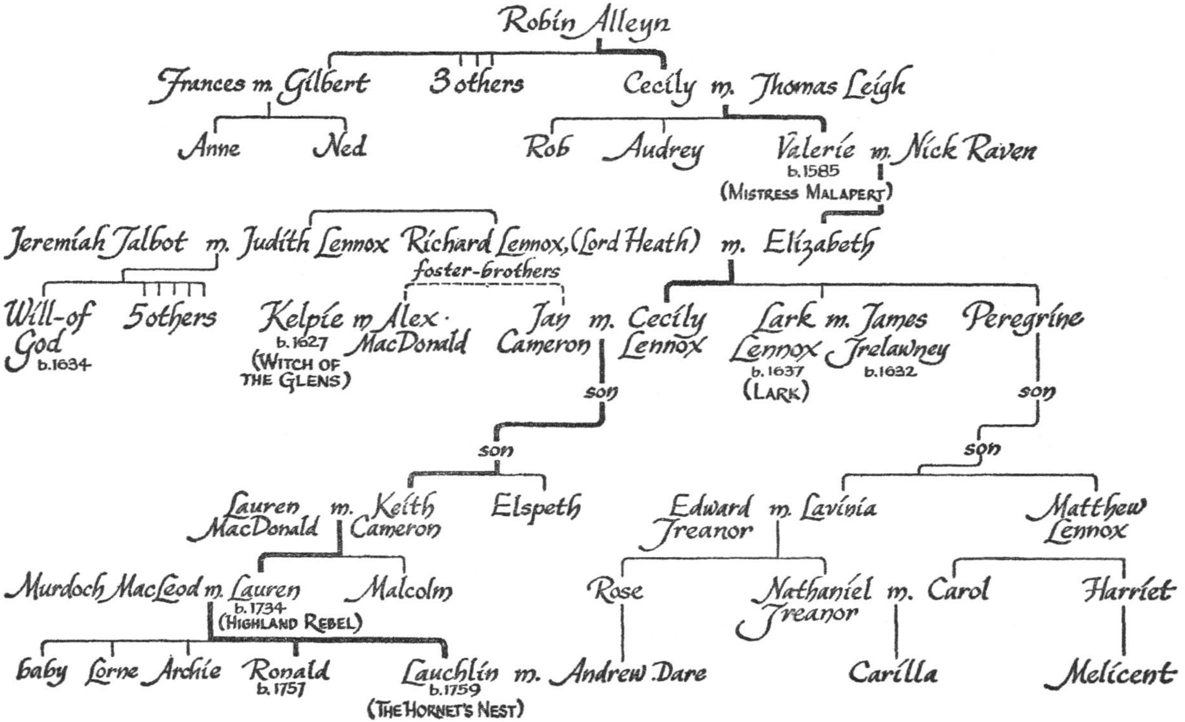

Robin Alleyn
Frances m. Gilbert
3 others
Cecily m. Thomas Leigh
Anne
Ned
Rob
Audrey
Valerie m. Nick Raven
b. 1585
(Mistress Malapert)
Jeremiah Talbot m. Judith Lennox
Richard Lennox, (Lord Heath) m. Elizabeth
foster-brothers
Will-of God
b. 1634
5 others
Kelpie m Alex MacDonald
b. 1627
(Witch of the Glens)
Jan Cameron m. Cecily Lennox
Lark Lennox m. James Trelawney
b. 1637
(Lark)
b. 1632
Peregrine
son
son
son
son
Lauren MacDonald m. Keith Cameron
Elspeth
Edward Treanor m. Lavinia
Matthew Lennox
Murdoch MacLeod m. Lauren
b. 1734
(Highland Rebel)
Malcolm
Rose
Nathaniel Treanor m. Carol
Harriet
baby
Lorne
Archie
Ronald
b. 1757
Lauchlin m. Andrew Dare
b. 1759
(The Hornet's Nest)
Carilla
Melicent

Author's Letter to Readers

Whew! And whoopee! Republication after only thirty-odd years.

It wasn't my fault it took so long, honestly. I did try. So did dunno-how-many friends of my books. All to no avail–until at last, some of said friends took action.

When I moved to Santa Rosa after twenty-five years or so living in England, I made friends with the local librarian, Darice McMurray, who not only was a delightful person, but *she had loved my books when young!* How very gratifying!

I was desolated when she was transferred. But it all turned out for the best when in San Francisco she went to cat-sit for some other librarians named Carla Kozak and Donna Trifilo, and found some of my books in their homes–and told them I was still alive and only ninety minutes away. It turned out that Carla at thirteen had written me a fan letter where I lived in England. (I remember it, too. It was particularly charming.) She and Donna both loved my fictional cats, and had got interested in things like Scotland and history, they say, because of my books. And they even had a whole group chatting on e-mail about whether I was dead and why couldn't my books get published again. So when they learned that I was (a) alive and (b) living 60 miles up the freeway, they all came up from San Francisco to visit me. And it was a wonderful visit. So many tastes in common!

Eventually things came together. Carla knew Joy Canfield of Image Cascade Publishing, and it seems they all talked to one another and also to Michele Blake, who wrote to tell me that she had loved my books too, and why didn't I phone Joy whose number she included? So I did–and as the English would say, Bob's your uncle!

Thanks very much to all of you! I couldn't have done it by myself. I'd been away too long. I didn't know where to start.

Contents

1.	THE SASSENACH SPY	1
2.	LAUCHLIN'S LUCK	12
3.	THE TARTAN SCARF	21
4.	THE HAGGIS	30
5.	REDCOAT'S WARNING	42
6.	REDCOAT'S THREAT	52
7.	LONDON INTERLUDE	64
8.	THE YORKTOWN DOCK	76
9.	CLAWS OUT	92
10.	THE FINE DAY	102
11.	BRAW WEE BATTLE	116
12.	WAITING	126
13.	MISCHIEF	131
14.	THE LEMON WAISTCOAT	142
15.	LORD DUNMORE'S DINNER	154
16.	WITCHES' BREW	164
17.	CARILLA'S CONQUEST	173
18.	THE SKETCH	180
19.	BY THE RIVER	190
20.	SHAKEN OPINIONS	203
21.	CONVERSATION IN A DRAWING ROOM	211
22.	THE WORLD TURNED UPSIDE DOWN	216
23.	ANOTHER HORNET	226
24.	POWDER MAGAZINE	231
25.	THE LAST WORD	240

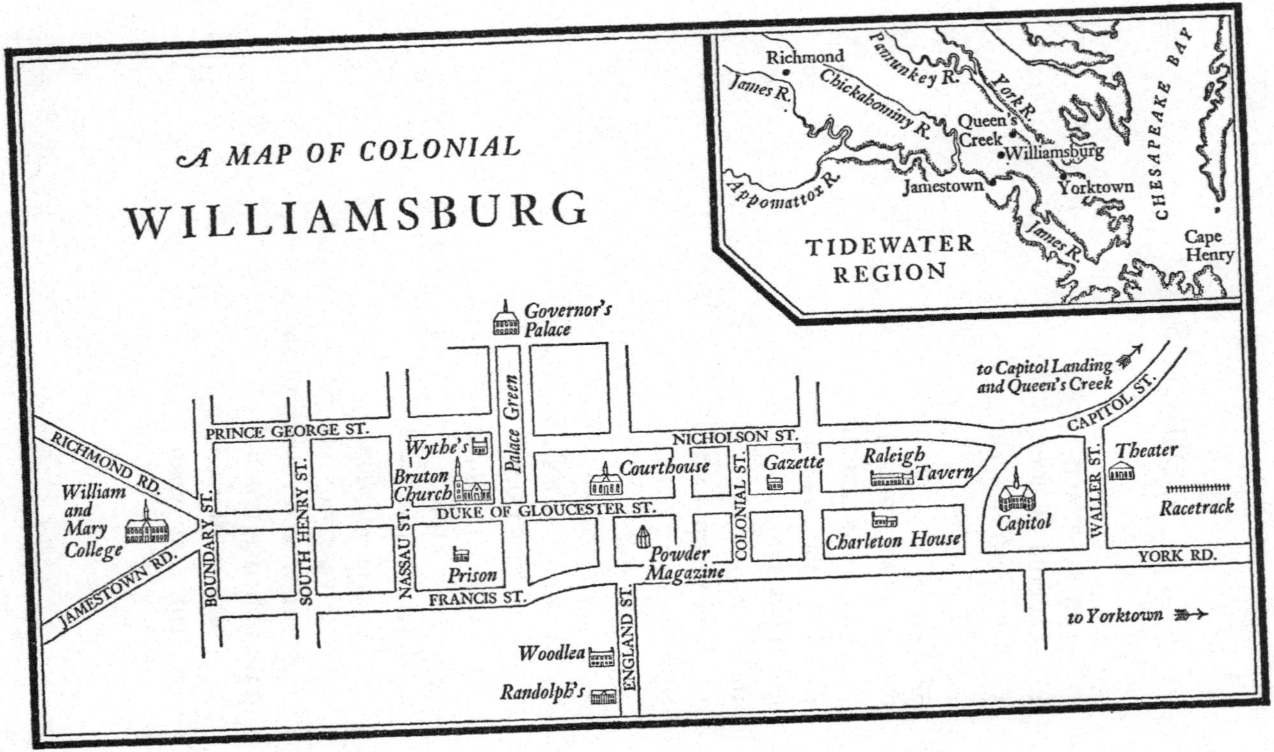

A MAP OF COLONIAL
WILLIAMSBURG
Richmond
James R.
Chickahominy R.
Pamunkey R.
York R.
Queen's Creek
Williamsburg
Jamestown
Yorktown
Appomattox R.
James R.
CHESAPEAKE BAY
Cape Henry
TIDEWATER REGION
Governor's Palace
to Capitol Landing and Queen's Creek
CAPITOL ST.
PRINCE GEORGE ST.
NICHOLSON ST.
RICHMOND RD.
William and Mary College
JAMESTOWN RD.
BOUNDARY ST.
SOUTH HENRY ST.
NASSAU ST.
Wythe's
Bruton Church
Palace Green
Courthouse
COLONIAL ST.
Gazette
Raleigh Tavern
Theater
Racetrack
Capitol
WALLER ST.
DUKE OF GLOUCESTER ST.
Prison
Powder Magazine
Charleton House
YORK RD.
FRANCIS ST.
to Yorktown
Woodlea
Randolph's
ENGLAND ST.

One

THE SASSENACH SPY

It was Lauchlin who saw him first.

She came frisking out of the big house like a kilted and fiery-haired Highland imp, and stood teetering on the step for a moment to savor the day and her own mischief. Late August it was, with heather just purpling the hills, and the Cuillin mountains blue to the south. A silver burn ran down the glen past a scatter of shieling huts to empty itself just out of sight in the deep blue of the sea. A chill salt breeze tugged impudently at the brown cloak which she had bunched over one arm as a careless sop to prudence—and because she was frequently cold.

The upper path curved around the hill and out of the glen. Lauchlin followed it, singing a wild Hebridean sea song in a voice that was sweet and silvery and wildly off-key. Hip-long bronze curls fine as massed cobwebs (looped up and tied in a boy's queue at the back of her neck) bounced as she ran; and she was dressed—in outrageous violation of maidenly propriety and English law—in her older brother's outgrown and prohibited kilt. Should a Redcoat see her, she would of course be in trouble again. But the risk, felt Lauchlin, just added spice to the satisfaction of wearing the doubly forbidden garment.

Anyway, she didn't really expect to see anyone in this

remote glen. Neither, clearly, did Seumas MacCrimmon and her brother Ronald, for from the mass of broom and juniper and heather on the hillside above came the thin, sharp notes of the chanter—the fingering pipe of the bagpipes, with bag and drones removed. Lauchlin grinned. Captain Fletcher, commander of the English garrison on the Isle of Skye, had caught them at practicing it only last week on a surprise visit to Kildornie. But he had let them off with only a terrible scolding, and would hardly be paying another call so soon, and Lauchlin felt altogether safe.

Therefore it was a very great shock to her to skip around a bend in the path and run almost headlong into a perfect stranger in a tricorne hat, who must be an Englishman—and therefore an enemy!

Lauchlin's dark eyes widened with dismay and defiance as the stranger stood there blinking his surprise. How like her own perverse brand of luck! Really, it was *much* too soon to be in a scrape again! She stuck out a pointed chin at the intruder, and belatedly wrapped the brown cloak over that bright incriminating kilt.

"Sassenach spy!" she hissed in English, all her sibilants sounding like enraged snakes. "Very well, then, go ahead and report me! But I will go on wearing the tartan, if I must weave it myself!" And her fierce chin jutted out at him recklessly.

To her surprise, the Sassenach spy looked intrigued and delighted. He was a funny, rosy-faced old man with a shock of white hair that escaped from its queue to stand straight up over his forehead, while his bushy eyebrows bounced up and down energetically.

"Good!" he said. "That's the spirit! Stand up to 'em,

m'boy, and don't be pushed around by any Sa—Sassenachs, or anyone else. . . . What *is* a Sassenach, by the way?"

Lauchlin stared, completely at a loss for the moment. She cocked her flaming head to one side, hesitated between suspicion and approval, then began to develop a cautious dimple.

"Sassenach," she informed him severely, "is the Gaelic word for Saxon. Englishman. Are you not one? You are no Highlander, nor even a Scot." For his voice had an accent she had never heard before, soft and drawling, with odd vowel sounds.

"Well, now, that's a mighty good question," said the old man chattily. "I've English blood in my veins," he conceded, "but I was born and raised across the sea in a colony called Virginia, and we like to call ourselves Virginians. Especially lately, with English taxes a mite unpopular over there. Does that make me a Sassenach or not? And why are *you* so fired-up against them, m'boy? What's this about reporting you? To whom and for what?"

Lauchlin simply stared at him with her mouth open. "*Oichan!* Don't you *know*?"

He shook his head cheerfully. "Reckon I'm mighty ignorant," he confessed without shame. "Tell me." And he perched his fine broadcloth breeches on a convenient boulder and waited as if it were the most ordinary situation in the world.

Lauchlin, who had a strong sense of the ridiculous, smothered a giggle and tried to look severe. She succeeded in looking confused.

"But—who are you?" She squinted at him as if to see an

answer that way. "And whatever are you doing here at all? Are you lost, then?"

"Well, now, I'm not right sure," mused the old gentleman, and then, as Lauchlin began to show growing symptoms of exasperation, he decided he had done enough teasing. "I'm looking for a Murdoch MacLeod of Kildornie," he said, and studied Lauchlin's face for an instant. "Reckon you must be his son," he guessed shrewdly.

It was Lauchlin's turn to tease. "Och no," she said quite gravely. "Not at all."

He stood up, perplexed. "Isn't this Kildornie?"

"Oh, aye." Lauchlin's eyes brimmed with mischief. "And my father is also Kildornie." She spoke with unconcious pride. The conquering English might try to ban titles, might call her father merely Mr. MacLeod—but to any Highlander he would always bear the proud name of his home and clan branch: Kildornie.

The old man paused, even more puzzled, while the distant chanter ended a bit of reel tune and fell silent. "But you said—"

"But I'm not his son, at all," Lauchlin continued demurely. " 'Tis his daughter I am. Who are you?"

The Sassenach began to chuckle. "Fair enough!" he wheezed. "Caught me out, you did! So you're a girl, eh? Splendid! We need more girls with spunk. Reckon we're quits now, hmm? Well, I'm a distant cousin of yours, Daughter of Kildornie. A third cousin twice removed, to be exact. One of my hobbies is tracing my family tree and visiting the branches that stayed in Britain. And I've always been intrigued by my great-grand-aunt Cecily, who married a wild Highlander. Just visited your Uncle Malcolm Cameron over on the mainland in Glenfern, and he sent me on here. Name's Matthew Lennox, by the way. Cousin Matthew to you."

Lauchlin suddenly discovered that it's quite impossible to curtsy in a kilt. Unabashed, she stuck out a tanned and not-too-clean hand, which Cousin Matthew shook vigorously. "Now tell me what I'm supposed to report you for, and after that, you can take me to meet your folks."

Laughlin's face darkened. One did get used to the ugliness of being under the rule of a harsh conqueror—especially if one had never experienced anything else—but only in the way one got used to a sore blistered heel when the shoe continued to rub. She set her teeth. "For wearing a kilt, just," she said between them.

He whistled soundlessly, stared at her. "Is that true? The English punish you for what you wear, after all these years? Why, the rising was way back in 1745!"

"And this is 1773! And they punish us even for wearing the kilt or the tartan, or for playing our music or dancing our dances, or bearing a weapon, be it even a wee *sgian dhu*." Scarlet flags of hatred began to fly in the creamy tan of her cheeks. "And that will be the least of it, and they occupying Scotland with their troops and spies, and charging us dear rent and fines for our own land, and prison or the noose or transportation for any offense. . . . 'Tis wicked devils they are, all of them!"

His eyebrows lifted skeptically. He thought she was exaggerating, and no wonder, since here she was wearing the forbidden garment just as if there were no harsh penalties attached. He didn't understand the seething rebellion that had to come out—at least with Lauchlin and Ronald it did—heedless of consequences.

"Well, well!" he said tolerantly. "And some of the folks

back home think *they* have problems with England! Still and all, most of the soldiers stationed here are probably nice enough fellows, you know, just following orders. The bunch that brought me here just now were right friendly and helpful; even lent me a horse. You—"

He broke off as Lauchlin turned on him, her eyes round with alarm and accusation. "You brought Redcoats *here*? Sassenach spy!" She whirled around to stare tensely up the path, where it wound upwards along the flank of the hill and out of sight. Was there movement there, through the birches and juniper at the turn?

Another movement from the other direction caused her to whirl back, and stare with sick dismay at the two kilted figures ambling out of the broom from the other direction. The tartans were on their bodies, the black oboe-like chanters in their hands, the black dagger called a *sgian dhu* tucked in Ronald's hose top. They stared with deep curiosity at this strange Sassenach talking to Lauchlin, and were clearly on their way to investigate.

"*Dia!*" whispered Lauchlin. And then, as the movement up the path quite definitely showed flashes of scarlet, she hurled herself up the side of the hill to where the boys stood some ten feet above. "Down into the heather!" she hissed, and could only pray that this strange and untried cousin wouldn't betray them.

"Bless my buttons!" exclaimed the strange cousin, staring at the empty spot where three young people had stood an instant before. The speed with which they had dived into the brush caused him to think again about the seriousness of the situation. And, having thought, he turned a bland face to the half dozen Redcoats who rode down the path.

Lauchlin, under some very thick broom and with her leg in a painfully prickly patch of gorse, listened with pounding heart, unable to see a thing. Ronald was glaring at her from beneath his shock of black hair, as if she were responsible for the whole thing, which she wasn't. Not this time, anyway. She made a face at him, and listened again, to the encouragingly innocent note in Cousin Matthew's voice.

"Well, bless my soul; imagine seeing you again so soon. Isn't it a splendid view from here?"

"Anything the matter?" Lauchlin recognized the hoarse London voice of Sergeant Tucker, whom she had met more than once—usually in disagreeable circumstances. She could easily visualize his burly figure and ruddy face, probably looking somewhat suspicious just at the moment. "Thought we 'eard pipes playin' up 'ere," he added invitingly.

"Pipes? Dear me, did you? I would have thought bagpipes were a thing you heard or didn't hear, and no uncertainty about it. And in any case, I thought they were no longer played around here?"

No one knew what Sergeant Tucker might have said to that. For Lauchlin got a sudden and unbearable cramp in her leg, and shifted position. She did it, she later swore, as slowly and cautiously as would never have cracked an egg. But somehow a large stone dislodged itself completely (it must have been hanging by a thread, just waiting for this moment, she complained afterwards), and crashed downward through the heather with a totally unnecessary amount of noise and fuss.

The party on the path below stopped talking and looked up.

" 'Oo's up there?" demanded Sergeant Tucker in the tone of one who already knew. "Come on out, now, 'ooever you are."

Many crises of this nature had taught Lauchlin quick wits. She cast one despairing glance at the boys. Ronald was, as she had feared, preparing to give himself up in order to save her—and possibly also partly because he always enjoyed a brush with the English whatever the consequences. This was all very fine, and even gallant—except that Ronald was also wearing his kilt. And this was considered a much worse crime in a lad than in a mere lass, who had no right to be wearing man's garments at all to begin with. Moreover, Sergeant Tucker was invariably harder on Ronald than on Lauchlin, however hard he tried to be impartial. No, it would be *very* much worse, and for Father, too, if Ronald showed himself.

She need not have worried. Seumas saw the situation as quickly as Lauchlin did, and came to the same conclusions. Instantly he rolled his stocky self neatly across Ronald's dark head and shoulders, pinning him down with his face buried in grass and heather and bog-cotton. At the same moment, Lauchlin pulled her long brown cloak around her shoulders, thanking her usually irresponsible guardian angel that she had happened to bring it because of that chill wind off the sea, and stood up with an air of injured innocence.

" 'Tis only myself, just," she called down, looking martyred. "What for are you so fierce? Is there a new law against being on my father's land?"

The usual look of suspicion came over the massive face. He stared with strong suspicion at those concealing folds of cloak. Having a secret soft spot for that particular bane of his life, he decided not to press too closely into it—and in any case, she had once deliberately fooled him that way. "Wot are you doing up there 'iding?" he demanded.

Lauchlin decided it was best to distract his attention from that particular bit of underbrush, which was heaving slightly. She moved down the slope and to one side, careful to keep her cloak well wrapped around her, and came to a halt just out of reach. "You frighted me," she murmured with what she hoped was sad dignity. "Every time I see you, you roar at me and bully me."

"Why, bless my buttons!" Cousin Matthew sounded deeply shocked. "A big man like you? Shame on you!"

Sergeant Tucker looked at him. He considered enlightening him about several things. He abandoned the idea. The old man was a Colonial, and it was said they were all rebels under the skin. Besides— He looked at Lauchlin, whose mouth was trembling in a way that might have been pathetic except that the glint in her eyes was altogether defiant and reckless.

"You ain't no actress, missy, and that's a fact," he commented sourly.

Lauchlin frowned, offended. But before she could decide how to answer this charge, the sergeant glanced up the hill again and smiled grimly. "Wot's that up there?" he demanded.

Quaking inwardly, Lauchlin followed his gaze and drew in her breath with sharp dismay. A bright yellow corner of tartan showed clearly from the boys' hiding place, utterly damning evidence.

Surrender wasn't a word in Lauchlin's vocabulary. She blinked, drew a deep breath, and turned artless eyes back to the ruddy face of her inquisitor. "Gorse," she said sweetly. "Or perhaps broom. Our hills are covered with gorse and broom, and they are having yellow blossoms."

"At *this* time of year?" inquired Sergeant Tucker with heavy sarcasm.

Lauchlin nodded stubbornly.

"And with black stripes?" The sarcasm grew even heavier.

"Oh, aye," returned Lauchlin, seeing nothing to lose. "We grow it that way on purpose."

And as they looked at it, the black-striped gorse twitched slightly, and gently withdrew itself from sight.

"Rabbits," said Lauchlin firmly into the silence. "Or squirrels, perhaps."

Her chin was well up and out. So was the sergeant's. Their eyes held, challengingly. And then Sergeant Tucker sighed. He had grown up in a corner of London where a child must be tough to survive. He remembered how it felt to stand at bay, game and stubborn, in the face of half a dozen enemies, and he felt a kinship with any small creature who faced disaster with unyielding courage . . . not that he knew this. He never let his mind suspect what his heart was doing. But somehow he could usually find a reason to be lenient with Lauchlin.

"Look 'ere, missy," he growled, and there was a ring of sharp warning in his voice. "I been awful easy on you, so I 'ave; and so 'as Captain Fletcher, 'oo's a kind and soft-'earted man." He included Cousin Matthew in his glance, and raised his voice a trifle. "This 'ere's a bit of good advice, like, and it goes for your brother, too, missy, just in case 'e should 'ear me. Captain Fletcher, 'e's leaving, end of November, and the new Commander, 'e's nobody to muck about with. 'E 'as no patience with lawbreakers,

Captain Green 'asn't. You'll make a pile of trouble for yourselves if you cross with *'im,* and don't ever say I didn't warn you."

He turned his horse around on the path, and nodded brusquely to the soldiers who had been silently watching and listening. "All right, men, we didn't see nothing—this time. Next time our eyes is likely to be a good bit better. And next time it's likely to be worse than a fine, too," he added.

And they rode back up the pass, leaving Lauchlin torn between relief and anger, laughter and apprehension.

There was dead silence from under the heather. Seumas clearly was taking no chances in letting Ronald up before the Redcoats were well and truly gone. Lauchlin hoped that he wasn't altogether smothered. . . . But she turned eagerly to Cousin Matthew, who was staring after the Sassenach, bemused by the situation in which he suddenly found himself.

"All for wearing a kilt!" he murmured incredulously. "Outrageous! Tyranny!" Then his face broke suddenly into wrinkles of laughter and he turned to point a lean forefinger at Lauchlin.

"Rabbits!" he chortled. "Striped gorse! Squirrels!"

The way he pronounced that last word sounded to Lauchlin like "squa'als." She tilted her red head to one side and laughed back at him. "Squalls?" she mimicked. "Would you be meaning squirrels?"

To Cousin Matthew it sounded like "squiddels." He said so. They were on the brink of a most enjoyable argument when they became aware of the two lads, out of hiding, standing and staring at them with greatly mixed emotions.

"I'm not wishing to sound inquisitive," remarked Ronald with perfectly heroic restraint. "But could one of you please"—his voice grew just slightly plaintive—"*please* introduce us?"

Two

LAUCHLIN'S LUCK

"I would have thought," said Ronald severely through the half open door into Lauchlin's bedchamber, "that when any stranger at *all* arrives suddenly—and *especially* a Sassenach on foot who clearly has *not* walked from Portree—that even a daft loon would think at once to keep a canny eye out for Redcoats. . . . Do hurry, Lauchlin!"

Lauchlin frowned as she straightened the folds of her full apricot skirts and flowered panniers, and ran a hasty brush down her long hair. Mother had, of course, ordered them all to make themselves presentable and come greet their new cousin properly in the drawing room.

"I was having just a *few* other things to think about!" she protested defensively. And then, because she was not one to stay on the defensive for long, she opened the door wider and threw a challenging look at her older brother's lean face. "And two of them," she pointed out, "were a pair of daft loons piping on the hills loud enough to be heard clear in the next glen."

Honors being even, they grinned at each other across

the carrot-red head of their small brother Archie, who as usual was stolidly ignoring their bantering, there being more important things to think of. "They will be having scones and shortbread in the drawing room," he reminded them. "Come away down."

Their parents gave them a judicial glance as they entered the wood paneled drawing room looking quite different people from the kilted rogues who had escorted Cousin Matthew in like a trophy-of-war less than an hour before. The lads wore their hair neatly queued, and their velvet jackets with neatly mended lace at wrist and throat. Lauchlin's damask dress, although an old one of her mother's made over, produced an unexpected glint of green in her dark eyes, and set off the bronze of her hair. The general effect caused her new cousin to stand up and bow gallantly over her hand.

"Bless my boots!" he said. "The fierce boy has become a charming young lady!" He shook hands with the boys and smiled at their mother. "I see where Lauchlin gets her hair, and Ronald his eyes and chin. Reckon you're very proud of them, aren't you?" He smiled at Archie, at five-year-old Lorne in her father's lap, at the baby kicking in his cradle. "May I be conceited enough to say they all do credit to their English blood as well as the Highland?" Cousin Matthew asked.

Lauchlin stuck out a dubious lip while she considered this most doubtful compliment, and allowed him to seat her beside him on the sofa, where she managed to look like a dignified young lady of fourteen for at least ten seconds. Ronald perched on the arm of his mother's chair, Archie plopped down on a hassock and stared unrelentingly at his new kinsman, Lorne stuck a shy finger in her mouth; and then Lauchlin reverted to normal.

"What English blood? Was it Mother's great-great grandmother, who was a Sassenach? Oh, yes, surely!" she remembered suddenly. "Lennox! But why ever did you decide to come visiting, and what is it like in Virginia? Are there lions and tigers?"

"Lauchlin!" Kildornie's frown was slight but definite. "Mind your manners! A great lass like you, and still behaving like a bairn! I am ashamed of you!"

She subsided, chastened but not really repentant. She had a running battle with her parents over matters like this, and her deplorable impulsive and irresponsible tendencies, and wearing that forbidden kilt. So far, scoldings and punishment failed to have any permanent effect at all—mostly because her mother and father were in their secret hearts on her side, and Lauchlin knew it. It gave her a tremendous advantage, and made their scoldings a bit half-hearted, however much they tried to be stern. This time, though, she had a feeling things would go hard. There had been no hiding those outlawed kilts, nor the nearly disastrous results. And there was a certain look in Mother's gray eyes. . . . Lauchlin sighed and looked at Cousin Matthew pleadingly. He was clearly as naughty and irresponsible as she and Ronald, and certain to be on their side.

He took the hint at once. "Don't want her too mannerly," he said with decision. "Like her the way she is. Liked her the minute she bearded me with her chin up and her eyes flashing. Good spirit there."

"We cannot afford overmuch of that kind of spirit in the Highlands these days." Father's voice had that brittle calm of tautly reined control, and Mother's eyes looked like two explosions not allowed to explode. The despairing anger that had stalked the Highlands for nearly thirty years entered the room and settled there. Wee Lorne felt it as a great black unseen beastie—a *uruisg*, perhaps—and whimpered against her father's neck.

"By George!" Cousin Matthew remembered that George could not be a very popular name in these parts, and hastily changed it. "Bless my soul! Never dreamed things were still this bad, after so long! You must have given old George II a smart fright back in '45. Invaded England clear down as far as Derby, didn't you? And then turned back and were defeated at Culloden?" He eyed his host shrewdly. "I take it you were supporters of your Stewart prince?"

He had touched the right chord. Lauchlin watched her parents lose their leashed look and become vivid with pride and loyalty. "We helped him escape, our Bonnie Prince Charlie!" said Mother softly. "He was a braw prince, Cousin Matthew. It may be true, as they say, that our Stewart kings of England were none so much to brag on—but the worst of them was surely better than the tyrannical German brutes whom England chose instead!"

Mother was sparkling, her face flushed, and the red-gold hair quite as bright as Lauchlin's. Her two eldest offspring glanced at each other hopefully. Once Mother's own feelings were roused, it was doubly hard for her to punish them for acting as she felt.

"We Highlanders would never accept the Hanoverian kings," Ronald put in, his chin squaring off in exactly the same way his mother's did, and his jug-handle ears exactly like his father's. "Would we, Father?"

Kildornie fell briefly into the trap. "Nay. My father's generation was out in 1715, fighting against George I, and thirty years later we ourselves went out against George II. Now—"

"Now 'tis another thirty years almost up, and another George on the throne, and another generation near ready to fight," put in Lauchlin irrepressibly.

Ronald poked her furiously to shut her up, but the damage was done. Her words fell on her parents like an icy waterfall, and they turned on her faces that were no longer lost in proud memory but filled with the bitterness of today.

"It is not!" rasped her father in a voice that caused Lorne to bury her ears in his wine velvet waistcoat. "It is never the time, never again. We are broken at last, the Highlands as a nation. Little *amadain,* where are your eyes and your brain? Look around you! There is an army of occupation settled on us, who keep us poor and helpless —those few of us who are left in the Highlands after the slaughter of Culloden and the deportation and hanging that followed. How rise when they forbid us the smallest fowling weapon or knife, and fine or imprison or sell as bond slaves or hang us for the slightest violation of their outrageous laws? We walk with our necks forever in a noose—and you and Ronald will be forever pulling at it until one day you will go too far!"

He had never spoken to them with such fierce intensity, and Lauchlin sat quite still, awed. Sharp silence fell, and the black beast of despair stirred and settled down again. Kildornie turned to Cousin Matthew, his face relaxing into a warm smile. "Forgive me, kinsman. But as you see, 'tis a serious situation, and dangerous to all of us to let them go on this way."

Cousin Matthew cocked his head to one side and waggled those bushy white eyebrows. "Well well!" He sounded oddly pleased, as well as distressed. "Well!" He looked at the chastened Lauchlin and Ronald. "Tut tut! Sedition, subversion, revolutionism, lawbreaking! Tell you what. You come on over to Virginia, all of you, and we'll have the next rebellion from there, hmm? Third time's the charm, y'know." He looked delighted with his notion.

Lauchlin and Ronald sat perfectly still with astonishment. Their parents looked at each other and at Cousin Matthew sadly.

"And our people?" asked Kildornie gently. "Small as my clan branch is, I am its chief and father, responsible to all my clansmen; standing as well as I may between them and the English; helping, advising, paying fines they cannot pay. Why, Cousin, I could as well desert my own wife and bairns."

"Moreover," added his wife, "we could not be happy away from the Highlands, however much a hell the English may try to make of it. It is our bones and breath and heart's blood, and our six years exile were a misery of homesickness."

Her eyes turned with love to the open casement, through which a shining white sea bird could be seen floating across the quiet purpled slopes, dotted with saffron-brown shagginess of Highland cattle and the low gray roof of a shieling hut here and there. A deep and abiding quiet lay over the heather, and the cry of whaup and the faint hush of waves upon the shore were part of the quiet. And over it all arched a pale blue sky filled with the austere light of the north.

Lauchlin sighed, partly because she loved it so much and partly because in an odd way she loved it not quite as

Mother and Father and Ronald did. If only the summers were longer, perhaps . . . if only it were warmer! On all but the hottest days the wind off the Minch was brisk and nippy, and Lauchlin usually carried a cloak and longed for a warmth that would penetrate her very bones.

Archie broke the spell by helping himself to more shortbread while everyone's attention was out the window. His mother rapped his fingers. Cousin Matthew sighed.

"Well, well, it's too bad. You're folks after my own heart, and I hate to see you oppressed here, when you could be over yonder in the Colonies helping oppose just that sort of tyranny. *We'll* never let things get to this state, I declare!"

"It helps to have an ocean between you and England," Kildornie pointed out dryly. " 'Tis a rebel you are indeed, Cousin, and best be very canny and careful indeed whilst you are here. Are all Colonials like you?"

"Well, I reckon not," he confessed, his puckish face crinkling with mischief. "Hardly any, in fact, save for a few fine fellows like Sam Adams up north, and young Patrick Henry right there in Virginia. Fact is, I'm downright eccentric. If you don't believe it, ask anyone in Williamsburg, especially my sister Lavinia." He chuckled. "Old Socrates is the man I admire most in history, and I aim to be a gadfly like him. Shake folks up and make 'em think. *I* figure I'm a public benefactor, but there are those who can't quite see it that way." He winked at Lauchlin. "Sure would like to see you folks in Williamsburg. You'd stir them up much more than any letters I can write."

"Be careful of any letters you write from here!" warned Kildornie urgently. "The laws against seditious writing are unbelievably severe, and they'll open and read anything they please. In truth, Cousin, you had far better wait until you're away home again before putting anything on paper."

"Aye, and even there, don't forget what happened to Socrates!" Mother's face, Lauchlin noticed with interest, was a battleground between amusement and seriousness. "Remember that one of the charges against him was corrupting the young, so take heed, Cousin Matthew!"

He looked startled. "Me? I'm *good* for the young! Stir 'em up, expose them to all sorts of ideas. I *couldn't* corrupt them, Cousin Lauren!"

"You could that," she contradicted him sternly. "Ours already have far too many ideas as it is, and the last thing on earth they are needing is stirring up! Och, stirring up will never be enough for Ronald, who would much liefer overthrow everything that doesn't suit him. And as for Lauchlin—" She shook her head. Lauchlin wriggled, not sure whether to be crushed or cocky, and looked for some sign of a twinkle on Father's face.

"What about Lauchlin?" demanded Cousin Matthew expectantly.

The twinkle appeared, was sternly subdued, popped up again. Kildornie and his wife exchanged rueful glances over Archie's head. Ronald grinned.

"She's hopeless," he explained. " 'Tis not the Evil Eye she has, but the Muddled Eye. Let her but open her mouth, and she cannot help saying the wrong thing—"

"Aye," chimed in Lauchlin, feeling that she may as well make a joke of it, "and bad luck fair haunts me. Let me drop a shoe and Archie will fall over it and break his arm, and let me so much as touch the kilt—" She saw her parents' stern eyes on her, and Ronald's reproachful ones, and prudently closed her teeth on the rest of that sentence. Punishment loomed ahead in any case; no need to remind Mother and Father....

"If she opens a window on a calm summer day," Kildornie contributed, as if the word "kilt" had never been invented, "a sudden windstorm will surely rise from the sea and wreck the room altogether."

"When she gave Mother a nosegay of flowers," Lorne remembered, "a bee flew out and stung her nose."

"And," concluded Mother wryly, "her most flattering sketches of people inevitably turn out to be caricatures of the most insulting variety, which she generously bestows upon the victims under the impression that they will be delighted, leaving us to explain that she *means* well. . . . I tell you what, Cousin Matthew, if you are wanting to see the *Each Uisghe*, the water monster who lives in Loch Ness over on the mainland, just you take Lauchlin along and let her be tossing a stone anywhere at all near the loch—and you can be sure 'twill be landing on the head of the poor beastie."

Cousin Matthew chuckled delightedly. "I see," he said. "Then I reckon if she hadn't been out in her kilt today, the sergeant and his men would never have thought to pop over the hill for a visit?"

They all nodded. "Very likely," they agreed. " 'Tis Lauchlin's luck."

Lauchlin grinned, quite unabashed, even smug. Her mother instantly applied a quelling frown, for the sake of her character as well as safety.

"At least two-thirds of Lauchlin's luck is due to her own feckless and madcap ways," she pointed out unanswerably. "And Ronald is as bad in his own way, surely. You really must *not* be encouraging them whilst you are here, Cousin Matthew, or I cannot tell what might happen."

"Who me?" He looked scandalously innocent and altogether wicked. "Wouldn't think of such a thing. I'll just keep them out of trouble now and again, as I did today, hmm?"

His hosts looked at each other with amusement and despair.

Three

THE TARTAN SCARF

Days went by, bright crisp days with a hint of autumn in the song of the sea, and a pale blue haze in the long twilight. Cousin Matthew made himself at home, visited the clansmen of Kildornie, and didn't do anything at all dangerous or revolutionary—unless one could count his conversation, which simply abounded in quotations from Socrates and radicals like John Locke and Rousseau, about the rights of man. Which was, brooded Ronald, rather hitting below the belt, considering the current situation....

"Bless my heart," said the old man on a pearly morning of sea mist as Lauchlin sat down at the breakfast table only ten minutes after everyone else. "What a picture you are, honey!"

The literal-minded Archie raised a carroty head from

his huge bowl of oatmeal. "What are you going to do today, Cousin Matthew?"

He beamed upon them all. "Thought I might ride over to Portree, to see if I've any mail there, and perhaps pick up a journal."

His hosts looked worried. Who knew what trouble he might get into, with the English garrison there? " 'Tis a long way," suggested Kildornie tactfully, "even with ponies. Could not Fergus go for you?"

"Nope." The snowy head shook with cheerful obstinacy. "Want to go myself. Look around a bit. May I take Ronald and Lauchlin with me?"

"Oh, please!" Two pairs of eyes stared pleadingly at their parents, who looked faintly apprehensive, and then remembered that for all his talk, Cousin Matthew had been a model of discreet behavior. "Let Fergus attend you, then, and take enough food for at least a small army," they agreed. And an hour later the four of them were riding up the winding path over the hill.

Cousin Matthew wore, in addition to a rich blue greatcoat and tricorne, an expression of great saintliness, which lasted just until they were over the hill. Then he pulled up his pony.

"Just a minute," he murmured. "Forgot to put on my favorite scarf." And from somewhere under his cloak he produced a voluminous scarf of blazing red tartan!

The three of them regarded it and him with deep emotion. "*Mis-an-dhui!*" exclaimed Ronald at last, awed. " 'Tis the Royal Stewart, too!"

"Yup. Figured it was. Fellow named Stewart's a weaver back home, and he made it for me. Pretty, isn't it?" He smiled with shattering innocence.

"Are you really going to wear it to Portree?" Lauchlin's eyes blazed with excitement and admiration. Cousin Matthew was indeed a kinsman after her own heart! He must, she decided, have Highland blood in him.

"Why not?" he demanded reasonably. "It's mine, isn't it? Fact is, I'm mighty interested in finding out more about these laws against tartans and such. Do they apply to visitors from Virginia, you reckon?"

Fergus made disapproving noises in Gaelic indicating that they were all too likely to find out, and most unpleasantly, too. It did no good, of course. Ronald just grinned rather wolfishly, Lauchlin told him not to be such an old grandmother, and Matthew Lennox wrapped the scarf around his neck with a flourish. And on they rode, a mixture of defiance, apprehension, and mischief.

Their path ran across tawny moors swelling to great breasts of hills, while the Cuillins gleamed hyacinth in the distance. Birches swayed against the sky, and dark patches of pine forest stood austere and still—undoubtedly haunted by fairy folk. As they neared Portree at last—after a wee nibble of oatcakes and cheese and buttered scones—Cousin Matthew reined in his pony, looking thoughtful.

"Tell you what," he suggested. "Suppose I just make right sure of getting my mail and journals taken care of before I test this law?"

"You mean you're going to take your scarf off?" Lauchlin's voice had the disillusion of one who sees a great hero fingering a white flag reflectively. Her cousin at once abandoned any lurking thought of prudence. "Not a bit of it, m'dear! But I was fixing to ask Ronald here if he would mind just nipping around on an errand or two for me. I've a letter or two I'd like put on that ship if she's for London." He cast a shrewd eye on the small merchant ship whose spars rose above the roofs of Portree, and the others nodded. It was about the right size to be bound for England, rather than across an ocean.

But Lauchlin looked reproachful, and Ronald stern. "England?" they demanded, pained.

"Now don't get your tails in knots, young'uns," he teased, so drolly that they were reassured at once. "I merely plan to visit some London cousins when I leave here. But in the meantime, I do want those letters safely on board before I come to grips with the Redcoats, and see if you can pick up any journals, from London or anywhere at all. Take Fergus with you, and Lauchlin and I will just rest here until you get back." He grinned. "Be glad to dismount for a bit, and sit my old bones on some nice soft ground. Tell you what, Lauchlin, I'll tell you all about my little great-niece Carilla."

Ronald and Fergus vanished into town, but Cousin Matthew was destined not to tell Lauchlin about his little great-niece that day. For he had got as far as noting that she was an adorable child, and Lauchlin's fifth cousin, when he was interrupted. The interruption was in the form of a pair of simply furious soldiers, who glared at the tartan scarf incredulously and whipped its wearer off to the garrison before he could so much as explain the Rights of Man.

Lauchlin scurried along at his side, very much in two frames of mind. On one hand, she rather doubted that Cousin Matthew fully understood the temperature of the hot water he was jumping into with such enthusiasm. On the other hand, Captain Fletcher really wasn't at all a bad sort for a Sassenach. . . . Moreover, any lingering uneasiness was dispelled by a most extraordinary sense of exhilaration that seemed to come at least partly from Cousin Matthew.

She stole a look at him. He was clearly having the time of his life. His blue eyes sparkled, his hair stood up like a snow-white halo around the face of a rosy and elderly pixie. The joy of coming battle was on him, and it infected Lauchlin, who gave a sudden skip of quite irresponsible delight. What fun to be in a scrape with Cousin Matthew! Much nicer than with Seumas, who had too much conscience, or even Ronald, who never enjoyed scrapes because he became angry at once. Just as well, really, that he was missing this one, she decided as the Redcoats marched the culprits into the Commander's office.

The thick-set, gray-wigged figure of Captain Fletcher sat there, and beside it a tall, sour-faced, black-peruked man who was undoubtedly the new Captain Green. Lauchlin eyed him with a strong sense that they were not destined to become fast friends. He, in turn, was eyeing the offensive scarf balefully, while Captain Fletcher regarded it with disbelief.

"Dear heaven!" he murmured, deeply moved by the very magnitude of the impudence—and also at the insouciance of the wearer, who was now looking about him with great affability.

"Good afternoon, gentlemen," he prattled. "Nice office you have here, though it could do with a woman's touch. You reckon they're fixing to offer us tea, Lauchlin?"

Lauchlin, quite intoxicated by his spirit, considered the matter most carefully. "Och, I don't think it," she decided with regret. "There's no tea things laid out."

"Too bad." He seemed disappointed but not really put out. "Matter of fact, I did think the invitation just a mite abrupt, but then it might be I'm just not used to their ways, hmm?" He looked benign, quite willing to make allowances. Lauchlin made a very small gurgling sound.

Captain Fletcher reached a tentative conclusion. "The old fellow's certainly a foreigner; quite probably dotty as well," he muttered with a perceptible air of relief, and bent a judicial eye upon the prisoner. "This is not a social call, sir. Don't you realize you've been arrested?"

"Bless my buttons!" Cousin Matthew looked profoundly interested. "You don't say! Think you might tell me what for? It can't be murder, because I can't recollect having murdered anyone just lately—" He paused, looked doubtful. "Have I, Lauchlin?" he asked anxiously.

"Not today," she assured him. "I know, because I've been with you all day, and I'm *quite* certain I should have noticed if you had. Likely you've done some other wicked thing." She frowned slightly, considered the possibilities, selected one. "Like breathing," she suggested blandly.

Captain Green regarded her with a profound dislike, which was destined to increase rapidly. Captain Fletcher covered his mouth with his hand, and beetled his eyebrows so that they looked like two gray caterpillars. Lauchlin longed to draw both of them, especially Captain Green, with his down-slanting eyes, and thin nose, and harsh lines beside an almost lipless mouth.

Cousin Matthew had produced a gold and enameled snuffbox from one of his huge coat pockets, and now offered it with the guileless smile of a clear conscience. "Reckon it's all a joke," he chuckled.

"It's not at all a joke!" Captain Fletcher waved away the snuffbox. "Sir, that scarf of yours is a blatant violation against the Act of Proscription, which makes all forms of Highland dress or tartan illegal on pain of extremely heavy penalties. Now, if you simply didn't know—"

Captain Green interrupted, his beaky face jutting forward like a bird of prey. "This insolent girl is a native, I take it?" He made "native" sound like "savage" or perhaps "cannibal." "And they were together? Then either he did know, or she's guilty of failing to inform him."

Even Captain Fletcher looked taken aback by this formidable logic. Lauchlin bit her lip as reality threatened to break through. The situation could easily become far from a joke, especially since Captain Green clearly felt in the mood for a good hanging or two. . . . Then Cousin Matthew twinkled at her gaily, and the reckless spirit instantly seized her again.

He didn't seem at all worried. He looked surprised, faintly amused. "Matter of fact," he confessed with a disarming smile, "she did tell me. But I reckoned she must be joking. I told her we English are decent, fair-minded folk at heart, however unlikely it seems at times. I said we'd always valued fair play and freedom above all else, and even if some foreign king didn't know any better than to pass oppressive laws, no Englishman would consent to enforce 'em." Both officers were looking uncomfortable. "I told her—" He turned his head to look right at Lauchlin, carefully chose his words to present her with a perfectly irresistible cue. "I told her that men who'd enforce that sort of tyranny weren't fit to be lackeys to a mad dog."

Any lurking notion of prudence fled Lauchlin's mind. Her heart-shaped face shone with virtue. "Och, but I stood up for them, just!" she cried. "I said they *were* fit to be lackeys to a mad dog. Or even," she added, piling lèse majesté upon sedition, "or even a mad German."

Even Cousin Matthew looked slightly alarmed at this. Captain Green sat still and cold, his eyes menacing. Captain Fletcher stared at her with deep anger. "You ruddy little fool; don't you know that remarks like that could hang you, young as you are?"

Shocked into complete sobriety, Lauchlin stared back, her eyes near-black circles of horror. What had she said? How *could* she? The fateful words had poured out so easily, and it was quite outrageous that she could not go back, now, just those few seconds, and unsay them! Would they really hang her? They hanged little children of nine or ten in London, for stealing even a shilling. . . . Her heart was choking her, crowding her lungs so that she couldn't breathe. . . .

And then Cousin Matthew's hand was firm on her arm, his voice was a blend of laughter and dismay. "Merciful heaven, honey, they've taken you wrong! You're thinking of that old mad German fellow Shmidt I was telling you about, back in Virginia, I reckon, aren't you?"

Lauchlin at once snatched at the straw, feeble though it was. She suddenly didn't feel in the least heroic. "Aye, then, to be sure." She raised wide eyes which she hoped were utterly guileless. "And who else would I be meaning, at all?"

Nobody believed them for an instant, of course. But they pretended to, for not even the harsh Captain Green really much cared for the notion of hanging so young a girl, or even imprisoning her. Instead, she and her miscreant relative were treated to an extremely long and severe lecture. Captain Fletcher pointed out that she and Ronald had been a burden and sorrow and source of worry to their parents for the whole three years of his assignment there, and were steadily going from bad to worse. Captain Green announced with grim meaning that once *he* took over, there would be no more leniency, and they were a lucky pair to escape with their necks unstretched this time. Captain Fletcher told Cousin Matthew that he was a wicked old man, and should be ashamed of himself, corrupting children in such a despicable way.

"Shades of Socrates!" murmured the wicked old man, much moved by this.

"Eh?" Captain Green had apparently not been raised on Plato, although his fellow officer shot a quizzical look at Cousin Matthew, who only shook his white head sadly.

After that, the scolding was repeated from the beginning, with variations, and then the offending tartan scarf was confiscated, and the two criminals, much shaken, found themselves standing outside the garrison, the shaggy ponies restored to them.

"Whew!" remarked Cousin Matthew, thoughtfully. "Well, now I know, don't I?" He began to get his cockiness back. He beamed, chuckled, and squeezed Lauchlin's cold hand. "I'd go into battle with you beside me any day! Girl after my own heart. If I were forty years younger, I'd marry you!" He looked regretful. "Well, how shall we amuse ourselves for the rest of the day? Bless my soul, but your hands are cold! Those Redcoats didn't scare you, did they?"

"Never the day!" lied Lauchlin, lifting her chin. "My hands are always cold," she added truthfully. "And 'tis in my mind that Ronald and Fergus will be tearing the place apart to find us the now, and ending up in yon same office if we don't find them first."

"Mmm, you just might be right," admitted Cousin Matthew, and they began to lead the ponies on toward the high street, their spirits almost completely recovered.

Four

THE HAGGIS

Ronald and Fergus were indeed searching Portee for their missing companions, and having what Cousin Matthew graphically called conniption fits. When they heard what had been happening, they were stricken very nearly speechless, and Cousin Matthew took instant advantage of this.

"So all's fine and dandy now," he commented cheerfully, "and it was a good thing you took those letters on, wasn't it? Did you get them on the ship all right?"

Ronald, his gray eyes brooding on Lauchlin, seemed to have trouble focusing on the question, finally nodded.

"Good. And did you find any journals?"

Ronald nodded again, and produced two. "From Edinburgh only," he said, and fell to brooding again. Lauchlin watched him with troubled eyes. Was he envious of her adventure, or worried by it, or angry? Certainly he was in one of his truculent moods, but with Ronald it was sometimes hard to know just why.

"Let's away home now," he said abruptly.

No one argued. No one really wanted to stay longer, especially Fergus, who seemed convinced that Redcoats were waiting at every corner to haul Lauchlin away to the gallows. He didn't care about Cousin Matthew; his loyalty was all for his own clan.

They turned back toward the edge of town, leading their ponies. Lauchlin looked anxiously at the others, struck by a thought. "There's no *need* to tell Mother and Father, is there?" she suggested hopefully. "It will only worry them, just."

Ronald eyed her with complete understanding. They had a long-standing agreement of silence about any scrape which wasn't discovered at the time. There was nothing dishonest about it, really, they now assured Cousin Matthew, who was only too willing to be convinced.

"We keep a note of our sins, and we always confess later, you see," Lauchlin explained earnestly.

Cousin Matthew chuckled. "A good bit later, I reckon?"

"Oh, that depends on how bad it was. We're waiting two or three more years to tell about the time we got caught in the tide and nearly drowned, and one or two other wee things, and I have it in my mind we could do fine waiting about ten years for this one." She looked inquiringly at Ronald, who merely nodded moodily.

She sighed, and it was almost a relief when they ran into their cousin Duncan from the southern end of Skye, and they all stopped for a chat. And then came Cousin Tearleach as well, eager to meet the Colonial cousin and ask about the New World.

But presently the conversation became all man's talk, about tobacco crops compared to potatoes, and whether cattle and sheep might do well in Virginia, and Lauchlin yawned. She felt suddenly deflated, and began to let her pony amble forward slowly, to crop grass further ahead, and also as a small hint. Then she forgot about the hint, because from down a side lane there rang the sound of young English voices. Lauchlin had never known any Sassenach children and she wondered what they were like.

She soon found out what these were like. The gleeful voices were pierced suddenly by the high screech of a kitten in pain. And Lauchlin, hurrying toward it, saw two boys tying a string firmly around the mouth of a squalling, struggling sack.

Eyes and hair ablaze, she left her pony to his grazing and marched down the lane in an extremely warlike mood. "What is it you're doing to yon poor wee beastie?" she demanded. "Stop it at once!"

She could hardly have been less tactful, or less likely to be obeyed. The larger of the two boys stood up, his fine marigold breeches somewhat stained by the damp ground on which he had been kneeling. He stared at her. "Why, you insolent little rebel!" he drawled incredulously. "How dare you talk to me like that? Who do you think you're ordering around?"

"Yourself is who," Lauchlin retorted, her reckless mood on her again. "Give me yon sack!" With a swift stoop and pounce she snatched it out of the hands of the younger boy, who had been watching with open mouth.

With an equally swift movement, the older one snatched it back, giving her a hard shove at the same time, so that she staggered backwards. The bag heaved and wailed piteously.

Lauchlin didn't often lose her temper. She did so now. Lowering her flaming head, she aimed it straight for the midsection of the older boy, and charged. Her head was hard as a young goat's, and in an instant her enemy was seated on the ground, gasping and holding his middle.

Lauchlin triumphantly seized her noisy trophy and turned back toward her pony. But before she had got halfway, her hair was seized from behind with a jerk which nearly tore it from her head. Ronald arrived at the top of the lane just in time to see his scapegrace sister drop to her knees, stubbornly clutching something, her head pulled painfully backward by a Sassenach lad as large as she, while another, larger yet, advanced with considerable menace.

Ronald suffered an instant and satisfying attack of that savage Highland fighting madness. He had been spoiling for a fight for nearly an hour now, and he waded into this one with a simply terrifying enthusiasm. By the time Fergus and Cousin Matthew arrived on the scene, both English boys had lost all interest in the argument—and in the disputed sack. One was in full retreat around a corner, and the other sat on the ground, a dazed hand to one eye, his lip cut and swelling. Ronald was bending over Lauchlin.

"What happened?" he demanded. "Are you hurt? What have you got here?"

He reached a hand toward the sack, which had subsided for the moment. It promptly came to life, let out a squawk, and shot out needle-sharp claws, one of which caught Ronald on his finger.

"*Mo thruigh!*" he said, withdrawing it and noticing that Lauchlin had similar wounds all over her hands and arms. "Is it all right you are?" he urged, noticing that she had her face lowered. He bent over to peer at her more closely, while Cousin Matthew recklessly trailed his fine broadcloth coat on the ground in an effort to see if she was hurt. Fergus stood by, swearing fine Gaelic oaths.

Lauchlin lifted tear-wet eyes and a wobbly grin. " 'Tis

not that I'm crying," she assured them earnestly. "Only, hair-pulling makes *anyone's* eyes water, just. They were tormenting the poor wee kitten," she added by way of explanation.

Ronald nodded, finding this a perfectly sound and solid reason for battle. He pulled her to her feet, while Cousin Matthew hovered and Fergus scolded, one eye on the visible Sassenach boy and the other on the corner around which the smaller one had vanished.

"Come away now!" Fergus urged anxiously. " 'Tis in my mind that the whole garrison will be down on us."

He was right. They had scarcely remounted their ponies (the sack now in Ronald's arms) when the smaller boy appeared. "There they are!" he shrilled, beckoning behind him. "Hurry!"

It seemed a splendid idea. Lauchlin had no desire at all to renew her brief and troubled aquaintance with Captain Green, and especially not just now. She dug her heels vigorously into her pony's flank, not needing Fergus's cry of "Away with ye!" Cousin Matthew, who seemed to share her feelings, raced just behind her up the lane and around the corner to the main road. Their retreat was without dignity, and at the moment neither of them minded.

Fergus and Ronald hung back for just a moment, to guard the rear, Fergus looking immensely large and dangerous. Then they whirled their ponies and followed just as a couple of annoyed looking Redcoats appeared at the bottom of the lane.

"*Dhiaoul!*" muttered Ronald, as he saw recognition in their eyes. Oh well, it was no great harm, and those boys had deserved it. He shrugged off worry and also the black mood that had dogged him earlier, and bent over his pony's neck as the four of them raced out of the town and westward in sudden and quite irrational high spirits.

There was no pursuit, and presently they fell into a walk. Laughter declined into silence. The captured sack was far from silent. It shrieked a protest and stuck out claws again.

Fergus watched as Ronald tried gingerly to find a position as little painful as possible for both himself and his passenger. "What's in yon bag?" asked Fergus dryly. "A haggis?"

"Yow!" said the bag indignantly.

Lauchlin gurgled. "Indeed, and I'd not like to eat a haggis as prickly as yon!" she exclaimed. "Poor wee Haggis! You're all right now, *mo chridhe*!" she crooned so sweetly that Cousin Matthew chuckled.

"What," he demanded with interest, "*is* a haggis?"

They looked at him with astonishment. "Do you not *know*?"

He shook his white head, bare to sun and wind, for he much preferred carrying his tricorne hat to wearing it. "Reckon we don't have such animals in Virginia."

They chuckled, regarded him with deep sympathy. "Och, poor man! We'll have Mother serve one soon!"

"Oh, it's to eat, is it?" He looked interested. "What is it?"

" 'Tis a braw dish," Lauchlin informed him, her pony alongside his. "First you take a sheep's stomach-bag, and then you take the lungs and heart and liver and the other insides, and perhaps a calf's, as well, if you are rich, and you mince them all up and mix them with oatmeal and blood, and perhaps an onion or two, and some suet, and then you stuff it into the sheep's stomach, and tie it up and put it in a pot to boil, and—" She paused, looking at Cousin Matthew doubtfully. For some reason he didn't look at all well.

"Is it ill you are, then?" she cried anxiously. "You're not having a rheum, are you? Would you like to stop and rest?"

Cousin Matthew swallowed hard and maintained that he wasn't at all tired. But Ronald insisted that they stop presently, just off the road on a southern flank of hill, where they could sit in the heather and stare across at the Cuillins and at a wee slab of sea between the hills to the southwest. "You can just glance at your journals," he suggested tactfully.

Cousin Matthew, still muttering that he could ride as far as anyone, opened them out with a flourish. One was *The Edinburgh Magazine* and the other, *Scots Town and Country*. While Fergus dreamed across the hills (a sharp eye open for any danger), the other three heads bent over the papers in the clear afternoon sunshine.

A letter signed "Patrioticas" went on at great length about Justice and Obedience to the Mother Country, and the Majesty of the Crown, complaining self-righteously about the ungrateful feeling of protest in the Colonies. Cousin Matthew snorted indignation, and Lauchlin chortled.

"Read this!" urged Ronald, handing them the other paper, in which a letter by one "Atticus" suggested strongly that Stern Measures be taken against the Upstart Colonists.

"One-sided!" sputtered the old man, really indignant. "It's the same with all of 'em! They only give one view, and that's a distorted one. How can there ever be justice, or even friendship and understanding between people in one place and another, if there's never any honest news or exchange of opinion? You—" He glared at his startled audience, "didn't know the first thing about Virginia or the other colonies until I came along—and all you know now is what I told you. For all you know, it could be all lies."

"Och, no!" protested Ronald.

"No?" Socrates couldn't have looked more challenging. "Well, either I'm lying, or these journals are. What makes you think it isn't me?"

Ronald didn't hesitate. "Well, 'tis you who says the Sassenach are wicked," he explained reasonably, "so 'tis you must be telling the truth." A simple matter of black and white, surely?

Cousin Matthew looked flabbergasted, and then began to laugh helplessly. "You poor boy, you're as one-sided as these! No, now don't get thorns in your hair," he went on hastily, as Ronald bristled. "Your version is a mite nearer the truth, I dare say. But you just demonstrated my point."

"But what *is* your point, just?" begged Lauchlin, completely mystified.

"It's that papers ought to give both sides of an issue, and not just the one they want people to believe. Or possibly they should just present the facts and leave out opinions, so folks can draw their own conclusions. But I suppose that kind of public-spirited fair-mindedness is too much to ask of human nature. . . ." He sighed.

Lauchlin and Ronald were silent for a moment, not really seeing why he was so upset, but quite willing to try.

"Well, it must be to *someone's* benefit to print the opposite of this." Lauchlin waved the paper. "They wouldn't have to be public-spirited, but only on the other side. Like a Colonial, for instance." She and Ronald looked at each other, the same inspiration popping into both minds.

"Like you," they suggested happily.

Cousin Matthew looked thunderstruck and then delighted. "By George! I mean, by gad! Or course! Just the thing! What's more, I'll tell them what's happening in the Highlands as well as the Colonies, make the English sit up and ask themselves what sort of government they've got, and if they really want it. . . . Call it the *Gadfly*, after old Socrates, you know, who stung people's complacency and ignorance for their own good. . . . Buy myself a publishing house in London . . . secretly, of course. . . ."

He beamed into their astonished faces. "Didn't think I'd take it seriously? Why not? It's a splendid idea, and I'm the one to do it. Lots of enthusiasm, lots of money, no heirs to leave it to. Anyway, I figure the best use for money is to broaden folks' minds. And I'm a good writer, you know. Got a way with words. I can turn out a lot of the articles myself, from first-hand knowledge. Tell you what; how about you two youngsters providing the ones about Scotland? Anonymous, of course. . . . You've got a flair for using words, too, Ronald m'boy; I've noticed. Ought to develop it. Reckon you might tend to be just a mite one-sided, but we can cure that."

He looked inquiringly at Ronald, whose narrow face and gray eyes were suddenly alight and who looked as if the world had suddenly opened before him—which in fact it had. His future was set: he was heir of Kildornie, and wouldn't have had it otherwise. But now he could do more than just endure, as Father did, hoping that some time soon the Act of Proscription might be lifted. He could raise his voice against tyranny, he could make himself felt, protest and be heard. He could *do* something! And there was no way he would rather do it, on the whole, than with his brain and pen.

Glowing, he said so. Lauchlin hooted.

"Och, the lying tongue of you! 'Tis with a sword you'd liefer be fighting, and you know it well."

"Only when I'm angered," said Ronald mildly, and grinned at her derision. It was true he was angered most of the time, in some way. But he was really of a peaceful nature at heart, he told her firmly.

Lauchlin hooted again and fell thoughtfully silent. Cousin Matthew looked at her inquiringly. "I'm not clever at writing like Ronald," she mourned. "Couldn't I do *something* to help? Find news—or—or draw sketches, perhaps?" She brightened. "Like that one I did of us diving into the heather that day, and you standing on the path, except I could be drawing all the things the Redcoats do here, and show how ridiculous it is. Could I?"

They were all on fire with enthusiasm now, all talking at once. "—smuggle the letters out by fishing boat . . . tell Mother and Father? . . . when I reach London . . . use made-up names . . . Now if I can just find someone to send me material from back home. . . ."

"What about your family?" asked Lauchlin. "I mean, your sister and nephew and great-niece Carilla and all?"

The old man chuckled wryly. "Reckon they might not write exactly the sort of thing I want, honey. Little Carilla's far too young, of course, and my nephew Nathaniel's a busy lawyer of very pacific political opinions, all for settling things by peaceful discussions around a conference table—even when the other side won't hear of it. As for my sister Lavinia—" He chuckled. "Lavinia's a loyal Englishwoman to the backbone, considers me a wicked subversive old radical. Wait until she sees the *Gadfly*! She'll be furious!"

Someone else was furious. The sack, which had been curled up asleep between them, now came to vigorous and noisy life again.

"Poor Haggis!" said Ronald remorsefully. "Still tied in that cruel stuffy sack whilst we enjoy the sun and air! Never mind; we're away now, and you'll just have to bide where you are until we get home. We've had a fine bit of trouble rescuing you," he added severely. "Stop skirling like an untuned bagpipe; you should be grateful."

"Waaagh" skirled Haggis ungratefully, and found Ronald's arm with a claw.

By the time they reached Kildornie, the sack was well into its second wind and was screaming to high heaven that it was being Kidnapped by Monsters. It could be heard from afar, and most of the household gathered at the door as the small procession wound down the path and up to the house. Fergus was having his turn at carrying the sack, very gingerly, by the top, at full arm's length. He looked as if he hated it, and muttered imprecations in Gaelic every time a claw found his hand.

"Whatever is in yon bag?" demanded Archie and Lorne, round-eyed, as Fergus handed it thankfully to Ronald and led the ponies away to the stable.

"A haggis," said Ronald solemnly, and chuckled at their expressions.

Kildornie appeared, looked at the writhing and screeching sack. "If that's my mail," he declared firmly, "I don't want it."

Everyone talked, though only Mother seemed able to make much sense out of the jumble, severely censored as it was. She raised a highly suspicious eyebrow and didn't pursue the subject. Doubtless she would hear a full confession one day, and she was in no real hurry to turn gray.

"Come away in, then," she told them, "and we'll let the poor beastie loose inside. It sounds very young."

"Hurry, Ronald!" cried Lauchlin. "I'm dying to know what our Haggis looks like!"

"Well, we know fine how it sounds and feels," he retorted, sitting down on the drawing room floor to untie the string. "There, wee Haggis, you can come out now," he told it.

There was a cautious pause. Then a black and white thunderbolt hurtled out of the bag, across the room, over a chair, and up the curtains to the very top, where it clung howling for someone to rescue it. But when Father reached up a helpful hand, Haggis changed his tune to ferocious threats, and clawed it. Father withdrew the hand with some haste. Haggis again began moaning to be rescued.

They stood looking at him, laughing and shaking their heads. He was a scrawny wee thing, hardly big enough to be out in the world alone. He showed, as Lauchlin pointed out, a fine fighting Highland spirit. Her father, sucking a bleeding finger, agreed with less enthusiasm.

It took half an hour to lure the kitten down with a dish of milk and raw rabbit. And by that time they had almost forgotten about how they got him in the first place—and about the tartan scarf.

Five

REDCOAT'S WARNING

They didn't for a moment forget the *Gadfly*. At the first opportunity Cousin Matthew explained the whole project to his fascinated hosts, and then sat back, beaming, to await their approval.

It was less than whole-hearted. "A braw idea, surely," admitted Kildornie, "and certainly much needed. There's just maybe one or two wee difficulties. Like how not to be arrested and hanged after the first edition or maybe the second."

Lauchlin and Ronald, seated demurely on hassocks, exchanged uneasy glances. Perhaps, after all, Mother and Father might not prove altogether delighted when they learned about the articles and sketches from Skye?

Nor were they.

"*Mo thruigh*!" exclaimed Mother. "What was it Murdoch and I were already telling you about helping our imps find mischief? They don't *need* help! 'Tis very naughty of you, Cousin Matthew! If you are determined to get yourself flogged or imprisoned or hanged, then I suppose we cannot stop you, but I have other plans for my own bairns! Besides, how could we be smuggling the articles and sketches off Skye safely?"

Her offspring winked at each other hopefully. Her husband looked shocked. "Lauren! I believe you'd like to help, too!"

Mother denied this with more spirit than conviction. Lauchlin put in her oar, despite Ronald's kick.

"You and Father were in all sorts of danger for the Prince when you were even younger than we!" she reminded her reproachfully.

Mother rallied instantly. "Aye, and in exile at your ages," was the unanswerable retort.

Lauchlin subsided. Ronald glared at her, wondering if she would ever learn when to hold her tongue. They both looked appealingly at Cousin Matthew.

"Thing is," he pointed out shrewdly, "they've got to do *something* to oppose tyranny. They can't just sit down and accept it, no more than you could at that age."

"We've had to learn," said Kildornie with bitterness. "We have to face reality, and what cannot be changed must be endured."

"Quite right for your generation," returned the surprising old man, no longer looking in the least like a pixie, but more like a sage. "You've had your battle; you've fought for an ideal. Now it's their turn." He jerked his chin at the enthralled Lauchlin and Ronald. "It's their natural right, to refuse to accept your reality, to change what cannot be endured, to put their lives at stake, if need be, for their own ideals."

Deep silence fell for a moment. The fire crackled in the enormous fireplace. Haggis, a sleeping black-and-white ball in Lauchlin's lap, stirred and stuck a claw right through six layers of petticoat. Lauchlin hardly noticed.

"You're right, surely," said Father at last. " 'Tis the right of the young to be embattled idealists, and heaven help the world if they ever do accept unquestioning the reality of their elders."

"I'm no *that* old, myself!" complained Mother. "Well, O Socrates, what more? What new ideals do our young fight for?"

He had an answer. "A new kind of justice, for everyone. I've got a notion, m'dear, that the old world is about to venture into a whole new way of thinking. Might be they'll look back after a thousand years or so and call it the beginning of the Age of Humanity. We've already got a few people thinking about the rights of the ordinary man. Some day we may even decide that folks like Indians and slaves and Jews and Highlanders and females are people too, hmm?"

"Hear hear!" cried Mother, quite carried away by that last bit.

"A braw dream," conceded Father. "And a braw lot of blood will be spilt over it, I'm thinking," he added a bit grimly.

"The more printer's ink now, the less blood later," urged Cousin Matthew. "Get the idea into people's heads. Especially the young, who aren't as fixed to their own prejudices."

"Very well so." Mother began looking stubborn again. "But *our* young—"

"—will go on getting into one scrape after another," said Cousin Matthew as virtuously as if it hadn't been himself led them into the affair of the tartan scarf, "unless you give them a legitimate outlet. I propose to give them one. And don't tell me you can't figure out a way to smuggle the stuff out, not with MacLeods all over the Scottish islands, and all of them your cousins, and half of them sailors or fishermen." He grinned at them engagingly, and dropped the subject there.

His future assistants didn't.

"Why just London?" demanded Lauchlin, huddling inside her cloak and shivering in the cold of autumn wind and spray.

They sat in their own private cove, looking across Loch Dunvegan to the gray gaunt Shoulder of Beinn Bhreac. Ronald, who never felt the cold, had no idea that his sister did. He looked at her now with satisfaction, knowing just what she meant.

"Aye, 'twas a thing in my own mind. We need a *Gadfly* here on Skye, giving news and information of the Colonies and *their* quarrel with King Geordie, and perhaps local news as well."

Lauchlin forgot the cold. "We can make just the one copy of each issue, and let it be passed on from one to another. . . ."

"Cousin Matthew could maybe be sending us more paper from London. . . ."

"And all in Gaelic, of course, lest it fall into Sassenach hands. . . ."

"And not put our names on it," grumbled Ronald in a reluctant concession to prudence. It galled him, but after all, he was the next chieftain, and had his duty to clan and family.

Lauchlin didn't care a whit, so long as it was done. "We'll start tonight, and we must get Cousin Matthew to tell us more about the Colonies. And I'll do a sketch of Captain Green."

For some reason it didn't occur to either of them that one of Lauchlin's sketches was as good as a signature any day.

It was about three weeks later that a burly, cloaked figure rode down the hill to Kildornie, head lowered against the swirls of sleety rain driving in on a western wind. Across a burn, along the narrow glen, and then he turned in at the big stone house which sat—as most Highland homes did—on the south slope of the hill.

Sergeant Tucker, by now, had no trouble seeing why. The north side of a high and steep hill might not see a ray of sunshine for eleven months of the year in this northern land. He shivered a little, remembering that London was not dark by mid-afternoon; not even in the dead of winter. Savage place, Scotland! He was not even sure he approved the midsummer nights, when it was never really dark at all, either. Unnatural.

Warmth and light and music came from the big house, even between drawn curtains. As he dismounted, he could just glimpse the big stone fireplace inside, with a roaring fire in it. The sound of bagpipes flowed and wailed about him; one could not, apparently, play them at anything less than full volume. He grinned wryly and pounded on the front door.

There was a brief pause, a raised voice, and abrupt silence from the pipes. When a maid appeared, looking flustered, the sergeant heard a faint scuffling from the drawing room beyond.

"I'd like to speak to Mr. MacLeod," he said firmly.

The girl looked more flustered than ever, and glanced anxiously at the closed door behind her. "Will you pe waiting here a wee," she said in her sibilant English, "and I will pe calling him."

Sergeant Tucker strode right past her. "You needn't bother; I'll just go in," he said. "And by the way, there's nothing wrong with me 'earin', you know," he added, opening the drawing room door.

The room, as he entered, fairly radiated innocent serenity. Old Mr. Lennox sat reading before the blazing fire. Lauchlin, respectably dressed in a rather shabby blue wool frock with scarlet ankles just showing above soft skin slippers, looked up at him with guileless surprise. The baby kicked in his cradle, Mistress MacLeod smiled over her knitting, Lorne curled beside her, and Kildornie rose from his chair.

"Well, Sergeant Tucker," he said without a great deal of cordiality. "What brings you here on a day like this?"

Sergeant Tucker looked around. He would have made a splendid detective, would the sergeant. He saw a corner of the carpet turned up, and the sofa somewhat displaced from the wall, and a suspicious bulge behind the curtains, in which a scrawny black-and-white kitten seemed unduly interested.

"You might as well come out," he suggested to the room in general. "I could 'ear you pipin' 'alfway up the glen. Besides, this 'ere's an unofficial visit, like."

If there had been any doubt in his mind, the kitten settled it by turning suddenly into a ferocious hunter and pouncing on a pair of small skin-clad feet under the curtain.

"Ow!" said Archie, and emerged, looking reproachfully at the ungrateful Haggis. From behind the sofa and the other curtains came the astonishing file of Ronald, Seumas, MacCrimmon the piper, Fergus, and two bagpipes; all tartan-covered, silent, and wary. Haggis, infected by the spirit of the hunt, promptly attacked the nearest, who happened to be Seumas. Seumas as promptly bent over and smacked the small behind, and Haggis fled, yelling loudly for his mother and the Redcoats, under the nearest chair. There he became a persecuted martyr and sat making small indignant yowling noises under his breath.

Sergeant Tucker, blinking a little, simply stood and looked at them. No matter how often he caught these Highlanders at a disadvantage, they always seemed to keep their self-possession. They did so now. Defiance, wariness, even amusement was in the faces turned toward him—but no apology or meekness. Kildornie gave a humorous shrug, Fergus and the MacCrimmons took dignified leave, and Lauchlin turned a mischievous face to the sulking kitten.

"You mind your manners, Haggis," she threatened, "or we will be giving you back to the Sassenachs!"

Sergeant Tucker sat down, unasked, on the nearest chair. "You should 'ave left 'im there in the first place," he remarked disapprovingly. "You're in a mort o' trouble over 'im, now." He glared at them. "I *told* you to take it easy and be'ave yourselves, and now look at what you've been and gone and done!"

"And what *have* we been and gone and done?" demanded Ronald aggressively. "Just rescued a poor wee beastie from torment by bully Sassenach lads."

"You know 'oo them bully lads was?" interrupted Sergeant Tucker. "They was Captain Green's sons, that's 'oo they was! And you beat 'em to a ruddy pulp, you did." The sergeant tried hard to indicate strong disapproval, but it was not easy, for it was his private conviction that the lads in question had needed being beaten to a ruddy pulp. " 'Ow do you think Captain Green felt about that, hmm? Well, 'e ain't forgot it, 'e ain't."

He paused to look around the circle of faces. Ronald

was wearing the modest smirk of a fox-hunter who finds he has bagged a wolf. His parents were looking deeply interested, quite perfectly concealing any dismay they may have felt.

"Dear me," murmured Mistress MacLeod. "*Two* of them, you say?" Her gray eyes gleamed with shameless pride, and the sergeant forgot himself.

"Ar, and good sized boys they was, too!"

He remembered himself. He scowled. "Didn't you know about it?" he asked accusingly.

"Och, well we may have forgotten just one or two little details," Lauchlin explained artlessly. "Ronald not wanting to brag, you know."

They all looked at her without comment. She subsided.

"And you!" said the sergeant wrathfully. He flung out a huge hand to include Cousin Matthew. "You two is worse, if anything! Wearing tartan right into Portee! And calling the king a mad German dog right in the Commander's office!"

There was a shocked silence. The culprits looked guiltily at their laps. It was quite clear that here were maybe one or two other little details they had forgotten to mention. Lauchlin, peering upward, saw that Mother's face was quite white, and Father's grave and set.

"She only meant—" began Cousin Matthew.

"I know! Chap in the Colonies. The Captains pretended to believe that, so's not to 'ave a little girl like 'er up on charges of sedition or per'aps treason. Real generous, they was; let you go with a warning. Might 'ave gone much 'arder if Captain Fletcher 'adn't still been in command. Well, 'e's leaving now, and Captain Green's taking full charge, and 'e knows *just* 'oo it was marched out of 'is office that day and went and 'elped attack 'is sons. And I'm telling you now, missy, and the rest of you as well, if you so much as blow your noses from now on, you've 'ad it."

There was no sound for a moment but the crackling fire. Mother had protective arms around her children, and was clearly ready to defend them with a claymore if need be. Cousin Matthew looked old and ill. And then Father stood up and walked over to the burly red-coated figure.

"You said this was not an official visit," he said quietly. "What would you be doing in our position, Sergeant Tucker?"

The soldier nodded briskly. "I'll tell you," he said readily. "I'd take the three of 'em, and I'd send 'em away for a long visit somewhere. The further the better. I might even pack up the whole blooming family and go out to the Colonies or somewheres, afore you get deported there as bond slaves, but. . . ."

He looked questioningly at Kildornie, who shook his head. "I'm Chieftain here," he said simply.

"Ar, I thought you'd say that," agreed the sergeant. "Well, you think about sending 'em away, then, or else turn 'em into saints, or keep 'em locked up. Because—Well, you've 'ad all the chances you're going to 'ave, see?" He paused, feeling strongly that he would like to say something else, but not quite sure what. He cleared his throat. They all looked at him. "Mind," he said gruffly, "I'm not saying them boys didn't deserve all they got, if I do say so as shouldn't."

He looked once again around the bright paneled room, the folds of carnation brocade enclosing it snugly against the winter wind. He felt that he had brought a worse wind in with him, blighting everything with a stricken air that was not here before. He was sorry about that; he had meant well. He stood up, alien and lonely and ill at ease amid these proud and clannish Highlanders, unbowed and unforgiving.

"That's all I've got to say," he ended heavily. "Got to get back to me duty now."

And then Mistress MacLeod rose swiftly and went over to him, her full jade skirts sweeping behind. "You'll no be going until you've stopped to sup with us," she said.

There was a breathless silence. Everyone knew the sacred unwritten law of Highland hospitality. To "take the salt" was a bond of friendship between guest and host. No Redcoat had ever been invited to eat at Kildornie. All eyes turned to the sergeant, wondering if he understood.

He did. His florid face reddened more deeply, and he cleared his throat. "I— Thank 'ee, Ma'am," he said, and sat down again.

Kildornie poured elderberry wine. There was a new feeling of warmth in the room that had nothing to do with the fireplace. Hospitality had been offered and accepted. From now on, nothing would change on the surface, but no act of personal enmity would pass between this particular Sassenach and the Kildornie MacLeods.

Except for Haggis, who had no morals or scruples, much less reverence for the laws of hospitality. Tired of being ignored, he came out suddenly from beneath the chair, turned into a fierce tiger, and attacked Sergeant Tucker's booted ankle.

They were laughing uproariously when there was a banging on the front door.

Six

REDCOAT'S THREAT

Catriona the maid popped a scared head in at the door, her black eyes circular. Whatever was going on, she did not know at all, at all, but a spell must be on the place.

" 'Tis the Redcoat captain and his troops, and asking for Himself!" she whispered in Gaelic. "He is wanting to come in."

"Cor!" said Sergeant Tucker, dismayed. "That's torn it!"

"Nonsense!" said his hostess, recovering her wits and remembering her duty to a guest. A loud voice and boots were already in the hall outside. "Quickly!" she said. . . .

Captain Green hardly noticed the small scuffling noise. When he strode, self-invited, into the Kildornie drawing room, it was to a scene fairly radiating innocent serenity. Old Mr. Lennox sat reading before the blazing fire. Lauchlin was drawing at the desk by the window. A studious Ronald concentrated on Latin. The rest of the family read or knitted or bent over toys. The baby cooed in his cradle, and a small black paw stuck out from under the low sofa. Everyone but the baby and the black paw looked up with expressions of guileless surprise.

"Mr. MacLeod?" asked Captain Green curtly, aiming his thin nose at the obvious candidate for this identity.

Ronald bristled inwardly at the omission of Father's title; he always did. Father never showed the least annoyance, and did not do so now. He merely waited in polite but not very cordial inquiry.

"I'm Captain Green, new Commander of the English garrison at Portree."

This news was received in noncommittal silence. Everyone sat and looked at him. No one invited him to sit down. A less thick-skinned man might have felt uncomfortable, thought Ronald, and wondered a little uneasily just how thick-skinned this man really was. He didn't *look* ill at ease. . . . His eye fell on Ronald and hardened. Ronald stuck his chin out, squared it, and returned the stare.

"I suppose you are well aware, Mr. MacLeod, that your two oldest offspring have a long record of criminal activity?"

Mother's chin went as square as Ronald's. "Have they so? And how are you defining criminal activity, Mr. Green?" She quite deliberately omitted *his* title. "You'd not include tormenting poor helpless wee animals, presumably?"

Captain Green ignored this thrust, except for an impatient frown suggesting an irritable wish that these Highlanders would keep their women in the subservient place where they belonged.

"They have had lenient treatment over and over, I gather, on the grounds of their youth," he went on harshly. "Far too often, I feel, since they seem to learn nothing, and are quite old enough to be considered as adults."

Mother's brows went up but she said nothing. No one said anything. It was up to Captain Green, if he wanted speech, to produce it himself.

"A few weeks ago they both—and this Colonial fellow as well—committed crimes punishable by severe penalties at the discretion of the commander." He glared at the three criminals, listed the crimes on his long finger. "The wearing of tartan. Seditious and treasonable utterances. Assault and battery upon Englishmen. Little English boys, to be exact."

Lauchlin could bear it no longer. "Little boys!" she jeered. "They were larger than we, whatever! Are they not adults too, then?"

"Lauchlin!" snapped her mother. Lauchlin lapsed into mutinous silence. A curtain twitched slightly. The black paw vanished altogether. Father looked quizzical.

"Apparently Scottish children reach adulthood at a far younger age than English children?" he suggested gently. "But never mind that. Do continue, er—Captain."

It was becoming quite clear that Captain Green did not intend to arrest anyone just at the moment. Lauchlin—although she had felt quite safe, really, with Father and Mother there—unclenched her hands.

Captain Green, who was finding this family extremely irritating and quite lacking the humility and respect proper from defeated barbarians, clenched his own fists and labored on. He was, to do him justice, a man of rigid self-control and he used it all now.

"Any further offenses from Kildornie will be dealt with extremely harshly," he said.

There was a small pause. "You need not have come all the way from Portree on a dark winter afternoon to tell us that," said Mother.

Haggis, now a fierce tiger, crept out from the sofa and began stalking a point in the curtain just behind the desk.

Lauchlin pounced on him, bore him to the sofa, and held him firmly, while he squalled that there was Something Hiding behind the curtain, and he was going to catch it.

The officer waited until Haggis had calmed down slightly. "I have reason to suppose the offense has already taken place," he said coldly, and produced a sheet of paper that caused Ronald and Lauchlin to stiffen imperceptibly and assume attitudes of incredible saintliness. Their mother shot them a brief, highly suspicious glance, and then donned an air of patient martyrdom. Lorne, not liking the feeling in the room, whimpered slightly, climbed into Mother's lap, shot a fearful glance at the frowning Redcoat, and buried her head. It created a madonna-like picture, domestic and faintly reproachful. Captain Green frowned more deeply and waved the paper. He was beginning, ever so slightly, to lose his sense of mastery over the situation.

"What do you know about this?" he demanded accusingly of his unwilling host.

"Not a thing," replied Kildornie truthfully. "How could I, in any case, and it flying past my eyes that way?"

"I fancy you'll recognize it with no great strain," Captain Green snapped irritably, and then pulled his temper back under leash. He handed it over. Ronald held his breath and Lauchlin said a small prayer. Cousin Matthew, who had been earnestly imitating a statue of Socrates reading, now moved just enough to peer at them both fixedly from beneath shaggy white brows.

Father took the paper, began to read it, at once chuckled.

"Let me see!" demanded Mother, and he moved over to her chair and held it down so that she could look. Lauchlin's sketch showed up clearly. It was a particularly wicked and insulting caricature of Captain Green, with drooping eyes and thin nose giving him an air of evil dissipation that was really quite unfair. He was a hard man, even a cruel man at times, but not evil or dissipated.

Mother choked slightly, looked up with quivering lip to meet his angry eyes. "Why, 'tis a very—disrespectful—sketch," she said unsteadily.

Lauchlin tried not to look smug. She did like seeing her talents appreciated! But what bad luck that their first issue should have fallen into English hands, to be sure! She thanked her guardian angel briefly that they had thought to write it all in Gaelic. There was nothing the Sassenach could prove. Nothing. He had naught but unverified suspicions. . . . Her eyes widened suddenly and her heart gave a great lurch as she remembered the sketch she had been working on when he came in. It lay this very minute on the desk where she had abandoned it when she snatched Haggis, face up, visible to anyone who bothered to look, utterly damning! What was she to do?

She looked at Ronald, met his stricken eyes, as the same realization came to him—and Cousin Matthew—and Mother and Father. Everyone perceived the danger, no one could think what to do about it. Any movement in that direction would just draw attention to it. And there were two good reasons for attention not to be directed there.

"Well?" demanded Captain Green, still staring at Father. From the corner of her eye, Lauchlin saw a tiny movement of the curtains just by the desk. . . . Was Captain Green raising his eyes? . . . Lauchlin instantly gave a sharp twist to the innocently sleeping Haggis's tail. Haggis, with an outraged howl, leaped straight into the air. Lauchlin leaped after him. Haggis lighted on top of Archie, who yelled. The baby woke up and cried. Haggis, clinging to Cousin Matthew, bawled that he was Being Attacked. Lauchlin protested tearfully that she didn't *mean* to upset the poor wee creature. Mother and Father looked patient, the captain offended.

When quiet was again restored, the desk lay bare, and the carnation curtains hung unmoving.

"Well?" asked Captain Green again, coming back to the subject, and quite unaware that he had just lost his case.

"An engaging bit of literature," Father said mildly, looking up. "I didn't know you could read the Gaelic."

The officer reddened slightly. "I can't. I don't need to. The drawing indicates clearly enough what sort of subversive document it is."

Father chuckled. "Are you so sure? Best you'd get a translation before you carry this too far, for 'tis in my mind you couldn't tell sedition from a nursery rhyme in the Gaelic."

"Some nursery rhymes began as sedition, too," muttered the captain, but his confidence wavered slightly. "You'll translate it for me at once."

"Never think it!" said Father gently. "Your authority does not extend quite so far, I think." He smiled, and Lauchlin suddenly perceived what he was about. For no Highlander would translate the Gaelic, surely, so the Sassenach could never prove what was written. And if he could not trace the sketch, either . . . she almost dared breathe easily.

The captain saw it, too. His jaw was grim, jutting out

even further then usual. He stood irresolute, glaring at the offensive *Skye Gadfly*. His eye fell on Archie, who stood stolidly watching.

"Can you read, little boy?" he asked suddenly, with what he clearly thought to be a winning smile.

Archie looked offended. "Fine I can!" he said indignantly. "And I nine years old!"

"Well well, how very clever of you!" His eye warned the family not to interfere, on peril of betraying their own guilt. Father's eye carried the same warning. It was quite unnecessary. They all knew their Archie.

Their Archie regarded the Sassenach with increasing disfavor. He simply hated that patronizing manner, which belied the flattering words.

"Fine I know it," he said uncompromisingly, and was clearly ready to call the conversation finished.

Captain Green detained him. "Well, then, see if you can read this writing for me, and I'll give you a shiny new sixpence," he cajoled, with a triumphant glance at the watching circle of faces.

The faces looked singularly unalarmed. Archie shook his carroty head violently. Did the Sassenach think him a fool, then? He said something highly unflattering in Gaelic, wrenched away, and marched over to stand beside his father with an air of militant defiance.

Captain Green straightened, looked at the solid ranks facing him, conceded a temporary tactical defeat. Lorne perceived his thoughts to be black spiders. "You think I can't prove it, don't you?" He spoke with savage restraint. "I shall, you know. And if not this time, the next. They're habitual criminals. They'll end up on the gallows."

He glared around, consciously striking a pose of military authority. Infuriatingly, they refused to look intimidated, or guilty, or even worried, except for the small girl with the flower face, who gazed at him as if he were Satan come to drag them off to hell. Her eyes were terrified, her soft lip quivered, but she was bravely silent. It was enough to make a man uncomfortable. And when he was being so extremely indulgent, too!

"I'm a fair-minded man," he told them, sincerely believing it. "I know as well as you do where this came from, but I'm not going to punish without further evidence. When that evidence comes to my hand, as it will, you need expect no mercy. We've been far too soft with you rebels as it is. The only thing you understand is force. Yes, and you cursed Colonials, too!" he snarled at Cousin Matthew. "All this talk of rights! You had best understand once for all that you have no rights but what England chooses to give you."

Invisible shafts of hatred ran like dull red spider webs between him and everyone in the room except the baby. Lorne could see them clearly, and she dimly perceived that to hate a person is to tie yourself to him. It was a dreadful thought, and she clung to Mother, who seemed to have the smallest hate-thread, and who was smiling—although not really warmly.

"So they say," she observed in the polite drawing-room tones one reserved for silly and garrulous old bores. "I feel sure your troops must be getting chilled out there, Mr. Green. Mind you don't get lost on the moors on your way back."

He left, a dangerous man.

There was a long silence when he had gone. The horses sounded up the glen, muffled by wind and waves, and

Fergus came presently to report that they had well and truly left. Then everyone breathed again, Lorne lifted her head, and Sergeant Tucker came out from behind the curtain waving the vanished sketch.

"Ruddy careless of you, missy," he told Lauchlin severely. "You ought to know better'n to leave this sort of thing 'angin' around."

Lauchlin instantly threw her arms around him and kissed him on the cheek. "Och, you darling man!" she cooed.

The sergeant's ruddy face slowly became bright scarlet, even to the ears. He put his hand to the kiss. " 'Ere now, missy, don't *do* that!" he brayed, tremendously pleased. " 'Tain't proper!"

He turned to his hosts, permitted his hands to be shaken, reddened all over again when Lorne reacted at once to this new atmosphere and insisted on placing her bunchy-skirted small self as close to him as he could crowd.

" 'S'all very well," he grumbled, "but you see what I mean? Sooner you gets 'em out of 'ere, the better. I 'ave to go back meself now." He shuffled his feet.

"Haste ye back," they told him, and no Highlander ever said that unless he meant it.

"Ar," he agreed gruffly. "Just to make sure you ain't in no more trouble." And he went, leaving a serious family conference behind him.

No time was wasted on recriminations. "In any case, I rather fear you've created your own punishment," said Father grimly. "The sergeant is quite right."

Ronald and Lauchlin looked at each other in dismay. Exile! They had not seriously thought it would come to this!

"Could we not visit Uncle Malcolm in Lochaber?" asked Lauchlin in a very small voice.

Their father shook his head. "You must leave the country, I fear. But—" The question hung thickly. Where, and with whom?

Cousin Matthew raised a snowy head. "I'm a mischievous old man," he mourned, looking really unhappy. "I *meant* well—but I'm an old fool, I reckon. It's up to me to fix things up now—if you'll trust me with them, Cousin Lauren?" He looked at Mother humbly.

She gave him a troubled smile and patted his hand. No one could remain angry with him. "But where will you take them, Cousin Matthew?"

"London," he said, looking much more cheerful.

"London!" They all stared. "But that's England! Surely they cannot go there! 'Tis not safe, whatever!"

"Oh yes it is! Safe as houses!" He began to sparkle again. "England long ago forgot that little rising of yours; it's just kept alive here in the Highlands. England's much more interested in the Colonies now. In any case, it will only be for a few weeks, likely, until I can send them safely off to my sister in Virginia."

They gaped. "Virginia?" they echoed faintly.

"Perfect solution. Lavinia and my nephew Nathaniel will be delighted to keep them, just as long as they'll stay. Years, if you like. We feel the same way about kinfolk there as you do here. And you needn't worry about the trip, for I plan to send them with my old friend Captain Duff on his *Jennifer*. He'll care for them as if they were his own."

They felt oddly as if they had been picked up by a white-haired and impish whirlwind. Lauchlin clutched at her father as if for protection. Ronald fought a hideous sense of unreality. Father, for once in his life, looked simply dazed.

Mother sat down suddenly, looking tired. "He's right, you know," she said. " 'Tis the perfect solution, and the only one. And we *have* hoped and planned this long time to send Ronald away to the Continent for a year or two, for education and experience. . . ." She sighed.

"But—'tis so far to send them to the Americas! And my wee lassie—" Father was taking it harder than Mother. "What of Red Indians and wild beasts?" he demanded.

"Posh and fiddle!" Cousin Matthew looked annoyed. "Williamsburg is as civilized as Portree. More, in some ways. They'll have a grand time, get experience, broaden their minds—and I reckon Lavinia will be good for them, too. Especially Lauchlin." And he chuckled.

There was more discussion, but it all came to the same thing, and presently Mother and Father became brisk and businesslike. Lauchlin and Ronald found themselves sitting rather close together for comfort, listening to plans for packing and preparations and probable weather conditions, and when various sea-going cousins were liable to be able to stop off Dunvegan Head and take on three passengers. . . .

They looked at each other bleakly, waiting for the future to stop this giddy zig-zagging and settle down into its new pattern so that they could come to terms with it. Ronald's chin was stubbornly square.

"Running away!" he muttered. "A Highlander running away to safety from the Sassenach!"

"Och, well, even the prince himself did so after Culloden," murmured Lauchlin, the realist. She was much more upset over leaving her home—and Mother and Father, Archie and wee Lorne, everything she knew and loved. And for months, or years, or even forever! She sobbed suddenly, and rushed over to climb into Father's lap as if she were Lorne's age, and burrow her red head into his velvet waistcoat.

"Cheer up, *mo chridhe*," he said softly into her ear. "Where's your sense of adventure?"

"Gone," she whimpered.

"Nonsense!" Mother was looking cheerful. "Imagine seeing the New World, and all the things Cousin Matthew has been describing to us! I could envy you, daughter! You must write often, and send lots of drawings, so that we can see and feel the forests, and mockingbirds, and fireflies, and those thousands of fragrant flowers, and the hot sunshine."

Lauchlin cheered up rather suddenly at these last words. And Ronald began to glow in the manner of someone who has a new and splendid idea—or perhaps just a variation on an old one.

On a dark but calm night in mid-December, a small ship bound for Liverpool made an unusual anchoring near Dunvegan Head, as near in as was safe to go. Torches flared briefly, and a small boat or two plied back and forth laden with boxes and trunks and an extremely noisy basket which began squealing with excitement the minute it touched the deck. Then came three people, much torn between tears and the sense of adventure. The small ship hoisted sail again, and the bay lay empty under the shimmer of Northern Lights.

No one knew it until much later, of course, but on that

same night, on the other side of the Atlantic, a number of very odd looking Indians boarded another ship, in Boston Harbor, and had themselves a highly unusual tea party.

Seven

LONDON INTERLUDE

A fine sleet blew over London as the stagecoach from Liverpool arrived after its six-day trip. The half dozen inside passengers climbed out stiffly, cold and tired and irritable. A basket, which had been complaining volubly the whole of the trip, went on complaining.

"Do hold your tongue, Haggis!" Lauchlin told it with asperity. " 'Tis yourself has had the most comfortable trip of us all, with a soft warm bed, and a space all to yourself, with no great fat Sassenach to squash you and blow snuff on you, whatever."

She spoke in Gaelic to avoid offending the great fat Sassenach, who had most unfairly been occupying all his own share of space and most of Lauchlin's. But the great fat Sassenach chose to be offended anyway. He raised a quizzing glass to one eye, surveyed them sourly, and waddled off, muttering something about savage barbarians from Scotland.

Ronald and Lauchlin stared after him, certain they could not have heard correctly. They were prepared to be called a good many things by Sassenachs: Jacobites, rebels, subversives, foes, knaves, even defeated enemies or haughty devils. But—they looked at each other, shrugged, and turned to Cousin Matthew, who had hailed a carriage and was ordering their boxes piled on the back.

"Never mind, honey. We'll soon be comfortable. . . . The Tudor Arms in Arlington Street, driver. . . . I always stay there when I come to London. Comfortable, clean, good service. We can all have nice hot baths, too, as soon as we get there."

Lauchlin, who had noticed the driver's sudden increased respect, was not surprised to find the Tudor Arms a genteel and probably exclusive place, with decor of a rich but quiet taste, and where Cousin Matthew was greeted with humble warmth by mine host in person. And if mine host wondered about the shabby children with outlandish accents who accompanied Mr. Lennox, he was far too clever a man even to flick an eyebrow. Instead, he showed them his three best bedchambers and a convenient private sitting room connecting them, and commanded a maid to take the young lady, who was clearly tired, to her own chamber at once.

The maid was far less tactful. She quite frankly looked down her long nose at this queer foreign girl, with no trace of *ton* or sophistication, no fine clothes or jewels, no proper accent—not even her own maid!

"Where's your abigail, miss?"

Lauchlin looked up from the fire—where she had rushed at once to warm her hands—puzzled as much by the tone and expression as the words.

"My what?"

"Your abigail. Your lady's maid. *No* lady travels without one."

Lauchlin imagined what Catriona, or perhaps Morag, might have made of this trip, and laughter danced in her eyes. "*I* do," she said, with an unconscious arrogance that came from knowing she was a Highlander and a MacLeod and Kildornie's daughter. She didn't deliberately set out to put this serving woman in her place—but she did so, for all that. "I should like a hot bath at once, please, and perhaps you can send a maid to help me dress for dinner." Her voice, soft and lilting, was the voice of Somebody speaking to Nobody, and the maid at once lost all thought of looking down her nose. Instead she curtsied.

"Yes, miss. . . ."

"Mistress MacLeod."

"Yes, Mistress MacLeod." She scurried out. Lauchlin contrived by sheer accident to go on looking serenely poised for at least four seconds after the maid left the room. Then she stood up, took a step, fell over Haggis's basket, and fell to the floor with a thud. When the maid rushed back in alarm, Kildornie's Daughter was lying full length on the carpet exchanging insults with an infuriated black and white kitten.

Ronald developed an instant loathing for London. It was big and dirty and crowded. Especially, it was crowded, with more people than either he or Lauchlin had ever seriously tried to imagine.

" 'Tis like a great ugly ants' nest," he told Lauchlin, staring up the street to the clutter and clatter of Piccadilly. "And all of them Sassenach, too," he remembered, appalled.

Lauchlin looked too, but with a much less jaundiced

eye. It was true that a little while in London streets made one feel battered and oppressed, desperate for the quiet empty spaces of Skye, and with a quite frightening desire to slaughter every human being within twenty feet. On the other hand, in small doses there was something very stimulating and exciting about it. Imagine, so many people, and all different!

"I'm thinking I could like it fine for maybe a wee hour a week, or even two," she decided.

"I could do fine wanting it," growled Ronald. "If Williamsburg is like this, I'll not stay there."

Nor did he change his mind in the weeks that followed. He endured London; he never enjoyed it. But presently he began to study it, his keen mind missing little that he saw. After all, knowledge was power, and it was only sense to study the enemy's capital. It would give him a background for his writing, too, and Lauchlin as well, and they spent long hours writing, sketching, and discussing.

"The daft styles of them!" sneered Ronald after a morning in the fashionable shopping centers, where ladies who all tried to look like Queen Marie Antoinette of France crowded enormous hoops and headdresses into town carriages or sedan chairs, and where men dressed like King Louis bowed their bewigged heads or strutted around on high red heels—all attended, of course, by supercilious servants.

But Lauchlin looked thoughtful, as she observed the difference between the fine gowns and her old wool dress, carefully mended by old Morag.

"So you don't think much of the *ton*, do you?" Cousin Matthew asked Ronald. "Tomorrow I'll show you a different London."

And he did. Here was the black filthy poverty, the grinding hunger, the hoarse whines of beggars, the furtive, greedy glances at Cousin Matthew's emerald ring and gold-headed walking stick, and pinched faces, the feeble wails of sick babies. . . . Here, surely, was Hell.

The first time she saw a chimney sweep Lauchlin burst into anguished tears, which dismayed her cousin and deeply mortified her brother. A Scot to shed tears before the Sassenach! Och, the shame! He turned a disapproving back while Cousin Matthew tried to comfort her.

"He's so *wee*!" She tried to shut out the sight of the miserable wizened child, with huge eyes of dumb misery in an old man's face. "He's no older than Lorne! Oh, 'tis cruel and monstrous! Can't we stop it? Can't we save him? We could take him home—"

"Honey, there's nothing we can do!" He was greatly upset, not having meant to distress her so deeply. "There are hundreds like him—and this one's gone." For the scowling master had hustled his boy off into the crowd.

Lauchlin raised a tearful face, set in a look of hate. " 'Tis very devils the Sassenach are! I've thought so all along!"

Cousin Matthew began leading them back toward the respectable part of town. "We'll go have a nice dish of tea," he soothed. "I couldn't take you any further into that section, anyway; not safe. And we must be fair, honey. What we've seen is bad—but the Continent is even worse, especially France. The poor here live in paradise compared with some of *them*." He considered this, while Lauchlin looked incredulous. "If *anyone* should rise in rebellion, the French should," he decided. "We Colonials are the best off of anyone, if it comes to that. . . . If you don't count our slaves, bond servants, and Red Indians, of course," he added a trifle too blandly. "But then most folks figure they aren't quite human, anyhow. Any more than chimney sweeps."

Ronald had been ready to accept that last bit as probable. So might even the warm-hearted Launchlin—until Cousin Matthew brought in the chimney sweep. She rounded on him in a passion of indignation.

"How dare they! How dare they treat people as if they were animals? 'Tis a sin! *Everyone's* human!"

"Even the Sassenach?" He looked mildly surprised.

Conversation languished.

Ronald, who preferred ideas to people, liked best their visits to places smelling of printer's ink, where thoughts were put on paper. His own, soon— They visited known publishers, and lesser ones, and others of a still more retiring disposition, who worked in the modest secrecy of unknown cellars.

It was with one of these latter that Cousin Matthew finally did business, and out of long conferences and much shrewd haggling, the infant *Gadfly* began to be born.

Unlike any newspaper ever heard of, it was to feature an astounding new feature: illustrations! This would add to the expense of printing, to be sure, but Cousin Matthew didn't care about making money, only stinging minds. So the *Gadfly* with illustrations would cost no more than others of these luxury items, without. They were all costly, in any case, so that people often clubbed together and subscribed jointly, and always passed copies from hand to hand, just as had been done with the late lamented *Skye Gadfly*.

"They'll lap up the drawings," predicted Mr. Fisher, the new and enthusiastic editor, grinning at one of Lauchlin's masterpieces. "Take her where she can see our splendid fat Prince of Wales and some of the rest of the Royal Family, Mr. Lennox. We could slip one of those in now and then, and keep them as a backlog in case mail from Virginia is delayed. Talented pair you've got there, sir." He mused over some of Ronald's work on life in Scotland under the Act of Proscription. "Strong stuff here. Be a shock to most people. I never dreamed things were like that, myself. And you have a good feel for words, Master MacLeod. You use one where most people would waste two or three. You should try to be more objective, though." He frowned at the second page.

"Ronald's maybe just a *mite* one-sided in his views," Cousin Matthew conceded, casting an amused eye at the page in question. "D'you really reckon *all* Englishmen to be devils?" he asked Ronald.

Ronald gave Mr. Fisher a sheepish grin and conceded grudgingly that perhaps there might be one or two, just, that were not.

"You'll find a few more in Virginia," Cousin Matthew promised. "Mind you two send me plenty of material. I'll count on you for up-to-date news." He pondered. "Hope the *Jennifer* won't show up before you've prepared me a nice backlog to cover your trip and any delays or losses —or interceptions—"

Ronald, accustomed to mail-searching, just nodded, unsurprised. "We can send duplicates of anything important —but mind your safety, sir. If they should be tracing you by the address. . . ."

"Don't worry, I've thought of that." The old man looked

cocky. "You'll address everything to one Socrates Raven, and send it to a highly respected Tory merchant I know here in London. Splendid chap. He'll slip them into my purchases, when I shop there, or Mr. Fisher's, or perhaps cousin Sarah—" He looked reflective. "And if anyone should come asking, he'll have a perfectly innocent story about a tall swarthy Mr. Raven who hasn't showed up lately."

"Well, and that the best you can do—" conceded Ronald, frowning. He had a feeling that should the Sassenach get that far, they might not easily be satisfied with such a story . . .

On the day the first issue came out, Cousin Matthew decided to take them all out celebrating—and then awoke for the first time to the deplorable fact that they had no clothes suitable either to fashionable London or Virginia.

"Bless my buttons!" he cried, deeply chagrined. "I've been letting you go around like that, never noticing!"

Ronald stiffened and Lauchlin flushed with offended pride—which he quite failed to notice. "Wait for me right here," he ordered. "You can be getting in a bit more work —and I'll be back presently."

He returned in an hour with a plump lady dressed in the height of fashion. Her heavily embroidered gown of cherry brocade draped over a wide hoop, with short panniers looped high toward the back, and a low square neck and a mile or so of rich lace. Her powdered hair was piled so high, with such an elaborate arrangement of curls, bows, rolls, ribbons, feathers, jewels, and a frothy tulle cap on top of it all, that both pairs of eyes fixed themselves to it in fascination. She had a dainty fan, which she flourished artfully, two chins, and a pair of bright eyes that quite belied the rest of her appearance.

"This is a distant cousin, Sarah Lennox," said Cousin Matthew. "She knows we're up to mischief, but not what it is."

"But he usually tells me in the end," she informed them, twinkling. "He's an incorrigible old man, in new mischief every time he visits London. You want to be careful of him."

Lauchlin grinned, liking her at once despite the headdress. "Fine we know it," she agreed gravely. "And we not needing help getting into trouble, ourselves."

Cousin Sarah chuckled richly, both chins sharing the joke. "Lennox blood without a doubt!" she said. "Look, Matt, you can even see it in the shape of her eyes, the way they tip upward a trifle. That runs in the family," she told them. "The old Lennox house—Silverstone—has a whole gallery of ancestors, and you can see those eyes over and over, in every color, on Valeries and Cecilys and Roberts and a dozen more."

"Goes back to Ravens and Leighs and Alleyns," Cousin Matthew added, unable to resist showing off his knowledge of the family tree. "Never mind that now. We're going to outfit these two for London and Virginia."

Ronald and Lauchlin had reached an understanding. "But we'll pay for everything ourselves, and get no more than we can afford," said Ronald firmly. "Father gave us some money."

Cousin Matthew was genuinely disappointed. "Don't be selfish!" he pleaded. "Spoil my fun like that! And after all I've done for you, too," he added cunningly, quite ruining Ronald's best argument.

They looked obdurate. Pride was pride.

"I haven't given you Christmas gifts yet," he discovered. "Need to make up for us spending Christmas in a stagecoach inn in Buckinghamshire. Besides, we can call it payment for your work on the *Gadfly*."

Eventually they compromised, and Ronald never did suspect that the bills gravely presented to him by the most exclusive tailors and mantua makers in Bond Street hardly covered the cost of the trimmings.

After that they saw a good deal of Cousin Sarah, who seemed to find them far more interesting than the usual social life of a rich widow. "Have you read this new paper everyone's talking about?" she asked one day over a dish of tea in their private sitting room. "They say it's seditious but amusing. I'm dying to see it!"

With the grin of a naughty imp, Cousin Matthew produced a copy from a table drawer, and Cousin Sarah let her tea grow cold while she read and chuckled and exclaimed. "La! It suits your opinions so well you might have written it yourself," she decided, trying to look shocked and disapproving. "And you, young cousins? Are you all for the rights of man, and freedom of the individual, too?"

They nodded, but rather vaguely. "We're against England, whatever," Ronald explained, being specific.

Cousin Matthew chuckled. "In the Highlands," he explained to their bemused guest, "it's all the same thing. These two haven't got around yet to noticing that there are any English but Redcoats, or any rights but the right to wear tartan and play the bagpipes. I'm aiming to widen their horizons a mite."

Cousin Sarah laughed, glanced again at the *Gadfly*. "La, I've no doubt you're all secret Jacobites—and not so very secret, at that—plotting to overthrow the government or start another civil war or something. You ought to let me help."

There were no servants in the sitting room, mercifully. Even so, Cousin Matthew glanced anxiously at the door, and Ronald went and opened it to be sure no one was in the corridor. Cousin Sarah's bright eyes widened.

"Why, I do believe I hit near the mark!" she exclaimed. "How mean of you to keep it from me! I vow, Cousin, you should know by now you can trust me!"

Cousin Matthew looked at her ruefully, and then at Ronald and Lauchlin. "Can, too," he agreed. "But you're much too respectable a lady to be mixed up in my shady doings, Sarah. Besides, you're a good royalist."

She shrugged. "Have you seen 'Prinny' lately, Matt? Our next king grows fatter, greedier, more immoral, and more wildly extravagant by the day. Not that it makes any great difference who rules, I suppose—" She pondered the way of the world briefly. "One king or another . . ."

"It may make a sight of difference should one of them drive the Colonies to rebellion," Cousin Matthew pointed out rather pithily, putting a restraining hand each on Ronald and Lauchlin, who were hotly resenting the notion that a Stewart was no better than a Hanoverian.

"La! Do you think it might come to that?" Cousin Sarah looked keenly interested, and not nearly as frivolous as she had first seemed. "I thought you said Colonists just wanted the tea duty removed so they could get on with their free trade and smuggling and all."

"Mostly—so far," he agreed. "But one thing leads to another. And there's strong feeling about that tea tax!"

"So I should think!" Cousin Sarah looked thoughtful. "This Boston Tea Party, now—"

"Boston Tea Party?" They all looked blank, and Lauchlin giggled at the silly sound of it.

"Must be a mistake," said Cousin Matthew quite decidedly. "Folks are boycotting tea all over the Colonies. Even my loyal Tory sister won't drink it. There's even talk of refusing to let ships unload it at all."

"That would explain it, then. Haven't you heard the story?" Cousin Sarah plied her fan briskly, paused just long enough to glance at Lauchlin. "Use your fan, dear; that's why I bought it for you."

"But I'm already too cold," Lauchlin protested, shifting a little out of the draft and nearer the fire. "I don't need to cool off."

"La, that's the merest incidental. You use it to express—"

"Sarah!" yapped Cousin Matthew, goaded. "What happened in Boston?"

"Oh yes. Why the news just arrived, and London is furious over it. Seems an East India Company ship—the *Dartmouth*, I think—arrived in Boston Harbor with a load of tea, and there was a tremendous row over whether it would be allowed to unload. They say two other ships at New York and Philadelphia were sent back still loaded, but in Boston some officials wouldn't allow the *Dartmouth* to leave without unloading, either. And it all ended up with some men calling themselves 'Children of Freedom' or some such thing—"

"Sons of Liberty," corrected Cousin Matthew, eyes

sparkling. "Sam Adams and his friends. Go on! What happened?"

"They dressed up as Red Indians and forced their way on board one night and flung all the tea overboard," said Cousin Sarah.

Cousin Matthew whooped. Ronald grinned widely. Lauchlin gurgled aloud, visualizing her next sketch, of a furious captain looking just like Captain Green, watching his tea sink. Haggis awoke from his place on the softest cushion, screamed what sounded like strong approval, and shut his eyes again. Cousin Sarah looked at them all. She sighed.

"La, *four* rebels!" she observed with an air of eager martyrdom. "You *are* going to let me in on whatever wickedness you're up to, aren't you?"

Three of the conspirators looked at one another, the fourth having gone back to sleep. "Och, aye," urged Lauchlin. " 'Tis herself would be a bonnie rebel, just, and yourself wanting her company once we're away to Virginia."

Eight

THE YORKTOWN DOCK

"Suppose they don't want us!" worried Ronald for the hundredth time, planting his elbows on the ship's rail and staring at that faint haze of land stretching ahead. "Suppose they wrote back saying for us not to come, or never got Cousin Matthew's letters at all? Suppose they refuse us or send us back! After all, they *are* Sassenachs, even if they're kin."

Lauchlin leaned beside him, dreamy and contented, the wind blowing warm and fresh from behind to tug her bright hair forward and belly the big sails above. It had been a wonderful trip, even the storm, when she and Ronald and Haggis spent a whole night in their cabin clinging for dear life as the ship pitched enormously. The mate had come in to bring reassurance, only to find two of them giggling at the acrobatics of the third, who was screaming for a lifeboat.

As for Haggis, he alternated between the roles of impressed seaman (with piteous moans) and ship's master, when he prowled up and down the deck making sour comments on the activities of the sailors. Just now he curled on a sunny corner of the deck, graciously permitting the caresses of one of the girls going out to be a bond servant for seven years, both of them enjoying an April sun already as warm as summer.

Lauchlin turned her own tanned face upward, grateful that she was the non-freckling type of redhead. She stretched out tanned forearms as well, and could have purred, herself. Why must Ronald raise worrying questions that properly belonged to the future? Tomorrow or next week they must face all the uncertainties and problems that doubtless waited in Williamsburg, but why sully the golden present with them? Now was to be enjoyed.

She turned her ruddy head sideways, pushed the tugging hair back, regarded her brother through lazy slitted eyes.

"Och, do not be tying a knot in your tail, whatever,"

she murmured, translating one of Cousin Matthew's remarks into the Gaelic. "Besides, he wrote two letters, did he not, in case one was delayed or lost?"

"Aye, and there's another thing worries me!" returned Ronald, determined to borrow trouble. "He had that wicked look in his eye whilst writing them, and chuckling all the time. And he wouldn't let me read them, either. 'Tis myself would feel better if I knew what he wrote, just."

" 'Tis yourself might feel worse, surely," Lauchlin pointed out realistically, but refused to disturb herself about it. Instead she stared down at the curl of sea below, and willed time to slow down.

Perversely, it speeded up. Land grew ever nearer, lush and incredibly green, and then the width of Chesapeake Bay, and then the banks of the York river, with alien trees and shrubs, and new strange smells, and fields here and there of what Captain Duff informed them was tobacco. And then, much too soon, they were actually docked at Yorktown and the future was upon them.

"You two just stand up here by the forward rail, out of the way," Captain Duff paused to tell them. "Mr. Treanor will be here for you presently, I reckon; and you can watch us unload until then. And keep that cat of yours in his basket, or he'll get squashed, sure!"

"Yaaah!" said Haggis insultingly from within the fine new basket Cousin Sarah had bought for him.

"Shocking manners he has," observed the captain indulgently, and went on about his busy day.

They obeyed his suggestion, wondering fitfully if they were dressed all right. Lauchlin's striped chintz was in rather deplorable condition due to more than five weeks at sea with no maid, no pressing iron, and very tight packing—but then nothing else she possessed looked any better. And although she had made a valiant attempt to scoop her red curls fashionably high on her head, they had instantly slithered sideways, giving her a faintly tipsy look, drooping slightly lower every time she moved. It wasn't her fault her hair was so fine, she told the critical Ronald crossly, and let himself be fixing it properly, then!

Ronald declined the invitation. His own black hair was tied neatly in back, but his jabot and ruffles were distinctly crushed, and so was the kilt which he had defiantly put on for the occasion. What with one thing and another, the two of them didn't look much better than the steerage passengers, those tired and shabby immigrants and indentured servants who stood on the lower deck looking helpless and bewildered.

Lauchlin regarded them with kinship and apartness at once. She shared their sense of bewilderment at being torn from their roots and exiled to a strange and possibly menacing new world. She could imagine the added terror of being transported by law, and sold as bond slaves. But those below didn't have the unassailable pride of Highland heritage to sustain them, and Lauchlin felt the difference without understanding it. Then she forgot them and lost herself watching the growing activity on the docks.

It was a cheerful bustle down there in the April sunshine. Slow-moving Negro longshoremen threw ropes to one another and passed boxes and trunks along from hand to hand in a chain, while overseers shouted orders. Sailors with tanned faces and far-seeing narrowed eyes laughed and called lurid oaths to each other. Captain Duff strode around, apparently able to be everywhere and see everything at once. Merchants in tricorne hats stood checking goods and talking to gentlemen in fine broadcloth or nankeen or taffeta coats, and more people were arriving on the dock every minute.

A group of young people caught Lauchlin's eye. She nudged Ronald, and they both stared with interest, for these were clearly of Cousin Matthew's social class, the sprigs of Virginia aristocracy, and therefore the sort that they themselves might soon expect to meet. Two pairs of critical eyes under identical level brows fixed themselves unblinkingly upon the sprigs.

They were all perhaps fifteen or sixteen years old, led by a tall, fair-haired boy with extreme good looks and an air of quiet assurance. There was a wide-shouldered lad with a funny face, all freckles and teeth and outrageous eyelashes that any girl would envy. And there was a stout red-cheeked boy with twinkling eyes; and a tall, pretty girl with brown curls; and a short one with a round dimpled face, enormous violet-blue eyes, and a pile of wheat-gold hair. The girls carried sunshades, and all of them wore a most astonishing air of serene superiority.

"*Mise-an-dhui*!" breathed Lauchlin, astounded. "They are bearing themselves as though they were Highlanders, just!"

Her clear contralto voice, with its lilting Gaelic vowels, carried easily to the group, who stood on the dock not too far from the *Jennifer*. They looked up curiously, staring at Lauchlin and Ronald as they might have stared at a couple of horses or slaves up for sale.

Ronald stiffened, and his grey eyes met the violet-blue ones of the fair girl. Hostility flashed between them. The girl drew back, offended, and turned to the stout boy.

"What *is* that barbarian language those immigrants are speaking, George?" she inquired in a sweet high voice that was probably meant to reach the ship rail.

The good-natured face glanced up, hardened briefly with the casual contempt due to obvious inferiors who failed to know their place, and smiled again as it turned back to fair-hair. "I reckon it could be Scotch," he drawled. "Some of our rebel bond slaves speak it. Father says the whole breed of them are traitors by nature, a lot of no-count trash overrunning Virginia—and trying to run it, too."

Only Ronald's rigidity and the increased pink of Lauchlin's cheeks showed that the black anger was upon him and the wee devil within her. Ronald looked down upon the group below as if they were some new sort of large insect, and quite probably nasty. As for Lauchlin, she had her own weapons. She gave a loud gurgle of astonished laughter. She spoke clearly in English.

"Och, listen, Ronald! The funny fat laddie sounds almost as if he thought himself as good as we!"

Ronald treated the funny fat laddie to a look of fastidious distaste. "And what would you expect from a Sassenach Colonial boor? They'll be a savage and illiterate lot altogether, and too stupid to know it, just."

The fair girl flushed crimson and the fat boy paled with rage, causing his ruddy face to take on an odd suety look, which Lauchlin commented upon instantly, gleefully, and loudly. The tall boy, who had been discussing a horse with the other boy and girl, took sudden note of what was going on. He looked embarrassed. "Really, George!" he said in a low voice. "One doesn't argue with— Oh, come on, do!"

But George found his tongue and took a massive step forward. "Look here, fellow," he said curtly, his good-natured face gone hard and pebble-eyed. "You be careful of how you speak to your betters!"

Presumably this reminder of class was intended to quell the upstart immigrants. Instead, it produced another peal of laughter from Lauchlin.

"Be careful, Ronald, of how you're speaking to your betters," she mimicked in a voice so like George's that the funny-faced boy forgot which side he was on and chuckled appreciatively.

Ronald looked George over, not at all admiringly. "Och, I will so," he agreed reasonably, "if ever I find any. I have it in my mind 'twill not be here." And he pointedly turned his attention to something else.

The group on the dock recovered self-possession, turned indifferent backs, and pretended Ronald and Lauchlin didn't exist. An interested audience of dock workers looked sorry the show was over.

"That's right, young sir!" called a grinning sailor to Ronald. "Let they young Tidewater peacocks know they ain't the lords of creation, after all." And a derisive chuckle rippled along the dock, causing Lauchlin and Ronald to feel the battle well and truly won.

They reckoned without Lauchlin's luck. She never knew how she managed to loosen the clasp of the traveling basket, but there was a sudden movement, a flash of black and white, a triumphant yell that he was free at last, and Haggis sprang lightly to the dock. Here he instantly turned into a Tidewater Aristocrat and began picking a complacent path among people and bales and horses.

"*Ochon,* Haggis!" bleated Lauchlin. "Oh, catch him,

somebody!" And before Ronald quite realized what was happening, she had dashed from the rail, scurried down the narrow and wobbling gangplank, narrowly missed decapitation by three startled longshoremen and a flying rope, and burrowed into the crowd after the kitten. Haggis at once stopped sauntering and became an escaped slave.

"Oh, catch him!" Lauchlin wailed again. She tried to dive between two fashionable hoops, stuck, tugged, tripped, and fell sprawling to her knees, with Haggis quite out of sight.

And then a strong hand hauled her to her feet again, its mate presented her with an infuriated Haggis, held by the scruff of the neck, and behind Haggis was a wide white grin in a freckled face.

"Yours, I believe, Mistress Firetop?" it murmured urbanely, and vanished briefly in a deep bow that was mocking in its courtliness.

Lauchlin gulped, suddenly and acutely conscious that she had behaved like a hoyden, that her hair had now fallen down completely and hung over her face and down her back, and that everyone was staring and those young snobs now able to look down their noses well and truly.

She flushed, torn between tears and a kind of despairing laughter.

"Och, I will be forever disgracing my family!" she mourned, taking possession of the swearing Haggis and dropping a deep curtsy which just did manage not to collapse in the middle. "Thank you," she added, pointed chin firmly up, while a mortified Ronald strode down the dock, kilt swinging, carrying the basket and wearing an air of wishing he had never met her and never would. Lauchlin wished so, too. Ronald's anger was a black, brooding, silent affair that usually lasted for hours.

He arrived beside her. He thanked the boy with the freckled face with cold courtesy, very much resenting the way those bright eyes stared at his sister's mane of gleaming bronze, hanging well below her waist like a gypsy's. He put Haggis back in the basket without affection. "Come away back and fix your hair, Sister," he said with great restraint, and led the way back to the ship.

It would have comforted them both very much to know that their retreat was one of imperial majesty that was quite stunningly effective.

Two hours later they still stood at the rail, drooping, dispirited, and very much worried. Ronald was still smouldering, and Haggis lamented tirelessly, and Lauchlin felt utterly forlorn and homesick.

And then Captain Duff appeared, smiling, with a tall, aristocratic man in a club wig and coat and breeches of the finest claret-colored broadcloth.

"Here's Mr. Treanor come for you at last," he said. "He thought you was some sort of package. This is what Mr. Lennox sent you, Sir; no mistake. Oh, and here's a packet of mail for you, too. It's been a pleasure having these young folk aboard, and I hope to be the one that takes them back some day." And he was off to speak to his bos'n with no further civilities.

Mr. Treanor was staring at them with a distinctly bemused expression that caused Lauchlin and Ronald to glance at each other uneasily. "Good gad!" he said faintly at last. "How like Uncle Matthew! How *very* like him!"

"I knew it!" said Ronald instantly and pessimistically. "You didn't expect us! I *knew* he was up to something when he wrote those letters!"

"I see you know my uncle well." Wryly amused blue eyes looked down—but not very far—into Ronald's. "He wrote for me to meet this boat without fail, because he was sending two very precious packages for Mother and me to keep until he came or sent for them."

"*Mo thruigh*!" said Ronald simply. Lauchlin's lip trembled.

"He said something about a third, smaller package—?" Mr. Treanor added inquiringly. Lauchlin pointed a despondent hand to the basket, which at once began to proclaim the evils of imprisonment.

"Oh!" said Mr. Treanor, startled. He looked at Haggis. He looked again at Ronald and Lauchlin. Suddenly he began to laugh.

Lauchlin, slightly heartened by this, stole a glance at Ronald, who was on his dignity, a proud Highlander to the core.

"I'm sorry!" said Mr. Treanor. "Do forgive me! But—Can't you see the funny side?"

If he could, Lauchlin certainly could! She at once began to laugh too, partly with relief. Ronald finally gave a reluctant chuckle, and suddenly there was a comfortable sense of all having shared a joke on themselves. Things were going to be all right, then.

"Well, let's have your boxes loaded on the carriage," said Mr. Treanor briskly. "A good thing I brought it down, not having any idea what size these precious packages might be. . . ." He shook his head, probably wishing for five minutes' private conversation with his deplorable uncle. "I'm still quite in the dark, you know, but I see he's sent another letter by this ship. Shall I read it first, or do you want to tell me about everything yourselves?"

"Best you read the letter at once," suggested Lauchlin anxiously. "And then if you're wanting to send us back. . . ."

"I won't do that, I promise!" He looked at her with kindness and sympathy. "You poor children, how you must have worried! Never mind, you're safe and welcome at Woodlea. Let's have those boxes loaded and start back at once."

"Well well!" said Mr. Treanor at length while the carriage rattled its springless way along the Yorktown-Williamsburg road. They had been altogether candid about everything except the *Gadfly*, which was Cousin Matthew's secret, and one he had asked them not to tell.

"He is staying in London, or perhaps traveling some more," Ronald explained, his sulks vanished and the prepared story easy upon his tongue. "But he's given us the name and address of a kinsman, Mr. Raven, and a great pile of paper, and he will be wishing us to send him great fat letters and stacks of sketches every week, with all the news. He said you'd not be minding, and that you'd send them off for us. . . ." He turned anxious grey eyes upon Cousin Nathaniel, as they were now to call him.

"To be sure," he smiled. "But I hope you don't think to find us all Jacobites here, young man. We're loyal Englishmen, you, know, and Uncle Matthew no less than any of us. It's just that he believes true loyalty consists in criticizing your country for its own good whenever you think it needs it."

"Oh—?" murmured his new cousins, faintly baffled.

They passed another grove of pine trees, and then a scatter of houses. Cousin Nathaniel leaned forward to speak to the driver. "Go right around past the Palace and College, Aaron, and back down Duke of Gloucester to England Street." He turned to his passengers. "I know you'll want to rest and freshen up, but this will take only a few minutes, and give you an impression of our town of Williamsburg."

Deeply interested, his guests peered out the windows; at the large Capitol Building on their right, where the House of Burgesses met, at the comfortable brick or white frame houses in the midst of green lawns and bright gardens, at the brick buildings of William and Mary College, marking the far end of town.

"Duke of Gloucester Street runs right through town from the College to the Capitol—just a mile from end to end," said Cousin Nathaniel, as they turned back down it. "There to the left presently you can see Governor's Palace, and there's the Courthouse ahead, and just beyond is the newspaper office—*The Virginia Gazette*—and beyond that is the Raleigh Tavern, where more politics gets discussed than in the Capitol. It's conveniently close, too," he added with a twinkle that reminded Lauchlin suddenly of Cousin Matthew.

"There's the Powder Magazine—in case of Indian attack or slave rising, but no one takes these dangers seriously any more. We're on England Street now," he added, as they passed the Powder Magazine and then made a jog to the left. "Here we are. That's the Randolph mansion at the end of the street, and here's Woodlea just this side of it. By the way, shall we have Aaron take your Haggis around to the back for the present? They can feed him out in the kitchen house—and anyway, it might be more tactful not to produce him quite yet. He and our cat Lady Seraphina might not take kindly to each other at first. Not that I think Lady Seraphina would actually descend to a cat-fight, mind; she's much too dignified."

"Haggis would," said Lauchlin positively.

The carriage drew up outside a neat box hedge and picket gate. Inside were wide green lawns, fragrant flower beds, mulberry and magnolia trees with a blue-grey bird singing in one of them, and a long, gracious white-painted house behind. It was astonishing for people accustomed to the gray stone of Skye or the brick or wattle-and-daub or half-timbered houses of England. There was, surely, much to be said for this kind of architecture. Wide wings north and south, and a deep cool veranda looked eastward across the front lawn.

"Sheltered from the afternoon sun, you see," commented Cousin Nathaniel casually. Lauchlin and Ronald blinked. At home, one built to get every possible *bit* of sun!

"Uncle did tell you about the family, didn't he?" asked Cousin Nathaniel as the slave opened the carriage door. "I've one daughter, Carilla, you know. My wife and father both died in an epidemic when she was two, so Mother has been running Woodlea and raising Carilla ever since."

Ronald and Lauchlin looked at him a trifle apprehensively. This would be Cousin Matthew's formidable sister Lavinia, and a terrifying sort of woman she sounded, too.

"Wonder what she'll say?" her son mused, getting out of the carriage.

So did Lauchlin. She braced herself as he led the way

through the gate and up to the front door, which a smiling liveried servant opened without a trace of surprise. She could feel Ronald tense behind her.

They were in a wide entry hall, with cream-and-green papered walls, green carpets, and comfortable cushioned settees along two walls. Straight ahead were tall French doors with slatted venetian blinds. A broad staircase rose to a landing where stood a tall gleaming mahogany clock. To right and left were paneled doors, painted white like most of the other woodwork, and through one of these there came a crystal voice.

"Is that you, Nathaniel my dear?"

"Brace yourself, Mother." Cousin Nathaniel led the way into a lovely drawing room, where a fragile and tiny old lady sat at an embroidery frame; a delicate porcelain old lady, all silk and lavender, with silver hair and velvet pink cheeks. Lauchlin, forgetting manners, stared. This could never be the redoubtable "Sister Lavinia"! Another of Cousin Matthew's jokes, surely?

She was looking at Lauchlin and Ronald now with an air of gentle waiting that would never be so ill-bred as to display curiosity. For some reason they suddenly felt themselves to be enormous awkward creatures, unkempt and filthy, belonging in a barn.

"These are our MacLeod cousins, Lauchlin and Ronald—the valuable packages Uncle Matthew sent." His eyes were filled with laughter. His mother's were not. They regarded the MacLeod cousins with clear blue outrage. Lauchlin's hand sought her brother's, which gripped hard.

"That's quite unforgivable of Matthew." The crystal voice crackled with anger. "He's disgraced our hospitality. Your rooms should have been prepared if we had known.

Please forgive us, my dears." And she picked up a silver bell and rang it, while Lauchlin and Ronald stood trying to recover their wits.

"Micah," she told the butler when he appeared, "have the east spare rooms made up fresh for Mistress Lauchlin and Master Ronald. Tell Cook we'll be two more at meals from now on, and you may serve coffee in here in an hour's time— Will that be long enough for you to bathe and change, my dears? Splendid. Send Rhoda and Jason to me at once, then, Micah."

Having finished that, she stretched out a slender wrinkled hand to each of them. "I'm so glad you could come, my dears. I hope you'll be very happy with us."

Surprises were not yet quite over. There was the novelty of being scrubbed and combed and dressed by skillful slaves who allowed no nonsense about wearing the kilt or the silver tissue dress Cousin Sarah had given Lauchlin as a going-away present.

"No, Master Ronald," said Jason firmly. "You'll wear the amber taffeta breeches and coat. They are being pressed now."

And in the next room—

"No, Missy!" said Rhoda firmly. "That's not proper for a young girl. You'll wear this pretty green silk and the ivory petticoat. Now hold still whilst I fix your hair, honey. It is the *beatenest* stuff!" And she shook her narrow, handsome head over the cobweb-fine masses that so stubbornly escaped from the pins.

"Ouch!" said Lauchlin, feeling crazily as if old Morag had suddenly appeared in a strange body. " 'Twill all just fall down again, whatever you do."

"Not when I've finished, it won't!" said Rhoda grimly.

Nor did it. When Lauchlin and Ronald appeared again in the drawing room, the bright curls were fixed in a charming cluster high at the back of her head, with two long gleaming ringlets hanging over her left shoulder.

The blinds in the western windows had been tilted upward to deflect the late sun, and a beautiful cat with long tortoiseshell fur and an air of calm royalty sat curled on a cushion near by. Cousin Nathaniel appeared in pale gray taffeta and fine Mechlin lace, Micah appeared with a silver tray, and an aura of civilized serenity filled the room.

"Where's Carilla?" asked her father, voicing Lauchlin's unspoken question. Even a very small girl would be interesting, and perhaps like Lorne. . . .

"Off riding with Melicent and Andrew." Mistress Treanor turned to Lauchlin and Ronald. "They're both cousins to Carilla, but Melicent's on the other side of the family, no relation to you. She lives next door, and Andrew around on Francis Street. Andrew's mother, my daughter Rose, is Nathaniel's sister. You'll all become splendid friends, I fancy."

Lauchlin looked hopeful, Ronald dubious. If they were anything like the sample on the Yorktown dock. . . .

"And what is the news from London, my dears?" Their hostess took a very small sip of coffee, with the air of one who would greatly prefer to drink tea, but for the principle of the thing. "Do they say anything about revoking this very ill-judged tea tax?"

"No, ma'am," said Ronald. "But when we sailed, Parliament had been called for March 31 to consider how to punish Boston for yon tea party in December."

Cousin Nathaniel looked startled, his mother serene. "And quite right, too. Samuel Adams is a shocking rabble-rouser. It seems to me, Nathaniel, that the New England Puritans are still fighting Cromwell's civil war, and trying to depose the monarch." And she bent an interested blue eye upon Ronald, who had suddenly choked. "I suppose you agree with them, my dear?"

"I'm a Highlander," blurted Ronald uncompromisingly.

"Indeed," she said kindly. "Never mind."

While Ronald was still deciding how to interpret that, there came a sound of voices outside the house, and a clear, high voice calling, and then light steps in the entry hall.

"Carilla!" called Cousin Nathaniel. "Come on in, honey, and meet the cousins your Uncle Matthew sent us."

"Cousins?" A short figure appeared in the doorway and stopped short. Violet-blue eyes stared aghast into dismayed dark and grey ones, but not a hair quivered on the golden head.

"I'm delighted to meet you, cousins," said Carilla sweetly, and advanced into the room.

Nine

CLAWS OUT!

Lauchlin awoke early the next morning, and lay quite still for a moment, trying to pretend she was still home, and that if she opened her eyes she would see the hills and braes and silvery water of the sea through the window. But it was no use. Her nose and ears knew better. This was no crisp and salty air from over the Minch, but warm and flower-scented. Instead of the sharp, plaintive cries of gull and whaup and curlew, there was a perfect clamor of other birds, all of whom seemed to be singing from the knobby-trunked tree outside her window.

"Kuh-yeek-uh, kuh-yeek-uh," said one, and another mimicked it, and a third seemed to be mocking the mocker. A wave of homesickness hit Lauchlin, turning her weak and empty for a moment. Then she pushed it back. She had found that she could keep it shut, for the most part, in a closet in her mind, and ignore it and go on and enjoy life. Sometimes it got out—but not as often as Ronald's did. Having disposed of the homesickness for the moment, Lauchlin opened eager eyes to the pretty periwinkle-papered bedroom, with blue hangings on the four-poster bed. Early sun, already deliciously warm, shone almost horizontally in at the window. Faint sounds from downstairs suggested that the slaves, at least, were up and busy. She lay staring upward for a minute, remembering last night. By tacit agreement the three young people pretended the meeting on the Yorktown dock had never happened; but this was no sign of accord or friendship, at all. It was merely self-preservation. And it seemed likely to be the only agreement they might ever have with their haughty cousin Carilla. Little girl, indeed! Lauchlin snorted and decided *not* to write and tell Cousin Matthew that his sense of time was at fault. With any luck, he might send a doll for Carilla's birthday. In fact, Lauchlin might encourage it, with a wee message, in one of Ronald's reports.

At the thought of Ronald, her eyes grew thoughtful.

Jumping out of bed, she threw a robe over her full nightgown and pattered next door to his bedroom, where she awoke her brother by the simple process of pulling back the bed hangings, losing her balance, and falling with her elbow dug into his side.

Ronald, who may not have been very soundly asleep after all, opened his eyes and grunted at her. Lauchlin grinned engagingly and sat down on the edge of his bed. "How do you think you'll be liking it here?"

Ronald's black brows leaped toward each other as the light of battle came into his eyes. "I'm thinking it may be interesting, just," he said with relish.

He was his most aggressive self, Highland pride sticking out truculently in all directions. Lauchlin prodded him a little. "These Virginia Sassenachs are thinking us Scots all wild barbarians, you know."

"Fine I've noticed," he agreed with a Satanic grin. "I have it in my mind that the most of them are needing to be taught a good bit about Highlanders." He looked extremely enthusiastic about the teaching. " 'Tis yourself will have to lesson Carilla, though, and she a lass and your own age." He sounded regretful.

"I'll draw insulting pictures of her, just," said Lauchlin. "I'll no be sending those to Cousin Matthew, though," she added, just faintly uncomfortable.

"We must be sending him some material back with the *Jennifer*," Ronald mused, wrapping his arms about his knees and wondering where to begin collecting information and impressions.

"The Treanors are *proud* of being English," observed Lauchlin, pained. "They even think Geordie a braw king. Did you hear last night they were saying 'twas just Parliament causing all the trouble with the Colonies?"

"Aye, I heard," said Ronald quite unnecessarily, since he had last night taken it upon himself to try to correct this mistaken idea and explain that the king was a wicked tyrant. This had not been received particularly well. Cousin Nathaniel had looked interested but doubtful, Mistress Treanor had turned to frozen honey, and Carilla had treated him to a look of perfectly blighting scorn. Ronald scowled to remember it, and longed to do something far more vigorous and aggressive and important than just being a journalist. " 'Twould be braw to stir up a wee bit rising ourselves," he mused wistfully.

"Och, 'tis ourselves could *never* do it alone," objected Lauchlin, the realist.

"We could maybe be wanting just one or two others," he conceded handsomely. "But we'll find them surely. There's Sam Adams, and that backwoodsman they were talking about last night—I can't mind the name. The one Herself was calling a wild radical and hothead and seditionist—"

"Patrick Henry," supplied Lauchlin. "And Cousin Nathaniel's friend Mr. Jefferson sounds a bonnie man, though perhaps a bit on the fence. But there'll be no Royal Stewarts here to lead a rising. And who could sit on the throne even if the Colonies did overthrow England?"

Ronald shrugged. "Och, well, they'd think of something, and it better than the German Geordies!"

Lauchlin bounced in agreement. At that, a small black whirlwind popped out from under the bed (where it should never have been, of course), leaped to the pillow, and reached out to take a furry swipe at Ronald's nose. Then it raced on up to the top of the bed canopy and clung there shrieking that it was Too High, and why were they just sitting there instead of coming to the rescue?

"Haggis!" chortled Lauchlin. Ronald stood up on the bed, his nightshirt flapping, and rescued the wailing kitten, who scratched him, swore that it was all his fault, and tore out of the room and downstairs, where a minute later they could hear him yelling to be let out.

"Och, he'll be feeling altogether at home now," Lauchlin declared gravely, while Ronald sucked his scratched hand. Their eyes laughed at each other as they remembered how earnestly they had pleaded to bring Haggis, on the grounds that the poor wee timid beastie was so fond of them that it would have been the greatest cruelty to leave him behind. He had, of course, been making liars of them ever since, showing no signs at all of affection and very few of timidity. So far, decided Lauchlin, his favorite roles were persecuted martyr and man-eating tiger. Last night he had been a martyr, hiding under the bed and whimpering dolefully. Now, clearly, he was pure tiger again, and off to explore his new jungle.

"And 'tis a braw idea, that," she decided, bouncing again. "I'm away outside to explore, myself."

"Best dress yourself first," advised her brother dryly, reaching for his own shirt.

Someone else was having an early stroll in the garden. Someone with thick guinea-gold curls tied high at the back of her head, and tumbling thickly down her back. Someone fresh and dainty in lilac silk.

They saw each other. They smiled sweetly. Carilla strolled over with the gracious air appropriate toward inferior people who must be kept gently in mind of their position.

"Good morning—er—Locklin," she said benignly.

Lauchlin laughed with the kindly indulgence due to

those unfortunate beings who lack breeding and culture. "Och, you Sassenachs all have such trouble with my name!" she cried " 'Tis not 'Locklin' at all: there's no 'K' sound but a 'KH' sound, like a soft cough. Do you not hear? Lauhkh-lin, the same as in 'och.' Try again."

Somehow Lauchlin was usurping Carilla's role. Moreover, Carilla was beginning to resent being called a Sassenach. She had a decided impression that the term was not altogether a complimentary one. Declining the lesson on pronunciation, she switched ground slightly.

"It's a *very* peculiar name, isn't it?" she pointed out. "The Scottish weaver in town has a son named Lachlan; isn't it a boy's name?"

"Oh, aye; Lachlan would be a lad's name," Lauchlin agreed, ignoring the implied slight. "But Lauchlin is a lassie's name. I know, for did not my mother invent it especially for me?" She looked distinctly smug. It was not everyone who had an original name.

"Really? How very—eccentric."

Before the outraged Lauchlin could lose her dignity and start calling names, a sudden screech made them both jump. Halfway up the mulberry tree a black and white kitten clung, hurling threats alternately at a mockingbird and Lady Seraphina. The mocking bird was yelling back, but Seraphina sat in the center of the lawn looking contemptuous. Her aristocratic tail twitched just a trifle, and then she looked pointedly in the other direction.

Haggis, infuriated at the affront, scrambled down the tree and rushed over to Lady Seraphina, shouting that he would carve her up and have her for breakfast, big as she was. Seraphina looked right through him. She had never yet admitted the existence of another cat, and she wasn't going to begin now. Haggis, dancing with rage, swatted Seraphina on the ear and then leaped back apprehensively.

"If that wild monster is yours," said Carilla indignantly, "you'd better keep it locked up! It isn't fit to be around civilized animals!"

"Are you feared my wee Scottish kitten will hurt your great fat Sassenach cat?" jeered Lauchlin.

Seraphina was still pretending Haggis didn't exist, and Haggis, encouraged, was clearly preparing another frontal attack. But before either girl could interfere, Lady Seraphina decided enough was enough. She rose to her feet and arched her back high in what might equally have been a threat or a bored stretch.

"Sssss," she remarked softly to no one in particular, and then turned on her heels and drifted off. The dignity of her exit was perhaps a trifle marred by the fact that the long fur on her hind legs looked ridiculously like full bloomers. Lauchlin shouted with mirth, but Seraphina—who had never seen herself from behind—was sublimely oblivious. And Haggis, thoroughly puzzled, peered after her, shouting once or twice for her to come back and fight like a man.

The girls looked at each other pugnaciously. It seemed up to them to carry on. " 'Tis a gey queer cat, yon," said Lauchlin, derisive.

"She's a *lady*." Carilla stared down her small straight nose at Lauchlin's unladylike tan.

"*Mo thruigh*!" Lauchlin looked deeply moved. "Is *that* what a lady is, in the Colonies?" she asked offensively.

"I reckon our cats are more ladylike than your girls, anyway."

"And was that view from behind your notion of a lady, just?"

They glared at each other with reluctant respect. Each had tested the other's mettle and found good defenses, strong artillery, plentiful ammunition, and superb marksmanship. It was clearly going to be a long war with no easy victory. A mutual strategic withdrawal was indicated, to plan the campaign.

"Are you having a pleasant conversation, my dears?"

The silver voice caused both armies to start guiltily, whirl around, and curtsy to the bluebell-clad figure on the veranda.

"Yes, Grandmother," said Carilla decorously, and her face confirmed Lauchlin's suspicion that they had best wear the mask of courtesy if they knew what was good for them.

"I'm glad to see you're such friends." The irony was unmistakable this time. "You'd best come in now and let Rhoda fix your hair before breakfast."

They nodded, curtsied again, and submitted to enforced and temporary truce. They went in together, arm in arm, gold and bronze heads touchingly close together—and whispering insults at each other before they were halfway up the stairs.

The war stayed underground throughout breakfast, and the three combatants were shatteringly polite to one another. Cousin Nathaniel sat at the bottom of the table eyeing the mail Micah had just brought in. Cousin Lavinia presided over the coffee urn, still giving the impression of a being composed of silver and velvet and fragile lace—with rather more solid silver than one might at first suppose, decided Lauchlin wryly, sipping creamy hot chocolate and eyeing the remarkable old lady over the rim of the cup. Nothing would ever shatter *her* poise: not runaway kittens or fallen-down hair, or hostile strangers on an alien shore—or having unknown kinfolk arrive without a moment's notice. One would have thought their visit the one thing she had most longed for all her life.

Lauchlin sighed a little. It would be grand, just, to have that kind of unshakable dignity.

And then a vision of rosebuds, brown curls, and dimples appeared in the doorway and froze, blinking in disbelief. "Awp!" it said.

"These are my cousins just arrived from Scotland, Melicent," said Carilla, putting a bold front on it, especially under Grandmother's eye.

"Mercy me!" said Melicent faintly, and then, with a lame excuse, bolted home to tell her mama and recover from the shock.

"I shall really have to speak to Harriet about Melicent's manners," Grandmother remarked severely. "Now I'm sure you'll like to get acquainted with Williamsburg, my dears, and Carilla will be happy to show you around. Mind you girls take your sunshades," she added, looking thoughtfully at Lauchlin's face, which had presumably never seen a sunshade. "You must learn to care for your complexion, my child. A milk white skin is very important to a young lady. Carilla will lend you one of hers."

The three of them had just got out on the veranda some five minutes later when three boys turned in at the gate.

It was the same three, of course; it had to be. Ronald looked at them with a kind of ferocious glee. He had once supposed that everyone, even the English, recognized the great superiority of the Highlander to any other being on earth. It had come as a great shock to realize that they did not, and he now felt it a sort of holy duty to enlighten them.

The boys stopped at the bottom of the stairs and stood staring upwards with varying expressions of blank incredulity. They weren't very quick at pulling themselves together, Carilla decided with morbid satisfaction, and clucked at them reprovingly. She had done *much* better last night.

It was Andrew who rallied first. He blinked at Lauchlin. "It's Mistress Firetop!" he discovered, pleased.

"You take that back, Sassenach!" demanded Ronald at once. He clenched his fists hopefully.

"Oh, it's a compliment," Andrew told him affably, sauntering up the stairs. "Fact is, as soon as I know what her name is besides Firetop I intend to ask her to marry me when she grows up."

"Och, I couldn't." Lauchlin looked at him gravely. "You're not a Scot."

"Now stop that, Andrew!" said Carilla rather crossly. And with really enviable aplomb, she introduced them all as if Yorktown had never been.

It never *had* been. This was understood at once. A most regrettable error due to a misunderstanding. They hadn't *looked* like gentry, protested George in good-natured chagrin, and if he had reservations about admitting even titled Scots to social equality, he stifled these for Carilla's sake. After all, one shouldn't be blamed for one's cousins.

The tall handsome boy, Edwin, first bowed over Lauchlin's hand with a gallantry that caused her to gurgle irrepressibly, and then held out a friendly hand to Ronald. Andrew drawled that he and Ronald had better get along, as they were destined to become brothers-in-law. Melicent, more or less over her shock, joined them breathlessly from next door. All was merriment and goodwill.

Only Ronald stifled a regretful sigh. He had been *so* in the mood for a good fight!

Ten

THE FINE DAY

"Disgraceful!" Mistress Treanor shook her frosted head over the hem Lauchlin had just put into one of the slaves' new dresses. "Quite impossible, my dear. Do it over at once. I should never ask our slaves to wear such slovenly workmanship."

Lauchlin, feeling the triumphant eyes of Carilla and Melicent without even looking, tossed her head just slightly. Cousin Lavinia saw it, of course.

"I do hope you'll be accepted into Mrs. Hallam's school," she added, implying clearly that the distressing nature of Lauchlin's needlework, manners, complexion, and singing voice made this highly doubtful. "Carilla, this seam is not quite as even as it might be. Melicent, at that rate you won't finish by next year. One day you girls will all have homes of your own, and you must learn to sew yourselves in order to supervise others."

Lauchlin resentfully began picking out stitches. Carilla flickered a jeering glance at her. Lauchlin just edged the tip of her tongue between her teeth. Cousin Lavinia saw that, too. Of course.

"Mind your manners, girls! Backs straight. Shoulders well back, and don't lean your head forward, Lauchlin, even when you sew, or I shall have you on the backboard for an extra hour. Carilla, keep your eyes on your work, young lady."

"Yes'm," said Carilla meekly. Lauchlin pressed rebellious lips together. If this was being a lady, she thought very poorly of it. Outside, a mockingbird sang in the delicious sunshine, and Haggis challenged him to mortal combat, and the radiant spring day was being wasted while she was submitted to tyranny by a silver hand in a lace mitt, as it were. She stole a glance at the tyrant, who was probably reading her mind this very minute. She sighed. In Carilla's grandmother, Lauchlin had met her match, and after one or two battles of the will, began to regard her with reluctant affection as well as admiration.

She sighed again, unresigned, and wildly impatient. And Ronald, lucky thing, was free to roam Williamsburg —and in his kilt, too, doubtless. True, he was to start at William and Mary College tomorrow, but right now he was probably either at the *Gazette* office or at the Raleigh, listening avidly to impassioned talk.

For the Assembly was to open in a few days, and burgesses were arriving early, and rumors from across the Atlantic were thick. It was said that Parliament was preparing to pass heavy punishment upon Boston for that little tea party. Even some English newspapers were moved to protest, and to hope that these "Coercive Acts" would not, after all, be passed.

Closer to home was the question of the wild lands of the Ohio. Everyone wanted them: Virginia, Massachusetts, New York, Connecticut, Quebec, and even the Indians, who kept insisting in a very narrow-minded way that it was *their* land both by possession and treaty, though no one took this claim at all seriously. And in the meantime, Virginia's Governor Dunmore kept giving huge chunks of it away to his friends, regardless of whether anyone had settled there or not.

Lauchlin sighed again, perceiving that politics here in the Colonies were a great deal more complicated than she and Ronald had supposed, and also feeling rather sorry for the Indians.

"Almost The Season again!" Melicent, who could be roused from her indolence by any thought of social life, sighed happily.

"What Season?" asked Lauchlin, curious.

"Why *The* Season. Public Times." Melicent looked scornful of such ignorance. "Every spring and fall when the burgesses meet, but especially spring. All the aristocracy and gentry come in from their plantations and open their town houses, and the streets are filled with fine coaches and there are lots of balls and things, and the theatre opens, and it's every bit as rich and gay and splendid as anything in London could be."

Lauchlin, forgetting her prejudice against anything English for the moment, indulged in a derisory snort, which Mistress Treanor chose to ignore. So did Melicent who had just remembered, belatedly, that Lauchlin had actually been to London, and had an unfair advantage. She shifted the subject slightly.

"Mother says perhaps I can make my debut next year,"

she bragged with a sidelong look at Carilla. She was ten months older than her cousin, and loved to rub it in. "Perhaps I'll even have a silver tissue gown, like Lauchlin's, only finer."

"I doubt it," said Carilla's grandmother equably. "For one thing, whatever Sarah Lennox thinks, it is not suitable for a young girl. For another, we get very few shipments of English goods these days, what with these ridiculous duties and taxes, and I doubt if your mother could find any silver tissue."

Melicent pouted briefly. "All this squabbling is so silly! The taxes can't be all that much. Why don't we just pay them and stop fussing with England?"

She received a sharp frown for this opinion. "My dear!" said Mistress Treanor, "It's not the amount, it's the principle. We are English citizens, and Parliament must be made to realize that we will not be deprived of English rights."

It was clear that Melicent did not at all see this, or even care. She sighed over the lack of silver tissue. "Well, then, are we going to have a war about it?"

"Heavens no!" said Mistress Treanor in a scandalized tone which settled *that* nonsense once and for all. "It is quite unnecessary for civilized people to resort to such unmannerly behavior over anything." (Lauchlin bristled.) "What an idea! War with our own people, indeed! You haven't been reading those radical pamphlets by that Sons of Liberty group, have you?"

"Mercy me, no!" Melicent looked horrified at the very notion of so much mental effort. "I just thought if we went on fussing this way, we might start fighting after a while."

Lauchlin thought this quite the most sensible thing

Melicent had ever said. She looked up, enthusiasm for the idea shining on her face. Cousin Lavinia gave her a quelling glance.

"Disagreements can always be worked out by peaceful means, given a little reason and good will on both sides," she said.

Lauchlin could hold her tongue no longer. "Aye, *both* sides," she said darkly.

Carilla unfairly used the reminder to make a point of her own. "Yes, and what about Lord Dunmore?" she asked her Grandmother. "It doesn't seem fair of England to send us a Governor who's a low-down, obstinate, cheating, drunken boor."

"*Carilla!*"

Carilla's white skin turned pink. "Well, that's what Father said; I heard him," she said defensively. "And he said Lord Dunmore looks *down* on us Colonials! Even," she added hotly, naming the really unforgivable offense last, "even us Tidewater Aristocrats!"

"That will do, my dear." The blue sparks in Mistress Treanor's eyes suggested that she would have something to say to her son later. As for Lauchlin, she studied Carilla with a deeply speculative expression—which materialized some few hours later in the form of a sketch.

It was a wicked sketch, showing a lady (strongly resembling Carilla) and gentleman of the Tidewater Aristocracy, innocuous at first glance. But the styles were subtly wrong, overdone, somehow suggesting boors trying to ape their betters. And the expressions were of such vacuous complacency that Carilla slowly became quite pale with fury as she studied it.

It was the only sign she gave that Lauchlin's shaft had

struck home. But presently she went up to her bedchamber and stayed quite half an hour, coming down at last with an unusually pleased expression.

When Lauchlin went to bed that night, it was to find a bit of deathless verse pinned to her pillow.

"The bonnie Young Pretender,
He had a thousand men.
He marched them down to Derby town,
And he marched them back again."

She stared unbelievingly for a moment. Och, it was most savagely cruel, to mock at the bitter tragedy of Bonnie Prince Charlie and the slaughter of Culloden Moor! All the blood spilled, and the hearts broken—

Heartbroken herself, Lauchlin marched into Carilla's room, boxed her ears, and marched out again, turning away quickly, so that the scalding tears wouldn't spill over in her enemy's sight. Then she sat despondently in her room, in the yellow flicker of candlelight and the warm night air, fighting against the conviction that she had brought this hurt on herself. She had used her art for malice—and it had come back with doubled venom.

As for Carilla, she sat for some time holding her stinging face and staring at the closed door. She *had* seen the tears, and been shocked. She hadn't known. She somehow hadn't thought of Lauchlin as someone vulnerable, who could be hurt. And she hadn't known that casual bit of doggerel could prove such a wounding missile, either. She almost wished it hadn't. Or that it had struck Ronald instead, whose air of scornful superiority galled and infuriated her.

Lauchlin was accepted at Mrs. Hallam's School for Young Ladies, despite her needlework, her outspoken radical opinions, and her unfortunate inability to carry a tune. (Carilla who had a true, sweet melodious voice seemed to be doing a *great* deal of unnecessary singing these last few days.)

On a brilliant morning, three demure young ladies walked down Francis Street to the place where they learned those things needful for young ladies. Music, dancing, drawing, needlework, deportment, and French conversation, Melicent told Lauchlin with a superior air.

Lauchlin, not missing the tone, glanced sideways at the brown and gold heads maintaining a definite apartness. In a way she was looking forward to school. It would be new and different for someone who had always been taught at home, with Ronald, by Father and Mother. Besides, there might be some girls with whom she could be friends. She was getting lonely, lately, with Ronald always busy collecting and writing his material, and at his own school.

"French conversation?" she repeated in mock awe. "Och, will ye not be straining your intellects that way?"

Melicent, missing the mockery, looked smug. "We'll help you with it," she promised graciously. "And we have a very good teacher, all the way from Charleston in South Carolina."

Lauchlin bit her lip.

At the corner of Francis Street, George and Andrew joined them, on the way to Edwin's, where they all shared a tutor.

"Morning, Mistress Firetop," said Andrew amiably. "You're not holding that sunshade right, you know. It's shading your shoulder, and the sun is full on your face."

"As ever was," agreed Lauchlin at once. "And no need to mention *everything* you see!"

Andrew looked delighted. "Will you marry me, Mistress Firetop?"

Lauchlin looked at him judiciously. She shook her head. "Too many freckles," she decided.

"Remind me to ask you again," he said, undaunted, and Carilla shot him rather an annoyed glance as the girls turned in at Mrs. Hallam's front walk. He was, she felt, carrying a joke rather too far.

The day began disastrously with singing. The teacher stopped them halfway through the first song and looked at Lauchlin with deep reproach.

"That is not amusing, Mistress MacLeod," she said coldly.

Mortified, Lauchlin didn't even try to explain that she couldn't help it. She stuck her pointed chin in the air and refused to sing at all after that.

Drawing was not really as successful as it should have been, either. Pretty watercolor paintings of flowers were simply not her strong point. She looked at the result with strong dissatisfaction, and then amused herself by giving every flower center an expression of bored disgust.

"Really, Mistress MacLeod!" said the drawing master, pained.

Mrs. Hallam herself took the dancing lesson, and here at last Lauchlin found recognition. "Why, you have perfect rhythm, my dear, and I have yet to see anyone more light-footed!" she exclaimed in a burst of praise quite rare for her.

Carilla, hitherto the unquestioned best dancer in the school, managed to produce what passed for an unselfish smile. After all, every girl in the class was looking at her to see how she'd take it.

Lauchlin, unaware of this, sparkled with pleasure. "Och, all Highlanders have wings on our feet," she explained. "You should see my brother do the Sword Dance —or me, for that matter," she added modestly.

Mrs. Hallam's approving smile dimmed a trifle. "I hardly think that sounds very ladylike, my dear. Surely females don't do it!"

" 'Tis a man's dance," Lauchlin admitted. "But now everyone knows and does it, in secret, you see, to keep it alive." She looked around at the puzzled faces. "All our dances are proscribed by law, you know," she reminded them. "Forbidden on pain of punishment. Surely you know that!"

But either they didn't know it, or it wasn't considered a fit subject for conversation. Even Mrs. Hallam's face closed against her, and the girls looked more inimical even than before.

"We'll confine ourselves to the lesson, Mistress MacLeod. Places, girls, for a reel. We'll begin with Sir Roger de Coverley."

The girls closed around her for the noon break, clearly hostile.

"Are you *really* from the Highlands? Is it true nobody wears shoes or proper clothes there? Is that your brother that goes around town in a wild kilt? Where did you get *those* clothes? How many people has your father killed? Are you really a Jacobite? Did they have to teach you table manners when you came? Is that your real hair? Who taught you to speak English?"

Lauchlin, who had never faced this sort of thing before,

quailed before it for a moment. Then she girded her loins for battle.

"We eat a Redcoat for breakfast every morning, just," she announced. "Or perhaps a Sassenach baby when we can get one. And then all dance barefoot over the sword to the pipes—and wait until you hear my brother play the pipes—and the battle-madness on us, and the long claymores in our hands!" She drew her brows together, made claws of her hands, moved forward menacingly. "*Tha la math ann an diugh*!" she spat.

The girls fled, squeaking in alarm, even Melicent. Only Carilla stood still, looking contemptuous and feeling uncomfortable. Lauchlin gave her one speaking glance, and then turned away, her nose very high indeed. Who wanted to be friends with a lot of silly, mean-minded, stupid Sassenach, anyway?

Enmity was thick in the air during Deportment and Needlework periods, as the young ladies silently gloated over Lauchlin's ineptitude, looking forward to her even greater humiliation when it came to French conversation.

Lauchlin looked forward to that last class, too. Not for nothing had her parents spent their long six-year exile in Paris! Their children spoke French as fluently as Gaelic and English. Lauchlin bided her time.

The French Master entered. He spoke. The class answered in chorus. He made a fairly lengthy remark, which Melicent answered haltingly. All eyes were turned to Lauchlin, hoping to see an expression of blank incomprehension.

They were not disappointed. Lauchlin stared unbelievingly at this dapper-faced, drawling young fop, who was turning now to give her a condescending smile. "Mademoiselle speaks no French, *n'est-ce pas*?"

It was too much. "But yes, I speak very good French indeed," she retorted in that tongue. "But you, I regret, Monsieur, do not."

Now it was everyone else who looked blank. With savage triumph, Lauchlin repeated her remark in English. "I do not know where you got that shocking accent, but there's no Frenchman at all would understand you," she added spitefully.

The girls looked scandalized. The French Master reddened. Lauchlin spent the rest of the hour in Mrs. Hallam's study, maintaining stubbornly that it was perfectly true, and she knew a Paris accent when she heard one. So did Mrs. Hallam, actually, and when Lauchlin had demonstrated her point, she didn't question it.

"But your manners, my dear!" she expostulated. "No lady would go out of her way to humiliate someone else."

Lauchlin reflected fiercely that everyone else had been going out of their way to humiliate *her* all day, but she couldn't say that, of course. She pressed her lips together tightly, forced the tears back from her eyelids, and met Mrs. Hallam's gaze unyieldingly.

Mrs. Hallam had very sharp eyes indeed, and a fairly accurate notion of what had been going on. She sighed. "Try to make some effort to get along with the others, Mistress MacLeod. You're going to find yourself very lonely if you don't."

Lauchlin started to say something, bit it back, and went on looking obdurate. What was there to say that wasn't whining and undignified?

"Very well. School is over for the day; you may go home now. I fancy Carilla and Melicent will be waiting for you."

Lauchlin doubted this, but didn't say so. She curtsied, left the room, walked through the hall and out the front door, where, as she expected, her enemies waited. No Highlander ever shrank from battle! She marched into their midst with a belligerent smile.

"My goodness, Carilla, we do feel sorry for you, having someone like that in your house."

Before Lauchlin could answer this remark which rose clearly, something happened that astonished no one more than Carilla Treanor. For Carilla found herself standing at Lauchlin's side, facing her tormentors furiously. How dare they? Lauchlin was her own private enemy, to be defended to the death against outsiders.

"How dare you! You are a low-down, sneaky, contemptible lot, aren't you? A lot of horrid little catbirds, pecking a swallow!"

They stared, quite taken aback. They rallied. "She's common trash," retorted one hardily, "and I'm not going to associate with her."

"I reckon *she* might not stoop to associate with *you*, Letty Stegg!" retorted Carilla. "*Your* grandfather was nothing but a common tradesman. And Lauchlin—" She remembered Great-Uncle Matthew's huge, detailed family tree and was inspired. "Lauchlin and I have Plantagenet blood!"

They looked daunted. Lauchlin recovered her wits, accepted the miracle, and made a contribution, Plantagenet blood was nothing to her.

"I've Royal Stewart blood, too," she said, not bothering

to mention the fact that many Highlanders could make the same claim.

They wilted further. Carilla finished the job. "What's more, her father's a noble lord."

They stared. Lauchlin looked startled. Carilla elaborated. "He has a title, hasn't he, Cousin?" And the huge, violet eyes looked commandingly at Lauchlin.

Lauchlin at once fell into the spirit of the thing. She adopted an air of quiet nobility, really rather above proclaiming itself, but willing to oblige a cousin. "Oh, aye," she agreed carelessly. "He is Kildornie, and Ronald after him."

The girls capitulated. "Oh," they sighed, humble. "You never told *me* that," accused Melicent, doubly aggrieved. Why had things been kept from her, and whatever possessed Carilla to change sides like that?

"It's supposed to be a secret," Carilla announced at once, with an eye to possible future consequences. "Lauchlin isn't the sort to go flashing titles around, but you all acted so downright rude—" She left the sentence hanging, and no one dared demand an account of her own behavior. "What's more," she added in a lowered voice and far more truthfully than she knew, "she and Ronald have political enemies."

"Oooh," breathed the girls, and Lauchlin's popularity was ensured.

She wanted none of it. Carilla had stood up for her against the pack; Carilla had needed no bullying or snob appeal; Carilla was her one true friend. They walked home together, arms entwined, hurling the most appalling insults at each other—to the complete mystification of Melicent, who didn't in the least understand the rules of this strange new game, and wasn't at all sure she wanted to. She stalked behind, a disgruntled swish of brown curls and primrose silk.

Lauchlin didn't even notice. She was racking her brain to think of something to do for Carilla. Something special. . . .

"I was noticing in class, 'tis yourself is no bad at dancing for a Sassenach. Would you maybe like to be learning the Sword Dance? Or—" She looked anxious. "Would it be too unladylike, just?"

Carilla looked delighted. "You can start teaching me this evening," she said promptly. "And," she added, just to keep things on an even keel, "maybe I can help you learn to carry a tune. You sound just like a seagull screeching."

"Mind," said Lauchlin at once, "I'm no so sure I should be teaching one of our fine Highland dances to a Sassenach clod-foot."

"Scottish savage!"

"Backwoods barbarian!"

They were both enjoying themselves hugely.

Melicent had a contribution. "Just wait," she said as they paused in front of her gate, "until Cousin Lavinia hears about you swearing at us this noon."

"Who, me?" Lauchlin produced a guileless face, and dancing eyes.

"Yes, you. When you cursed us in Gaelic." Melicent looked injured. Carilla stared at Lauchlin with hopeful curiosity. She had wondered, herself, about that awful sizzle in the alien tongue. But Lauchlin put on a face of holy innocence that would have done Haggis credit.

"Och," she explained virtuously, "I was only saying 'twas a fine day, just."

Eleven

BRAW WEE BATTLE

Ronald went for a full week to William and Mary College. Then he was requested to leave on the grounds that he was corrupting all the other boys with subversive ideas and talk of insurrection.

"Dear me," said Cousin Nathaniel mildly when he heard this, and regarded Ronald quizzically. "Is it true?"

"Aye so!" bragged Ronald, and looked to see if he had shocked and offended his host.

But Cousin Nathaniel failed to appear alarmed. He had, he said, no objection at all to exposing the young to subversive ideas.

Ronald looked rather deflated, and Cousin Nathaniel went on.

"After all, it's surely an important part of education, to meet all sorts of ideas, good and bad. And if your own beliefs won't stand up to a good stiff challenge, the sooner you find out, the better. And that," he added unfairly, "goes for you, too, my boy. You're quite as intolerant and one-sided in your views as John Randolph or any other extreme royalist. I'd like you to be exposed to some Tory ideas—and really listen to them and think about them as fairly as you can. I wonder, now—" He lapsed into deep thought and went presently to pay a few calls, he said, leaving Ronald vaguely uneasy.

The next thing Ronald knew, he found himself sharing

lessons and tutor with Edwin, George, and Andrew. He found it highly disconcerting. For one thing, he didn't want to be friends with a bunch of Tory Sassenachs. For another, he was rather shocked by the whole notion of liking a person whose beliefs you simply loathed. You couldn't, he told his sister angrily, be social friends and political enemies with the same person at the same time.

"Och, why not?" asked Lauchlin, busy with a sketch of Duke of Gloucester Street at the start of The Season.

Ronald glared at her. He had not missed the change in quality of her feud with Carilla, and he detested Carilla. "Well, how can you be loyal to both, just?"

Lauchlin drew an Indian striding majestically through the thick dust, with no one paying much attention. "Och, why not?" she repeated, and began to sketch a kilted Ronald striding even more arrogantly than the Indian, and one or two sunshaded ladies looking just faintly startled.

Ronald frowned. The trouble with Lauchlin was that she could never remember to hold a grudge, however justifiable. Let the enemy so much as smile and she'd make friends at once. It was foolishly trusting. He told her so, with some asperity.

Lauchlin stuck her tongue between her teeth, added a bit more swing to the kilt, and then looked up with puzzled eyes. "Why not?" she asked for the third time. "I *like* liking people, and if everyone did it, perhaps we'd have no need of wars and risings and such. Besides, I can't *not* be nice back, if people are nice to me."

It was true that the boys displayed a warm casual friendship that was endearing and hard to resist. Edwin's affable courtesy, Andrew's teasing, George's rollicking good nature—Ronald frowned. "What about Geordie?" he asked his sister.

Lauchlin dropped troubled eyes to her drawing. George really was *so* nice, now; full of fun and gallantry . . . and yet, she could never quite forget the pebble-eyed George she had first seen at Yorktown, who looked at them as if they were mangy curs to be kicked instead of fed. "I am always wondering how he treats his slaves, just," she confessed. " 'Tis as if he's one person to his equals and another to his inferiors." And then she frowned again, uneasy about that word "inferiors." It was not a common concept in the Highlands, where there were clansmen and their chief, and he the leader, but no man considered inferior as a man unless he behaved badly. In England, with a class system like the layers of a cake, it was different. Lauchlin remembered London, and the chimney sweep, and the maid in the hotel, and felt more uncomfortable than ever.

"They're all like that," Ronald told her darkly. "With the two faces of that Roman god Janus. You cannot be trusting them, Lauchlin; and that goes for Carilla, too."

"And her grandmother, and Cousin Nathaniel, as well?" demanded Lauchlin, indignant. " 'Tis yourself is daft, Ronald MacLeod, to be inventing enemies who might be friends! Besides, I thought we were wanting the Colonists to be our friends, and all of us having a rising some day, perhaps, to throw off the king."

This unanswerable logic quite floored Ronald for a moment. He sat considering it, frowning with an annoyance he couldn't quite explain, but had to do with his sister pointing out the obvious to him.

"Why can't we be starting a *Virginia Gadfly*?" suggested Lauchlin hopefully. "We could tell all about Scotland, and London, and Carilla can write wicked verses, and perhaps—"

"No!" Ronald snapped angrily. "She's a Tory, you daft loon, and an enemy! Have you *dared* tell her about the *Gadfly*, you wee traitor, after swearing secrecy? If—"

"Indeed and I would never be doing so, daft loon yourself!" Lauchlin stood up, knocking her chair over and causing her hair to slip sideways with the energy of her movement. Wounded and wrathful, she glared at him through those slightly tilted dark eyes. "And the shame upon you, Ronald MacLeod, to be thinking it! But Carilla is my friend and cousin, and she talks to me while you are at the Raleigh Tavern where I cannot go, or off with the boys, or away in your room writing for Cousin Matthew, and I not free as you are to go and get material. And I've never sworn not to be starting a *different* paper with her. I shall ask her about it whenever I feel like it, and if you're not wanting to help, you need not!"

They glared at each other. Lauchlin, who usually made up a quarrel at once because she could never bear to stay angry or endure one of Ronald's black silences, held her ground. She had Carilla to turn to.

Ronald, sensing this and angrier than ever, stalked out of the room, and went to try to pick a fight with the boys.

It wasn't easy. Edwin had been taught that political arguments were not at all in good taste, and he could seldom be drawn into one. George had far too much lazy good nature, and would *not* turn again into that aggressive lad of the Yorktown dock. As for Andrew, he was hopeless, for he loved to turn ideas upside down and inside out for the mere sport of it, and kept switching arguments disconcertingly in mid-air.

Ronald found the boys easily enough, for they were just drifting in at the gate in search of him. They all draped themselves on the grass under the heart-shaped leaves of the mulberry tree, and within five minutes Ronald had contrived to make at least three offensive remarks about the English.

Infuriatingly, no one rose to the bait. George's eyes hardened for the briefest instant, and then he grinned jovially, yawned, lay back on the cool grass. Andrew merely surveyed him under those ridiculously long lashes. Edwin considered the comments and discarded them as irrelevant.

"After all, we all call ourselves Virginians, now, anyway."

"*I'm* not!" Ronald squared his chin aggressively.

Andrew chuckled. "Reckon you'd like to take up arms against the lot of us tomorrow."

He was so near the mark that Ronald scowled doggedly. "People oppressed by the Sassenach ought to stand up for their rights and liberty, if they call themselves men at all," he said insultingly.

"Well, we do, in a civilized way," George pointed out from his prone position. "We boycott tea and most English goods, don't we?"

Ronald snorted. Andrew switched to his side. "That's no use. What we need is to get high waterproof boots and march on London."

Ronald looked enthusiastic, George and Edwin startled. Then they realized that Andrew was joking as usual.

"You Scots really did rise in rebellion, didn't you?"

Edwin looked thoughtful, faintly astonished, distinctly disapproving.

"We did that!" Ronald boasted. "Twice!"

"And did it solve your problems and give you freedom?" wondered Andrew, his face guileless.

Ronald turned an incensed shoulder on him and attended to Edwin, who was saying that Virginia aristocracy would *never* descend to brawling. "We simply don't *do* things that way."

"That's for low-class backwoodsmen and immigrants," added George, taking a stalk of grass out of his mouth. "You've been listening too much to rabble-rousers like that Mr. Henry, Ronald. He'd have you thinking such rabble was human and fit to have a say in government, and own property, and heaven knows what else. Filthy swine!"

Edwin seemed to agree with the sentiment if not the choice of words. Andrew looked noncommittal behind freckles and eyelashes. Ronald, who had indeed been listening to Mr. Henry in the Raleigh Tavern, turned on George with a glittering eye.

"Perhaps 'tis the backwoodsmen will run out the Sassenach, after all," he said, his Highland lilt very pronounced. "And when that's finished, 'tis in my mind there'll be wanted a wee bittie change, or maybe two, in the way the Colonies are run. There's you aristocrats running the land altogether for your own benefit, and never caring a whit for the lesser folk. 'Twill never do, at all. The poor people and slaves have got to be freed and educated, and given an equal voice whether they own property or no, or they'll be having another rising themselves one fine day, and you not liking that at all."

They stared, speechless.

"Are you— Are you suggesting a *democracy*?" George could hardly say the word, which was considered rather worse than swearing. Even radicals of the worst sort rarely went so far as to use it right out loud in public.

Carilla came out on the veranda just in time to hear that last bit, and see their faces; and George's eyes hardened for an instant. Then— "He *must* be joking!" he said with relief.

Carilla, who knew better, looked hopefully at Andrew, who seemed to be choosing his words with some care.

"Reckon Ronald's the one to teach us, all right," he drawled. "Tell us how you do it in the Highlands, Heir of a Noble Lord, and how all the shaggy, barelegged clansmen in their stone huts come up to the big house and tell your father how to run the clan."

Lauchlin appeared just in time to see her brother toss back the dark hair—half escaped from its queue—and issue a challenge to battle. Andrew promptly accepted the invitation, which, he explained later, *no* red-blooded Englishman could resist. In an instant the two were having a small but enthusiastic war of their own. Since there were no established rules, they simply made up their own, punching, wrestling, pummeling, and generally trying to do as much damage as possible.

Edwin shouted at them to stop; this was not the way gentlemen fought! George watched with detached interest. Carilla cheered Andrew on, but rather faintly, not being used to this sort of thing. Lauchlin yelled encouragement to her brother, but with a cheer for Andrew every time she remembered Ronald's constant snubbing of Carilla. (Although, to be fair, Carilla was just as horrid to Ronald. It was a regular feud.)

Lady Seraphina came to see what all the fuss was about, and sat on the top of the veranda steps disapprovingly. Her front paws were placed neatly together, her full tail curled around her, and she looked rather like a goddess surveying the foolishness of mortals.

Haggis arrived on the scene in quite a different frame of mind. He shot recklessly into the midst of the battle, shot out again, and swarmed up the mulberry tree, where he clung with a bushed-out tail and eyes like saucers, shouting for everyone to look at the Monsters down there.

And then a fragile figure all snow and lavender walked out of the front door, just at the moment when each boy was still perfectly certain of victory, but beginning to suspect that it might take just a little longer than had at first appeared.

"A gentleman," she remarked, her crystal voice cutting through the sound of combat, "never resorts to violence. Stop it instantly."

They did. Sheepish and considerably battered, they picked themselves up and bowed a bit dizzily. "Your servant, Ma'am," they mumbled rather indistinctly. "Apologies, Ma'am."

Mistress Treanor surveyed them fastidiously. Their hose and breeches were grass-stained and torn. Buttons were missing, shirts ripped, waistcoats gaped open. Their queues had quite vanished, so that black and brown hair strung wildly over their shoulders, and their faces were already beginning to take on quite an interesting variety of odd shapes and colors.

"I cannot think," observed Mistress Treanor quellingly, "why anyone should suppose a dogfight to be intellectually convincing. Really, if the aristocracy cannot conduct themselves in a relatively civilized manner, I hate to think what the world may come to. I should suggest that you come inside and try to repair the damage to some degree before anyone else sees you."

She held the door open, and the shamefaced boys filed in, still murmuring apologies for having caused her any slight inconvenience or annoyance. It was to be noted that neither of them indicated the slightest regret for fighting. They had enjoyed it very much.

They grinned painfully at each other over washbasins filled with cold water that a clucking Jason set for them.

"You're a bonnie fighter," Ronald admitted generously.

"You're not so bad yourself," chuckled Andrew. "If we ever do rise against the English, I wouldn't mind having you beside me."

"Fine that, and soon the day!" Ronald's still-open eye brightened and he at once began to wonder how soon Andrew could be completely converted, and what was the best argument. Andrew grinned fiendishly, reading his mind with no trouble at all. Ronald grinned back. They shook hands and went back out to the garden, where Haggis was now shrieking from the tree that he couldn't get down and the mockingbird was after him. George was preventing Lauchlin from climbing the tree, and Edwin was preparing to do it himself.

"Might as well let us," suggested Andrew practically. "Couldn't get much more messed up than we are now." And by the time Haggis had been hauled down, squalling and clawing, and at once begun to brag that he had won that, hadn't he?, it was quite clear to everyone that the fight had been a sort of blood-brothers' initiation.

"Literally," murmured Lauchlin with a mischievous

glance at their sundry wounds and a look in her eye suggesting that there had better be no more nasty remarks about her friendship with Carilla. And she made up her mind then and there that she *would* start the *Virginia Gadfly*.

No one noticed that George was looking like someone assailed by a sudden doubt.

Andrew lay down under the tree again, in precisely the same spot and position which he had abandoned half an hour earlier. His eyes glinted blue mischief.

"Once upon a time," he murmured, apropos of nothing whatever, "there was a governor called Little Red Robinhood, who lived in a palace with his Merry Redcoats, who were all named Will Scarlett. And this Mad Merryman was a splendid chap who used to steal from the poor Indians and give most generously to his rich friends, and—"

He was interrupted by two peals of delighted gurgles, a shout of laughter, one reluctant grin (from Edwin), and a deeply shocked look from George, who found that the talk about democracy had already strained his broadmindedness quite enough for one day.

"After all," he pointed out uncomfortably, "there's such a thing as class loyalty, Andrew."

But Andrew just looked wickedly at him from half-closed eyes and went on with his disrespectful fairy tale.

Twelve

WAITING

Now that May was here, and The Season had started, Williamsburg looked very different from the sleepy little town of a month ago. Delegates to the Virginia Assembly had come, many with their families. So had the plantation owners who weren't delegates, just for the social season. Gloucester Street, ankle-deep in fine dust, thronged with people and coaches. Silks and brocades, laces and plumes, were everywhere. Pretty young belles strolled along or stood talking with as many handsome men as they could collect, using dainty fans quite as much for flirtation as for cooling purposes.

It was Ronald who needed a fan—or a brisk Skye wind. Lauchlin might revel in the warmth, but he found it oppressively hot, and didn't find it at all encouraging to be told that it had not yet started to get hot, and just wait 'til summer!

"I could do fine without it," he grumbled, and went off to write to Cousin Matthew, promising more news to come. For under the fine polished surface of life these days was a sense of uneasy waiting. Like one of their famous thunderstorms waiting to break, said Andrew ghoulishly.

Lauchlin at once went and drew a sketch of a thundercloud looking vaguely like the Houses of Parliament, with one huge thunderhead at the top which had the profile of

George III. It loomed ominously over a carefully copied map of the colonial coast, and anyone with half an eye could see it was meant to show the apprehension with which everyone awaited news of what Parliament was doing.

"It's terrible!" said Carilla at once, chuckling at it. "Only you should put in Ronald in a too-short kilt, and Mr. Henry in mussed-up coat and breeches, shaking their fists at it. Is it for our *Virginia Gadfly*?"

Lauchlin hesitated only an instant. She could make another for Cousin Matthew this evening. "Aye," she agreed. "And you can be doing some verses about Sassenachs licking German boots, and how everything in Williamsburg gets hotter and hotter along with the weather."

For this was exactly the case. Patrick Henry was now saying openly that England had no rights at all in the Colonies, and there should be a complete separation. This was an appalling idea to moderate people like Mr. Treanor and Peyton Randolph, who merely wanted English rights for all English citizens. Legislative debates grew more and more heated. So did the informal ones in the Raleigh. So also did Governor Dunmore, who was scarlet with fury most of the time these days, at the incredible impudence of these upstart Colonials.

"I am thinking he sounds just like King Geordie, only perhaps not quite so bad," remarked Lauchlin. "If you're having enough sense to loathe yon Lord Dunmore, why are you daft enough to stay loyal to the king?"

"I keep telling you, stupid," retorted Carilla. "It isn't *him*. I don't care who's on the throne. It's the Crown itself, and England, and all the fine old traditions they stand for, like the dignity and freedom of the individual." She sounded exactly like her grandmother, whom she was quoting, and she felt a sudden thrill of pride in her own heritage.

Lauchlin just snorted disrespectfully. "Och, dignity and freedom for *whom*? Not for the Scots, and not for the Colonies, and not for slaves, or for the poor folk in London or the wretched wee chimney sweeps. A fine dignity and freedom *that* is, whatever!"

Carilla frowned, feeling there to be a great flaw in this argument somewhere. It was not fair, somehow, to couple Colonies, which *should* be free, with slaves, who quite obviously should not; and to throw in, moreover, those other groups which fell somewhere in between. It made it very hard to answer, especially since Carilla herself was lately suffering a great deal of uncertainty about such things. Better, doubtless, to shift to a new line of attack.

"I suppose you think things would be any better if we had your horrid old Stewarts and their Divine Right of Kings?" she suggested pointedly, and had the great satisfaction of seeing Lauchlin at a loss. For there was no denying that three of the four Stewart kings who had ruled England could only be called disastrous.

"*Mo thruigh*!" said Lauchlin, considerably shaken by this point of view, which had somehow never occurred to her before. Instead of getting on with the battle, she retreated from the field without further ado, and sat considering the matter with a perfectly fearsome frown. Carilla sat and waited, tapped a silver-buckled foot, yawned, wrote some lines of doggerel, chuckled over them, and at last jumped up.

"If we just sit here, Grandmother will find us and either give us some sewing or put us on our backboards. Come on, Lauchlin, do! Show me some more of the sword dance, up in my room."

"Very well so," agreed Lauchlin, gladly abandoning thought. And a few minutes later they were at it. Their full silken skirts were pulled up and out of the way to show a quite indecent amount of stocking. Rhoda watched, scandalized but fascinated, while Lauchlin nimbly demonstrated the complicated footwork.

"—and now I spring over this blade, and turn, and ready to touch my toe across in yon square—" Her toes flashed over the crossed sword and scabbard filched from Cousin Nathaniel. "Keep high, mind, and as close to the blades as you can without touching, and—" She stopped short. The strains of bagpipe music wailed suddenly through the open window. Not just the chanter this time, but the full volume of bag and drones as well.

"*Ochan*!" cried Lauchlin, clasping her hands and taking a deep breath, almost as if she could smell the tang of salt and heather and larch. "Oh, it makes me so *homesick*!"

Her saucy nose crinkled with delight and grief. But Lady Seraphina, who had been curled on a chair, flattened her ears slightly in outrage and swept majestically from the room. Rhoda looked alarmed, and Carilla more than a little startled.

"What on earth *is* it?" she demanded. Her ears felt assailed, and her body battered by the sound, and it felt rather like the time she had been caught and tossed in the sea breakers.

"The pipes, lass! The bagpipes! Have you never heard them, then? Ronald has been learning against the law at home all these years, and now . . . Och, isn't it a *grand* sound, Carilla?"

She looked at her friend a trifle anxiously. Cousin Matthew had said some folks considered bagpipes an invention of the Devil to torment the ears of Christians. Lauchlin had not believed that anyone could be so daft, and had said so. Could anyone *possibly* fail to thrill at the wild haunting sounds which went to blood and bones, filled the head and twitched the feet with joyous madness? . . . A glance at Rhoda's face now suggested to Lauchlin that they could.

"Lord preserve us!" said Rhoda simply.

But Carilla's fair head was tilted slightly to one side. Her violet-blue eyes focused on something beyond the wall, and her feet began to tap the rhythm that her ears had not yet distinguished. She smiled. It *was* grand! "A person could almost get tipsy on just the sound," she discovered. "Even if it *is* Ronald playing. This is the best thing Scotland ever produced, I reckon."

Lauchlin promptly hugged her. Carilla, carried away, hugged back. Rhoda beamed over this pleasant change from the eternal bickering.

"Och, we'll make a bonnie Highlander of you yet!" promised Lauchlin.

"Over my dead body you will!" Carilla squawked.

"Very well so," Lauchlin agreed nastily. "Better a dead Scot than a live Sassenach any day."

They glowered at each other happily. Things were back to normal, thank goodness.

Thirteen

MISCHIEF

A brilliant Saturday morning. The hot May sun beat down upon massed blossom, causing the scent to rise in waves, warm and sleepy. The drone of bees filled the air. Mockingbirds sang in the trees, and catbirds mimicked them. From the kitchen house around in back came the murmur and song of slaves at work; and Haggis, a prowling lion, stalked an invisible something across the lawn. On the cool veranda sat one porcelain-and-lavender figure and two of restless blue silk, all plying their needles.

Lauchlin yawned, tried to stifle it, and of course knocked the scissors into Carilla's lap. Carilla squeaked and tried to kick Lauchlin without moving her full skirts. Then they both turned sheepish eyes to Mistress Treanor.

"A lady," said that lady, "should always be perfectly controlled in all ways. You sadly lack self-discipline, Lauchlin my dear, and you are far too impulsive. Act with deliberation and forethought, always."

"Yes'm," sighed Lauchlin, hanging her head. Carilla looked smug.

"As for you, Carilla, this silly feud you are carrying on with Ronald is quite puerile." She considered this and changed her mind. "No, not puerile; children never carry on such silliness for so long. It is a habit, I fear, of irrational and petty adults, and I am very much ashamed of you. I had thought you above such idiocy."

Carilla turned crimson, was tempted to protest that it was Ronald's fault at least as much as hers and probably more, and thought better of it. One simply *didn't* resort to excuses or tale-telling, however unjust the accusation. She stared resentfully at her sewing, ready to cry. Her grandmother released her from the blue javelin of her gaze and spread it to take in both girls.

"And what is this nonsense Mrs. Hallam tells me?"

They looked at each other, uncomfortable. "Mrs. Hallam?" they murmured.

"Don't repeat like that, my dears; it sounds half-witted. She says fully half her young ladies are forgetting to be ladies at all, and are spraining their ankles right and left trying to learn *men*'s dances. The Highland Fling, I believe she mentioned, and something with the unlikely name of—Sheen Trooze?"

She looked hard at Lauchlin, who giggled impenitently. "Spelled S-e-a-n T-r-i-u-b-h-a-s," she pointed out with an irrepressible twinkle in her dark eyes.

Mistress Treanor considered this irrelevant fact in silence, while the two needles, not daring to falter, toiled on. Haggis sat at the foot of the magnolia tree hurling threats at his pet enemy the mockingbird. Lady Seraphina opened a contemptuous eye, yawned, moved from a patch of sunshine to a patch of shade, and curled up in it. Time stretched interminably.

Then reprieve came, and from an unexpected source. Three boys came loping up England Street, tore in at the gate and up to the veranda without even remembering to bow to Carilla's grandmother. "News from England!" they panted. "You'll never guess what Parliament's done!"

The needles stopped—or at least two of them did.

Cousin Lavinia would never display anything as vulgar as curiosity. Lauchlin stared in great surprise at Andrew, whom she had supposed never got upset about anything. He had too strong a sense of the ridiculous, so that he always saw the funny side of things. But he wasn't amused now. His freckled face was red with indignation, and his jaw stuck out.

"You'll never guess, Grandmother! They've passed an Act saying that the men who were in the Tea Party will be sent back to England for trial!"

Lauchlin's dark eyes widened and she felt sure she had turned pale. Many men had been taken from Scotland for trial in England—and invariably ended as grisly heads stuck up over London Bridge as a warning.

But Cousin Lavinia seemed unaware of this. She merely plunged her needle into the bit of embroidery in her hand. "Well, why not?" she said. "The tea they destroyed was English property, wasn't it? And where are your manners, boys? Andrew, I'm surprised at you."

They bowed, belatedly and rather absent-mindedly. "But Grandmother!" Andrew protested, redder than ever. "That's all very well, but how can they possibly get a fair trial in England?"

"Never mind them," said George. "There's worse, Ma'am. They've passed an Act that takes away most of Massachusetts's chartered rights—"

"And another," finished Edwin, "that closes the Port of Boston on June first. They say there'll be English warships stationed there to make sure that not so much as a row-boat goes in or out."

Now Carilla's eyes widened in dismay, and her grandmother's needle stopped. "That," she said severely, "is as foolish as it is unjust. Parliament is punishing the shipowners, who had nothing to do with that deplorable Tea Party, and who abhor violence quite as much as we do. If England persists in antagonizing those who are loyal and moderate, whom do they suppose will support them against the extremists?" Her needle stabbed into the cloth as if she had Parliament at the end of it. Lauchlin longed for the skill to draw her as she looked now, longed even more to be at the Raleigh, where Ronald undoubtedly was, sketching the debate that was most certainly raging there.

"That's just what we thought, Ma'am," began Edwin gravely. Andrew, who really was extraordinarily worked up about this, interrupted.

"Bother the shipowners! They're rich; they can stand losses. How about the shipbuilders and sail makers and carpenters and small merchants and sailors, and all the others who depend on shipping to keep alive? How about their families? And most of them just as loyal and moderate as any one of us. . . . Or at least they *have* been," he added darkly. "I reckon *this* will make good radicals of them."

This last was a telling point. They considered it gravely. Lauchlin was busy considering Andrew. Who would have dreamed he had such a passion for justice and for helpless common folk? Doubtless it was because of his habit of arguing all sides of a question. He was very much like Cousin Matthew, now she thought about it, and might make a fine braw revolutionary. He might, even, be just what was needed for the still-unborn *Virginia Gadfly*, since Ronald wouldn't hear of working with Carilla. . . . Och, of course!

George laughed suddenly, and shrugged. "Why worry about the rabble? They'll always follow some low fellow like Patrick Henry, who's already yelling about wanting to secede from England."

Andrew favored George with a not altogether amiable smile. Edwin shook his blond head.

"That's all very well, George, but this time Mr. Lee agrees with Mr. Henry about secession. He was visiting my father when the news came, and I heard him say so."

"Henry Lee?" Mistress Treanor looked pained. He was a Tidewater Aristocrat, who had no business at all supporting radical and seditious notions.

George clearly agreed. "Traitor to his class," he muttered.

Unexpectedly Lauchlin's eyes met Andrew's and a spurt of amusement flashed between them. Then it was gone, and Lauchlin couldn't have said what it was that was funny. But Andrew was looking at his grandmother with the air of someone just about to pull the cat's tail.

"Colonel Washington wants to raise a militia and take it to Boston's defense," he announced casually.

They stared, incredulous. "Nonsense!" said his grandmother firmly. "George Washington has never been interested in political rights. All he cares about is land."

Andrew's large teeth showed in a positively sardonic grin. "Mmm," he agreed silkily. "And he's been hoping to get several thousand square miles of Ohio Territory—and we forgot to mention just now that Parliament has also passed an Act ceding all that land to Quebec."

There was quite a long silence. Then Mistress Treanor picked up her needle again. "I dare say common sense will prevail in the end," she remarked calmly. "Run along, now, all of you. . . . Fold your sewing neatly, Lauchlin; how many times must I tell you that? And remember your sunshade, my dear. You can't be using it properly, for your skin is getting just like an Indian. And have Rhoda pin up your hair again."

At last even those sharp blue eyes were satisfied, and they were off down England Street, with a brief stop for Melicent. Lauchlin fingered her pocket, bulging just now with a wad of paper and some pieces of charcoal. Her back looked determined. Carilla's round face had the scared but pleased look of someone about to assist in mischief. No one noticed because other things were so interesting.

Up ahead, England Street divided the green expanse of Market Square, with the octagonal Powder Magazine on the right and Maupin's saddlery beyond it. A couple of red-coated English soldiers pretended not to notice the groups of indignant citizens clustered everywhere, angry and alarmed. Peyton Randolph and his brother John passed, turning right on Gloucester Street, toward the Raleigh Tavern. A man with too much gold lacing on his pink satin waistcoat and too many beauty patches on his florid face, was trying to talk to a gentleman with a head like a Roman coin, who gracefully excused himself and walked on.

"That fellow from Georgia," said George scornfully. "Pretending to be a gentleman when he isn't! I wonder Mr. Lee even bothered to be civil."

"Because Mr. Lee *is* a gentleman," suggested Edwin dryly.

Andrew favored the pink satin waistcoat with a narrow glance. It was said that Georgians tended to be brutal to their slaves.

They turned into Gloucester Street just behind an impeccably dressed, fine-featured aristocrat and an awkward fellow who clearly cared little about clothes. They were talking animatedly. Edwin's eyes widened and he glanced at the others, jerked his head sideways.

"Look at that!" he whispered. "Carter Nicholas and Patrick Henry on speaking terms!"

"Mercy me!" exclaimed Melicent, who had been very much inclined to take the whole thing lightly. "Why, this silly old blockade business *must* be serious, then!"

Andrew grinned. "Stands to reason. Private squabbles just vanish if there's a common enemy." He grinned at Lauchlin who had stopped short, struck by this blinding revelation. Of course! England herself was doing a better job at starting a rising than she and Ronald, who had been making a great mistake, surely, in talking against England. That made people want to defend it. The trick was to reverse it. She walked on again, thoughtfully.

"Wonder what the Assembly will decide to do?" mused George. "After all, Boston's in Massachusetts, and none of Virginia's business at all."

"Fine that," agreed Lauchlin instantly, trying out her new theory. "Who cares what is happening in some other colony?"

They paused, turned to stare at her in surprise. This was altogether unlike Lauchlin! Andrew looked deeply disappointed, and Melicent blinked at hearing such a sensible remark from that source. Edwin frowned.

"Won't do," he said. "All the Colonies must stand together, now." And Lauchlin grinned so fiendishly that Andrew gave her a puzzled glance.

They had reached the Raleigh now, a long, white, gabled building with many windows, and a lead bust of

Sir Walter over the door, and a generally hearty air about it. More horses than usual were tied to the hitching bars in front, and the benches under the taproom windows were full. Two more men in cool broadcloth coats headed toward the door, and Lauchlin nudged Carilla.

"Oh, *look*!" squealed Carilla instantly, and turned to wave a distracted hand in the direction of Charlton House across the road. Lauchlin did not wait to hear whatever fiction would follow. She slipped into the door of the Raleigh behind the broadcloth coats.

The public bar led into a handsome parlor, all of it darkly crowded to eyes fresh from the blazing sunshine. Lauchlin, blinking, edged along the wall trying to be invisible.

Two gentlemen talking about passive resistance saw her, paused in their conversation with raised eyebrows. Then another. And then—

"Hoy, young missy, you can't come in here!"

Now everyone was staring. Lauchlin took a deep breath and displayed her most winning smile. "Och, 'tis all right," she explained. "I don't want to *drink* anything."

There was laughter. The barman frowned. "Wouldn't serve you if you did," he retorted. "And that don't matter. Females aren't allowed."

"Why not?" demanded Lauchlin reasonably.

"Don't be silly, miss. They just aren't. Everybody knows that."

Lauchlin tilted her chin at him. "Och, that's no answer at all! What harm am I doing, whatever?"

"Well, you're causing a right distraction, for one thing," he retorted with truth. For burgesses were ceasing their talk about the Acts of Parliament, and were listening with considerable interest. It was a wonder that Ronald, who must be in the next room, hadn't heard and come out to see what was happening.

"*Seadh*!" said Lauchlin in disgust, turning a severely reproachful eye on the barman. " 'Tis yourself causing the distraction, not me! *I* never said a word. I was minding my own business, just, and you it was started an argument."

There was more laughter. "Touché!" said an elderly man with a magnificent sweep of forehead over a Roman nose. Lauchlin at once produced her paper and charcoal, and began to draw him.

"Here, what are you doing?" demanded the barman, incensed. "You can't stay here, I tell you."

"Shhh," said Lauchlin abstractedly. "Stop bothering me; I'm busy. If you'll be keeping your head so, sir, you can be going on with your conversation, and I not minding."

"That's very handsome of you," said her subject, neglecting this suggestion. He exchanged amused glances with the tall, red-haired young man at his shoulder. "So you're an artist? But I thought young ladies only drew flowers in vases?"

"Ou, aye," agreed Lauchlin, concentrating on that prominant and courageous chin. "But 'tis myself is no proper lady at all. Both Cousin Lavinia and Mrs. Hallam say so. Although," she added fairly, "they are both trying very hard to make me one."

"Look, missy!" said the barman. "Look, Mr. Wythe and Mr. Jefferson, she can't stay in here!"

Lauchlin tilted a defiant chin at him. "You keep saying that, and if you can't think of a good reason, just, then you should be quiet and pretend I'm not here at all."

The door opened, an oblong of blinding white light.

Someone came in. "Firetop!" cried Andrew joyfully. "I should have guessed sooner! Are you being thrown out?"

"I'm trying to sketch this gentleman and some of the others," she said crossly. "I don't see why everyone is making such a fuss. There, sir. If I was having more light and less bother, I could be doing it better."

She handed the sketch over. Mr. Wythe stared transfixed at it. So did Mr. Jefferson and several of the other gentlemen, who gathered round. Then they began to laugh.

"By gad, she's caught you, George!" said someone. "Look at that nose!"

"It's not *that* big," complained Mr. Wythe, looking over the sketch with a quizzical look in his grey eyes. "Did you mean to flatter me, young lady?"

"Look, miss—" pleaded the barman without much hope. Everyone ignored him. Lauchlin cocked her head and regarded Mr. Wythe sadly.

"Och, I always mean to draw people exactly as they look," she explained, "but they always say I've insulted them. And I don't see why, for everyone can *always* tell who 'tis meant to be. Have I insulted you?"

Andrew had managed to get a glimpse of the sketch. He grinned. "Most awfully," he assured her. "Best let me take you home at once."

"Please do!" begged the barman.

"On the contrary," said Mr. Wythe. "I'm delighted, and I mean to keep this sketch. Can you do Tom Jefferson here?"

"Please, Mr. Wythe!" The barman looked ready to cry.

"Tell you what," suggested Mr. Jefferson. "There's nothing very improper in a very young lady sitting—well escorted, of course—in the small parlor, is there? With, perhaps, a glass of lemonade?"

The barman looked doubtful. "She come in alone—"

"But now she has Mr. Dare here, and Mr. Wythe and myself, and Mr. Lee and Mr. Nicholas who want their portraits done; and I haven't a doubt in the world that the young lady's brother is here somewhere. And the light is much better in there. Come along. You won't mind if we talk politics whilst you draw, will you?"

"Och no!" said Lauchlin eagerly. " 'Tis myself is wanting to hear it! You see—" She tossed her head at the barman, felt her hair begin to slither downwards, and laughed resignedly as Mr. Jefferson held out a gallant arm and led the way toward the small parlor. "No matter, 'tis always falling down. . . . You see, ideas here are so very *complicated*! At home in Scotland 'tis all very simple; if one is Highland, one hates the Sassenach. But here—" She shook her head in bewilderment, and felt her hair slip further.

Mr. Lee turned his classical head, smiling. "Here, what?"

" 'Tis a very patchwork of in-betweens," she complained. "A body can be for England but against King Geordie and Parliament and Governor Dunmore, all; or for Geordie but against Parliament, or for the Crown but against the king, or for English Rights but against English Rule, or for English Rule but against English taxes, or—"

She stopped, not because she had run out of ideas, but because the men were laughing, and Andrew was grinning, and Ronald was looking across the room at her with an astonished face, and it all made a picture she wanted to put on paper at once. Without any further fuss, she sat down and began to do so. It was perfectly certain that once Cousin Lavinia heard about this, she would never have such a chance again, and best make the most of it.

Andrew sat beside her, watching with deep joy while one caricature after another sprang to life.

"And to think I never knew you had an imp in your fingers!" he mused. "Why didn't you ever tell me? I say, Firetop, I have a splendid idea! Will you marry me?"

Lauchlin peered at him from beneath demurely lowered lids. "Och, no," she said gravely. "How could I, and you not even able to play the bagpipes?"

Fourteen

THE LEMON WAISTCOAT

"But you told me to act with deliberation and forethought, and I was doing so." Lauchlin's pointy face was demure, her eyes almost impudent.

Cousin Lavinia spoiled this splendid argument by declining to argue. "Since neither of us is a fool, my dear, there's no point in your talking like one, is there? I think there's no more to be said on the subject. You've promised never to do it again, and neither of you is to go anywhere but church and school for a week unless Rhoda or another adult is with you, and there'll be an extra hour on your backboards tomorrow. . . . Carilla my dear, I shouldn't eat any more biscuits and honey if I were you; your mother's family ran to plumpness, and I heard you complain only yesterday that your stays were cutting you in two. Lauchlin, it was doubtless kind of you to leave the door open a crack for Lady Seraphina, but both of you know she's not allowed in the dining room."

Lady Seraphina did, at any rate. Her furry, snub-nosed face in the doorway wore the expression of a princess on the doorstep who thought it might be nice to come in, but was far too proud to ask.

Lauchlin sighed. The other subject was clearly closed, and she had gotten off easily, though it seemed hard on Carilla. Cousin Nathaniel and Ronald were maintaining a prudent silence, and it was best to leave well enough alone. In any case, a gentle creaking of the front gate suggested that the boys and Melicent were arriving for an evening visit and to hear all the details of Lauchlin's adventure.

Presently they were all sitting out in the warm dusk of the veranda, with light from the drawing room shining through while they examined the now-famous sketches.

"They kept some of the best ones for themselves," Lauchlin grumbled, but only half-heartedly.

"They're good," said Edwin, surprised. "A pity you're a girl. You could get some of them published."

In the dim light Lauchlin and Ronald exchanged glances, tempted but cautious. Only three days ago a packet of mail had arrived, with a letter from home (that had Lauchlin in tears of homesickness) and several copies of the *Gadfly*. But it wouldn't do to tell anyone, of course.

Andrew, who had been with her at the Raleigh, was

now looking over some of her older drawings, chuckling. George guffawed at the one of Mr. Henry looking impassioned. But Melicent frowned.

"I don't think they're very good at all!" she announced. "They're horribly exaggerated, and not at all like the people."

Lauchlin bristled. Andrew looked wicked. "Like this one better?" And he handed her one of a hopelessly awkward, wrong-footed class of girls blundering through a Highland Fling, while Mrs. Hallam looked horrified. It was easy to pick out Melicent. The nose was a little too sharp, the eyebrows too arched, and there was something unmistakable in the angles of head and shoulders and wrists.

"No I don't," said Melicent crossly. "It's not a ladylike sort of drawing at all, and Mama says she's a disgrace. Imagine, walking right into a tavern, like that! The whole town's talking."

"The more daft they, then, if they can think of nothing better to talk about!" Lauchlin put her nose in the air.

"Mr. Wythe and Mr. Jefferson didn't think it was awful," said Carilla with triumph. "When they escorted her home, they told Grandmother she was delightful and refreshing and had a great deal of talent, so there."

George laughed. Edwin looked disapproving. But for some reason it was George who drew an uneasy glance from Lauchlin. That was the same laugh as when he was looking at the sketches, with, somehow, a faint hint of the Yorktown dock—as if he had discovered or decided that she and Ronald were not worthy, after all, to be considered social equals. And surely she had glimpsed the pebble look in his eyes several times lately? Was it since the fight? Or later? Did it exist at all?

And what did it matter, demanded Ronald, when she slipped into his room later to tell him about it. "Let him think what he likes, so long as he minds his manners. He hasn't been rude or tried to snub you, has he? If he does, I'll just be teaching him a wee lesson."

Lauchlin shook her bright head, laughing and then wistful. She and Ronald were no longer as close. Ronald was so wrapped up in his own affairs and the *Gadfly*, and she with Carilla—and he resenting Carilla. She thought of asking him again to help with the *Virginia Gadfly*, and then changed her mind. He'd already said Cousin Matthew was more important, and that he wouldn't work with Carilla anyway; and the idea of their doing it without him annoyed him quite unreasonably.

Besides, Carilla and Lauchlin had already asked Andrew to come see them Monday after lessons. Andrew was what they needed, anyway. Was it disloyal of her to think that he would be better in a way than the single-minded Ronald, who wrote with passion and force, but lacked the gift of ridicule?

"Och!" said Andrew in a perfectly awful imitation Highland accent. " 'Tis a grand idea, just!" He looked at the material they had placed before him, matching up sketches with some of Carilla's most satiric doggerel. "Reckon you two talented ladies don't really need me at all."

"Well, but we do!" protested Carilla. "For one thing, we need help in copying it all out, and we want you most especially to write some of those idiot fairy tales of yours. You know, like Little Red Robinhood, only with news." Carilla looked at him expectantly.

Andrew's freckled face lighted with fun. He thought for a moment, deep-blue eyes dancing, and then chuckled. "I've another idea," he announced, and picked up a quill. "How's this?" he asked presently, and read it aloud.

Now it came to pass that when Parliament heard of the Boston Tea Party, they waxed exceeding wroth, and they sat them down and devised many grievous punishments which were called the Coercive Acts.

And it came to pass that when the Virginia Legislature heard of the Coercive Acts, *they* waxed exceeding wroth, and they sat them down in the Capitol of Williamsburg and devised a drastic measure with which to punish Parliament, and this drastic measure was called A Day of Fasting and Prayer, and it was to take place upon the first day of June to mourn the start of the blockade of Boston. And the burgesses were mightily pleased.

Now it came to pass that when Governor Dunmore heard of the Day of Fasting and Prayer, *he* waxed most exceeding wroth of all, so that clouds of smoke arose from his nostrils, and he came forth from his Palace like Beelzebub, trailing Red Rage and Red Flames and Redcoats, and he hied him to the Capitol, whither he smote the table and swore mightily and spake wrathful words, saying that Fasting and Prayer were Wicked and Treasonous. After which he smote the table again, and said also that the burgesses were disloyal and subversive, and rebellious and seditious and revolting.

But lo, the burgesses arose and said they might be those other things, but they were *not* revolting.

And Lord Dunmore said they were, and he dissolved the Legislature, saying that now they couldn't have any more Revolting Meetings.

But at this the burgesses, waxing wrother by the minute, betook themselves right over to the Raleigh where they have been having Revolting Meetings ever since. And they have come to pass motions inviting all the other Colonies to be Revolting, too, and to meet together in a Continental Congress in September, to debate more drastic actions against Parliament and to annoy the King's Governor.

And lo, it shall come to pass that the Day of Fasting and Prayer shall take place upon the first of June as planned.

Andrew stopped reading and cocked his brown head at them. Lauchlin was dissolved in giggles, Carilla staring with startled eyes.

"Mercy, Andrew, is that all true?" she demanded.

Andrew grinned. "Is it what you want?"

"Och, aye!" exclaimed Lauchlin at once. But Carilla stamped a small buckled foot in annoyance.

"You stop teasing me, Andrew Dare! Did all that really happen today?"

He nodded. Lauchlin, who had been reading *A Midsummer Night's Dream,* was strongly reminded of a smug and mischievous Puck saying the lines about what fools these mortals be. "I saw some of it myself," he said, with an impish grin. "They're all simply *furious*—and dead serious about it all, too. It would make a perfectly splendid satiric comedy," he added disrespectfully, causing Lauchlin to choke with new laughter.

Carilla frowned. "That's my father you're talking about," she pointed out rather crisply. "And I don't think it's a bit funny. What's going to happen now?"

Andrew became sober. "Reckon it could get serious enough," he admitted. "I heard George's father say the burgesses were skirting mighty close to treason."

"Nonsense!" cried Lauchlin instantly.

"But you see, Firetop," Andrew pointed out, "you aren't

the governor. And it's the governor who's His Majesty's representative around here, and in command of the king's army, and if *he* chooses to decide that it *is* treason. . . ."

Carilla surprised herself. "Why don't they leave us alone?" she spat. "Why should England appoint our governors, like a nurse for the children—or an overseer for the slaves! We *aren't* children or slaves, and I think we ought to govern ourselves!"

Lauchlin hugged her ecstatically. "Och, 'tis just what we Scots have been saying all along!"

"Yes, well I don't mean we should be completely separate from England," Carilla amended hastily. "I mean, like Mr. Jefferson wants, with all of the colonies, and countries like Scotland and Ireland and Wales having their own governments, but still joined in a kind of friendly alliance under one flag."

"*Dhiaoul!*" said Lauchlin disgustedly.

"Don't you two start a fight now," Andrew interrupted them. "Do you want me to help copy this *Virginia Gadfly* or not? And do you want my little news item or not? Because if not—"

"Oh, we do!" they cried, and presently three quills scratched away busily. Andrew polished his bit of prose, Lauchlin gleefully produced an irreverent illustration for it, and Carilla scowled over a new and impudent bit of parody. At this rate, they told each other, their first issue would be ready for distribution by tomorrow evening, easily.

But it wasn't.

It was just her luck, complained Lauchlin later. She

had *intended* to be a perfect lady; she always did. And it wasn't Rhoda's fault, either, because the whole thing was over before she knew it. It was nobody's fault at all, but Fate that put them just at that spot at that time—and then what else could anyone have done?

That spot happened to be on Francis Street, and the time was just as Rhoda was escorting the girls home from school, grumbling a little because everyone in town knew why they had to be escorted, and Rhoda felt personally disgraced.

And then, just at the corner of Colonial Street they came upon a scene of great violence. There was a coach with one large wheel almost off. And there was the florid man from Georgia in the pink satin waistcoat—only now he was in lemon taffeta—and he was beating his coachman with a horsewhip.

Carilla gasped and paled at the savage crack of the whip and the muffled cry. Nothing could be lower than to flog a helpless slave! Rhoda's eyes were anguished, and Melicent looked revolted.

Lauchlin felt none of these things, nor did she stop to consider the matter with deliberation and forethought. She merely lowered her flaming head as she had once done in Skye, and treated the florid man to an even more vigorous imitation of a goat, in the center of his lemon waistcoat.

"Oof!" said the Lemon Waistcoat, and sat down abruptly.

Lauchlin, a small fierce warrior, stood triumphant over her foe, while he wheezed painfully and the coachman cowered and Melicent screamed and several figures began running toward them.

"Wicked coward!" said Lauchlin. "*Mallaichte slaoightire*! I hope I hurt you very much, just!" she added earnestly.

And then she backed up just a tiny step, because the *mallaichte slaoightire* was getting up, and the look on his face suggested that he was indeed no gentleman, and might not be at all above hitting a young lady with a whip. Lauchlin's eyes widened slightly with apprehension, but she stood her ground, her hair a blazing bronze mane tumbled around her. That sight caused at least two approaching figures to run even faster.

The Lemon Waistcoat jerked her painfully by the arm, shook her with great violence, and raised a savagely purposeful whip—and then Rhoda threw herself heroically in front of her, and Carilla, with a sob of sheer courage, snatched the whip and pulled with all her might. An instant later a white-faced demon brushed Rhoda aside and confronted the Lemon Waistcoat himself.

"How dare you touch my sister, you dark-hearted *beasde!*"

The Lemon Waistcoat, goaded beyond endurance, let Carilla have the whip, clenched his fist, and hit Ronald in the eye with it.

Melicent screamed louder than ever. Lauchlin twisted around and bit the arm holding her. Ronald staggered slightly and then retaliated just in the spot where Lauchlin's head had first hit that taffeta paunch.

And at that moment, to everyone's relief, Mr. Jefferson arrived on the scene. "Be quiet, all of you!" he commanded with such authority that Lauchlin decided on the spot he'd make a splendid King Thomas of Virginia. "No, never mind telling me, sir; I saw the whole thing, including the disgusting and cowardly spectacle of you whipping your slave."

"It's my property!" snarled the Lemon Waistcoat. "I've got a right!"

"Legally, no doubt." Mr. Jefferson's voice was grim. "But you'll find it's not an acceptable form of behavior around here, and you're going to be extremely unpopular—with Society and tradesmen both—if you do it."

The heavy jowls reddened, the small eyes narrowed. He looked, decided Lauchlin, like a great ugly-tempered pig. "I know you! You're that fellow who tried to get a law passed about freeing slaves! Skunk!"

"I tried to have it made legal for an owner to free his slaves," retorted Mr. Jefferson. "True enough, and I'm sorry it failed. In the meantime, Mr. Slave-beater, we don't like brutality in Williamsburg, as you may have noticed, and best you remember it."

He turned his back on the cursing Lemon Waistcoat, and bent a rather amused eye on the participants in the small drama. "*Do* stop crying, young lady; or at least do so in silence. Mistress Lauchlin, you're all right? And you, Mistress Carilla? What a pair of doughty Amazons! I fear you're going to be in disgrace with Mistress Treanor again. And you, too, young man. That eye is going to be a beauty! Shall I see you all home and try to soften the repercussions?"

"Oh, please!" begged Lauchlin, and slipped a trusting hand through his arm. She carefully kept her other arm at her side, because she didn't want anyone touching it; and she didn't move her head much because of the violent shaking it had got. There was no need, she felt, for either of these things to be mentioned. After all, she *had* brought it on herself, and there was going to be quite enough fuss as it was. And if her shoulder developed large purple finger marks—as she rather thought it would—then no one but Rhoda need see them, and Rhoda wouldn't tell. . . .

Nor did she. From that moment, Rhoda was Lauchlin's scolding but devoted friend. She fetched a special (and magically treated) herb ointment for the bruises, and she massaged the poor wrenched neck, muttering darkly all the while that such behavior was *not* ladylike. She spent so much time fussing over Lauchlin's hair and Lauchlin's clothes that Carilla began accusing her plaintively of gross neglect, and threatened to join Haggis in his role of persecuted martyr.

"We're all persecuted martyrs," sighed Lauchlin. For Mr. Jefferson may have softened the consequences, but he had by no means averted them entirely. They were all in disgrace, this time—even Andrew, for regretting audibly that he had misssed all the fun.

Ronald was still looking like anything but an advertisement for passive resistance when Wednesday the first of June came around. Mistress Treanor looked critically at his purple eye when the family left for Bruton Parish Church. Shameful enough, her silence said, on an ordinary Sunday. But on the day of fasting and prayer for Boston—Well!

Ronald simply grinned at the old lady with what Carilla considered dreadful cheekiness. And to her great annoyance, Grandmother melted at once and smiled back at him with quite unnecessary warmth. Carilla's cheeks were unusually pink all the way to church, and she flirted noticeably with every boy she saw.

Then her attention was distracted, for Lauchlin was nudging her and nodding toward the governor's pew—significantly empty. It was clearly another declaration of war between Lord Dunmore and Williamsburg. What would happen next? Eyes met questioningly, all over the church. How far could things go without one side or the other resorting to violence?

"Suppose somebody should start shooting or something?" Carilla whispered apprehensively to Lauchlin.

Lauchlin shook her head, feeling a bit uneasy, herself. She was not as sure as she had been that a rising would be a grand and glorious thing. "Och," she whispered back hopefully, "No one could *really* be starting a fight. Your grandmother would never permit it."

But the ominous emptiness of that pew shadowed their minds all the way home—and at Woodlea a note awaited them from Lord Dunmore!

"An invitation to dinner on Tuesday," said Mr. Treanor with an oddly noncommittal expression. "All of us."

They all looked at the ornate sheet of heavy paper as if it might be a snake. Carilla swallowed. Lauchlin shuddered a tiny bit. She had glimpsed the governor only briefly, but it gave her the same horrid feeling that spiders and rats did.

"What for should he be wanting that?" demanded Ronald, lapsing into pure Gaelic idiom in his surprise.

"I don't know," mused Cousin Nathaniel. "He never struck me as the sort to give friendly little family dinners. I wonder what it is all about?"

His mother handed her cloak to the waiting Micah and began to take off her bonnet. "Well, I rather fancy we shall all find out on Tuesday evening, won't we?" she said serenely.

Fifteen

LORD DUNMORE'S DINNER

Governor's Palace quite dominated the north side of Williamsburg. A wide and gracious street led north from Duke of Gloucester Street past the church on the left and the expanse of Court House Green on the right, and straight to the elaborate balconied palace, where liveried slaves admitted the dinner guests.

Accustomed as Carilla was to fine and rich things, she felt somehow overwhelmed by the glittering solemnity here. Nor was she the only one. Ronald's chin squared as he walked in the massive door, and his kilt—especially donned for the occasion—swung rather more than usual. Let no Sassenach lord think he could awe a MacLeod!

Lauchlin—who invariably found solemnity funny—looked around with irreverent mirth brimming from her eyes. "Och, shouldn't we all be entering on our knees?" she murmured to Carilla, who bit her lip suddenly. The sad-faced slaves doubtless thought both girls to be overcome with the grandeur; actually it was the giggles. But only for a moment. They stopped abruptly, as if the house itself forbade laughter or mockery. Their eyes met, startled and questioning. They both felt it. It was a hateful place, with an ugly, muddy feel about it; a bullying, craven sort of feel, not greatly unlike the Lemon Waistcoat. And it all came from Lord Dunmore, jeweled and pompous, with ruddy cheeks and mean eyes and horrid quivering jowls.

At least he did seem to be more or less sober, and he did make some effort to conduct a conversation, in a forced and stilted fashion. The girls and Ronald sat silently, with bright observant eyes, as the talk toiled its way through tobacco crops, weather, the newest styles, and the English company of actors now playing at the theater behind the Capitol Building. But no politics, Ronald noticed shrewdly. He noted the fact for his report to Cousin Matthew. Lauchlin was memorizing the scene in general and their host in particular, while Carilla tried to think of a rhyme for Dunmore.

The dinner dragged. The slaves were rigid, poker-faced, nervous. Lord Dunmore was unbearably condescending, his wife a peahen, the food too rich and overseasoned. And their host did drink a great deal of fine canary wine, Carilla noticed.

He got to the point with the final course of fruit and cheese.

"I fancy you've been wondering why I invited you, eh?" he announced, clearly implying that he wouldn't have stooped so low without a special reason.

"Candidly, yes," Mr. Treanor replied, implying something quite different.

"Frankly, it's these—er—Young Persons you have staying with you." His Lordship leaned forward so that his gold-laced satin paunch pressed revoltingly against the edge of the table. His smile quite failed to be engaging. "You make no secret of your Highland origin," he accused Ronald, staring pointedly at the bright tartan of his kilt below a fine new dress jacket.

"Fine we're proud of it!" Ronald scarcely bothered to conceal his contempt.

Lord Dunmore looked startled and offended, not being

at all used to having a young sprig of a lad look down his nose at him. "Hmmm," he grunted, looking as if he had a bad taste in his mouth. "And I make no doubt that your parents were involved in that treasonous Rising back in '45, eh?" Ronald bristled at the choice of adjectives. "And you share their political opinions, eh?"

"Aye," said Ronald shortly. His chin was truculent. Lauchlin, across the table, stared with angry eyes. Mr. Treanor was frowning, and his mother seemed to be developing a layer of frost.

"Treason." Governor Dunmore seemed to savor the word. "Disloyalty to England."

This repetition was too much for Lauchlin, who flung her head back like a wild young foal, so that several pins flew out of her hair. "It is not, then!" she cried. "We're not English, so why *should* we be loyal to England? Are you loyal to Scotland?"

"Lauchlin!" said Mistress Treanor quellingly. Lauchlin subsided, quelled for the moment, one lock of hair slipping sideways.

Cousin Nathaniel was all lawyer now, crisp and incisive. "May I ask precisely what Your Lordship is implying, and upon what grounds?"

Lord Dunmore maintained astonishing self-control, considering that he had probably never been so directly confronted before in his life. He merely turned from red to purple, and swelled by several inches.

"Sedition is what I'm implying!" He flung two copies of a small newssheet on the table, tipping over his wine glass. "This filthy rag! This contumacious—" His vocabulary failed him. "It came in my last packet from London, along with a letter from Lord North wanting to know where it gets its material!"

The governor had had just enough wine to make him tell more than he really intended. "Half of it purports to describe conditions and events in Williamsburg," he fumed, "and seen through the eyes of a newcomer, at that. and the *other* half—" He glared at Ronald. "—is a pack of lies about the English occupation of Scotland."

Lauchlin opened her mouth to say they weren't lies. Then she shut it again under a cross fire of glares from Ronald and Cousin Lavinia. Lord Dunmore looked at her sharply.

"I am not a stupid man," he announced aggressively, "whatever some people appear to think."

This time it was Carilla who made a small choking sound, and he spared her a poisonous glance. Outrageous that he must suffer the impudence of these Colonials and Scots, who entirely failed in the reverent submission due an English Lord! The veins swelled in his forehead. He controlled himself.

"I don't believe in coincidences, and there is here an obvious and direct link with Williamsburg and Scotland."

He hadn't needed to point this out; his guests were well ahead of him. Lauchlin was wearing her impenitent look, Ronald had retreated to a place behind his eyes, and Carilla was staring at the newssheet with shattering realization. The heading read clearly *Gadfly*, and the cartoon under it was drawn in a perfectly unmistakable style. Everything clicked into place. Ronald's perpetual letters to Uncle Matthew, Lauchlin's careful duplicates of her best sketches, even the name....

She turned a reproachful gaze on Lauchlin, who sent back one of helpless apology. She *couldn't* share the secret; it wasn't hers!

Carilla nodded slightly, and Lauchlin sighed with relief. Then she looked searchingly at Cousin Nathaniel and his mother, each of whom had a copy, and who were reading them with considerable interest. Not by a flicker of an eyebrow did either indicate surprise or recognition.

"Mmm," said Mr. Treanor presently. "Very interesting. Rather a strong bias at times, but then what paper isn't biased—one way or another? And this at least labels opinion as such, presents reasonably accurate facts, and invites the reader to consider all views and form his own opinion. You say this is seditious, Milord? In what way?"

The governor spluttered wrathfully. "In what way? You're putting your own loyalty in doubt, Treanor, if you can ask! Every line questions the king's authority to govern as he sees fit!"

"That authority was questioned back in 1215, as I recall, and settled with the Magna Charta," retorted Cousin Nathaniel. "And again in the last century, when Charles I lost the decision and his head. Absolute authority does not exist in the English monarchy, and if you do not know that, Milord, you are unfit to hold office as governor of Virginia."

Lauchlin fully expected Lord Dunmore to fly apart, throw things, perhaps order them all arrested. But he had got himself on boggy ground, and had enough sense to shift it. "Do you, young MacLeod, deny that you had something to do with these papers?"

Ronald had no intention of doing any such thing. On the contrary! His black brows one straight line across his forehead, he flung back his head to proclaim the connection—and then in answer to a compelling look from Cousin Nathaniel remained bellicosely silent.

"Since this is not a court of law, Lord Dunmore, Ronald is not obliged to answer that question or any other. If you have real evidence of seditious behavior on his part, by all means produce it. In the meantime, it seems questionable that this paper *is* seditious, and you've no proof that he has any connection with it. And may I point out, sir, that *you* are doing more to create rebellion in Virginia than all the subversives in all of the colonies. In one day you gave Patrick Henry more supporters than he has ever had before, and you seem determined to turn every man against England."

He paused. The three young people were regarding him with profound admiration. Lady Dunmore and the slaves looked as if they expected thunderbolts to descend from heaven.

None did. Instead, Mistress Treanor carried on the attack where her son left off. She had been perfectly silent all this time, merely radiating a ladylike disapproval of such bad manners. Now she decided it was time to speak her mind.

"May I add, sir, that you have committed an incredible breach of manners." Her voice was icy, her manner that of an offended queen. "No gentleman—titled or not—would dream of inviting guests to his home and then insulting them. I am deeply ashamed for you."

And now, surely, he would have them all thrown in prison, perhaps sent back to England for trial as traitors? But he didn't, rather to the surprise of his household. He was of a color that defied description, but there was something about this old lady. . . . In any case, the events of the past few weeks had given him a rather unnerving glimpse of steel in these Colonials. He found himself defending his actions against this deplorable and intimidating female.

"It is my duty, Madam, to defend Virginia against subversion—"

This was a mistake. "Tell me, Lord Dunmore," inquired Mistress Treanor in her most sweetly acid voice, "do you look under your bed and in the wardrobe for subversives before retiring at night? Are we not all traitors according to your definition? It must make life very frightening for you, Governor. Do you visualize, say, my granddaughter and me, armed with muskets and perhaps dragging a cannon or two—"

"Don't leave me out!" clamored Lauchlin, who had been maintaining a truly heroic silence. "*I* shall steal all the ammunition from the Powder Magazine, just, and help load the cannon." She looked delighted at the prospect, and another lock of hair fell down.

Cousin Lavinia gave her a repressive glance, and turned again to their speechless host. "Had you better not jail us all at once, sir? No? Why, then, in that case I think we shall not impose longer on your gracious hospitality. Nathaniel, my dear?"

Everyone rose, the rustle of silk taffetas and brocade fortunately drowning out Lauchlin's gurgle of delight—although perhaps that would not have mattered much at this point. The atmosphere could not, by the wildest optimist, have been called amicable.

Late as it was, a serious conference was held in the cool, candle-lit library as soon as they got home. For the matter was not likely to end there.

"We were not wanting to involve you at all!" Ronald said unhappily. "That was why we said nothing—and it being Cousin Matthew's secret, besides—" He and Lauchlin looked at each other with misery and shame. Suddenly it seemed so dishonorable not to have been frank with the man who took them into his home! And yet—

"I know Matthew; he undoubtedly made you promise not to tell," said his sister crisply. "Never mind that now."

"But we were never dreaming—" Lauchlin was near tears. "And you putting yourselves in danger to protect us, too!" she told them accusingly.

Ronald was scowling blackly at the red-carpeted floor, his loyalties badly torn. Until lately the realm of ethics and loyalties had been such a clear-cut matter, and now it was most unfairly becoming more and more complicated. How had he come to be so fond of these Loyalist Sassenachs, who ought to be his enemies? And what did they mean by treating him as if he were a son of the house?

He regarded them with reproach, and Cousin Lavinia stared back severely. She had *never* intended to let herself become so attached to this fire-breathing young scamp of a rebel!

"I don't think we're in much danger," decided Cousin Nathaniel. "All of us burgesses are already on Dunmore's blacklist, anyway, and there's not much he can do against us if we give him no more excuse than he has now." He frowned. "The danger may be for you two, if he does get more evidence to connect you with the *Gadfly*. I could wish you hadn't distributed your drawings so lavishly at the Raleigh, Lauchlin."

Lauchlin hung her head and refused to meet Cousin Lavinia's gaze. But that surprising old lady stood up for her. "It's hardly likely that any of them will be displayed to the governor, Nathaniel. There's a far greater likelihood that he may try to intercept mail going to London. Can you arrange to have all their reports and sketches from now on given personally to ship captains you know we can trust? Or perhaps they could be taken to Richmond. . . ."

Ronald and Lauchlin looked at her in surprise. "You mean— Och, you mean we can go on sending them?"

"Certainly you'll go on sending them!" she said tartly. "I don't agree with your opinions, my dears, but I certainly shall not permit anyone to silence you! That kind of tyranny is just as bad as physical violence; perhaps worse, in a way." She looked thoughtful. "I must admit Matthew has rather a good idea, there. I must send him a dispatch or two, myself, just to balance your revolutionary views, my dears."

They stared at her, astonished.

"Och!" said Ronald. " 'Tis yourself is a rebel, too!"

"Impudent creature," she told him tolerantly. "Now run up to bed, all of you."

"Yes Ma'am," they said, curtsying and bowing.

In Carilla's bedchamber of white and rose, two bright heads conferred together while a patient Rhoda waited.

"What about the *Virginia Gadfly*?" demanded Carilla, alarmed. "If he sees that, he'll know for sure, what with the name *and* your cartoons! And I *do* think it was horrid not to tell me about Great-Uncle Matthew!"

"I *couldn't*," pleaded Lauchlin. "You know I couldn't! And anyway, yon serpent will never be seeing the *Virginia Gadfly*. Who would show him?"

Carilla fixed her with a gloomy eye. "With your luck, practically anybody," she predicted darkly. "A wind would blow it in his window, if nothing else. I think we ought to see if Andrew can get it back from whoever has it by now. And I don't think we ought to have any of your drawings in any more issues."

"*Seadh*!" Lauchlin bounced indignantly on the edge of the bed. "I like that! Whose idea was it, in the first place? If you and Andrew—"

"Oh, hush!" begged Carilla. "Grandmother will be in! I reckon we'd best just forget the *Virginia Gadfly*, and perhaps you'd let Andrew and me send some things to Great-Uncle Matthew. After all, if Grandmother is. . . ."

Lauchlin simmered down with a chuckle. "I've already sent a copy of your verse and Andrew's fairy-tale," she confessed, unblushing. "Yesterday, with that last packet. Och, just wait until we're reporting tonight's dinner, just!"

They looked at each other. Their eyes danced. They both fell at once into an abstracted mood which the apprehensive Rhoda recognized at once as the throes of creativity.

"Now you two behave yourselves!" she scolded, dragging Lauchlin off to her own room. "You're just *fixing* to get yourselves in more trouble, as if you hadn't already got in more of it than Miss Melicent will in the whole of her life!"

Lauchlin peered up at her mischievously through thick lashes. "Aye, but you don't love Melicent, all the same, and you do love me," she murmured, and rubbed her cheek affectionately against the dark one.

After which she sat down and produced a simply devastating sketch of Lord Dunmore, complete with paunch, jowls, and small cruel mouth. He was surrounded by menacing eyes fixed on him from under doors and beds, behind pictures and curtains, and even from a suspicious lump beneath the carpet. And he was glaring in great alarm at a tiny old lady and a round-faced girl with enormous eyes who defiantly aimed a large cannon at him.

In her own room, Carilla sat sucking her quill. "Little Lord Dunmore, he sat in a corner . . . No . . . There was an old Dunmore who lived in a stew . . . No . . .

Old King Troll was an obstinate soul
And an obstinate soul was he.
He drank and he lied and he swore and he stole—"

She chuckled wickedly.

Sixteen

WITCHES' BREW

Williamsburg was a witches' brew, simmering with uneasy conflict all through the heat of June and July. Burgesses went on meeting defiantly at the Raleigh, and everything seemed to wait for August first. Lord Dunmore continued to sulk and fume. And while Lauchlin and Ronald reluctantly became less one-sided in their opinions, the rest of the Colonials moved inexorably to more extreme views on one side or the other. It was, said Mistress Treanor austerely, the normal progress of any quarrel: quite deplorable, of course, but apparently inevitable. And she looked hard at George, who was spending a great deal of time visiting Carilla these days.

George smiled, but uncomfortably. He was moving rapidly to something not very different from the Governor's viewpoint, but he hated arguments, and there was a tacit agreement not to mention politics when he was there.

As for Ronald, he was so shattered by the heat that he no longer had the energy to be a fire-breathing seditionist. He had even been heard to concede (in a weakened condition brought on by an almost perpetual headache) that *if* the English were prepared to be reasonable, it might not, perhaps, be necessary to exterminate them altogether. Moreover, he added on a particularly ghastly day, it might serve them right just to let them *have* this outpost of hell. And Carilla, who also suffered a continuous heat headache, would have been inclined to agree with him if they had been on speaking terms.

Even the sun-loving Lauchlin was rather floored by it, and actually found herself, on a sweltering afternoon, wistfully describing to Carilla and Melicent the cold salt winds from the Minch.

"Stop it!" said Carilla pettishly. "You're just torturing us!" She waved a languid fan, but all it did was stir the hot stickiness of the air around a bit. Even here in her bedroom on the shaded north side of the house there was no breeze.

Melicent twirled her own fan coquettishly, imitating the dazzling belles of Virginia. Lauchlin giggled.

"Just you wait," said Melicent. "My mother's going to organize a special party season for the girls like us who haven't come out yet, and all the Tidewater boys will be there, *and* all the junior officers and midshipmen of the English army and navy who are around. They're all aristocrats, you know," she reminded Lauchlin, who had produced a scornful snort. "And won't you look silly when you can't even use a fan properly!"

"I can, just!" Lauchlin picked up the large one which she had been using for purely practical purposes, and flourished it. "Oooh, Lord Percival!" she trilled in a high voice, batting her lashes over the top of it. "Och, aren't you the most adorable man, just!" She vanished behind the fan with a simper and reappeared at one side with an outrageous wink. "Hee hee hee!" she giggled. "Ooooh, you naughty *thing*, you!"

"I dare you!" challenged Carilla at once, delighted.

"Don't you dare!" cried Melicent, trying not to laugh. "She'd *do* it, and she's already scandalous enough as it is! And my Mama says young gentlemen may be amused at a hoyden, but they'll *never* propose to her." She crossed the room to Carilla's large mirror and peered into it, quite reasonably certain that she would be the prettiest girl at the junior balls.

Lauchlin remained singularly unperturbed. "Och, I don't care. Anyway, Andrew does almost every day. And," she added wickedly, "I'm thinking George has romantic ideas in his head about Carilla."

"Oh, well *Andrew*—! He's only teasing!" Melicent sniffed as Carilla firmly moved her away from the mirror and peered in, herself. Was it true that George had ideas? So far, the world had deplorably failed to notice that Carilla was working very hard indeed to become an enchanting, adorable young lady, and she was rather worried about it. Did she lack charm? Did boys, perhaps, not care for short girls with round faces, even when furnished with large violet eyes and golden hair?

She stared, hopefully. Nice white skin with no tan or freckles or spots, and faintly pink cheeks, and reasonably long lashes even though they didn't show up very well. . . .

"Of course, *you'll* never be a classic beauty," said Melicent smugly. She was, and knew it.

"Carilla's *mignonne*," drawled Lauchlin, flaunting her French deliberately. "*And* she has golden hair, just. 'Tis in my mind she'll have more beaux at her feet than you, Melly."

Carilla dimpled at the thought. *That* would show Master Ronald MacLeod! Not, of course, that she cared a thing what *he* thought, anyway. He was just a barbaric Highlander, rude and mean and conceited and overbearing, and a revolutionary, and she didn't like him at all. In fact, she was totally indifferent to him. And to prove it, she began visualizing his annoyance if she should turn out to be the belle of Williamsburg.

"Master George is downstairs to see you, Miss Carilla," announced Rhoda at the door. "Here, let me fix your hair before you go down," she added, and Carilla flushed a little. Rhoda had never before spruced her up just for the boys.

Lauchlin stared after her small vanishing figure with a tiny sigh. She was being silly. George was everything that was charming and amiable and amusing—to his own class, of course—and doubtless he would make a grand husband, just. . . . She sighed again, and then wondered why.

"You get prettier every day, Carilla," said George with frank admiration, and bowed over her hand.

"Silly!" dimpled Carilla. "It hasn't been all that long since you were pulling my hair and calling me Shortie!"

He looked at the shining pile of curls with open admiration. "I wouldn't mind pulling it now," he admitted. "It sure is pretty stuff, Carilla."

She flushed with pleasure, fluttered her lashes. "Do you really think so?"

Seraphina, curled up on the sofa, opened and shut one

scornful topaz eye, and George laughed. "I always have, and you know it. Stop trying to flirt like Melicent, Carilla, or at least save it for someone who doesn't know you so well."

"You're horrid," Carilla told him without rancor. "Just you wait until Aunt Harriet's ball! I'll save *all* my dances for those handsome young English officers!"

At this moment the now fully-grown Haggis, who had recently discovered the role of Superior Being, stalked into the room and at once turned into a disapproving chaperone. "Waaah!" he said sourly. Then he leaped up on a small end table, scattered a portfolio of material once intended for the *Virginia Gadfly*, but now being prepared for Cousin Matthew, squalled indignantly, and jumped off.

"Oh, you wicked thing!" cried Carilla, and stooped to retrieve the papers.

"Let me," said George with that new-found gallantry of his, and dropped to one fine turquoise knee. "I haven't seen most of these," he discovered, studying one of Lauchlin's satiric sketches. "She is clever, isn't she?"

Carilla regarded him doubtfully. He sounded rather like someone praising a precocious slave. "I believe you think a mere female shouldn't be able to draw this sort of thing at all," she challenged him.

George rose to his feet, studying the picture of Lord Dunmore and the subversives. It was a new improved version, more suitable to publication in the *Gadfly*, and Carilla's bit of verse underneath was far more scurrilous than "Old King Troll" had been. He grinned, but not altogether in amusement.

"To tell the truth, I don't think a real lady would do this

sort of thing," he told her, clearly attributing it all to Lauchlin. "They must have a mighty funny notion of gentry in Scotland, Carilla. No, now don't blow me to bits. I know what you think of Ronald! And you know, if they weren't your kin, we'd none of us have accepted either of them socially."

This was probably quite true, and therefore unanswerable. Carilla stuffed the sketches back into their portfolio in a rather peevish silence.

"I wish you wouldn't be so stuffy," she muttered.

"I'm sorry," George said good-naturedly. "But I can't help caring about standards, you know. And I wish you and your family wouldn't listen so much to all this disloyal talk we hear nowadays. It could contaminate you, so you end up supporting the rabble."

"I won't! Don't be silly!" Carilla turned on him fiercely. "We aren't for revolution or separation or anything like that, and you know it. But there's such things as English rights, you know!"

"And English duty." George was more serious than she had ever seen him. "We owe loyalty and obedience to England, and it's treason to defy the king's appointed representative here. England would have every right to send troops over here to enforce order."

"They'd stir up a right smart hornet's nest if they did!" snapped Carilla, surprising herself almost as much as George. "Oh, please let's not argue politics, George," she pleaded. "We both hate it; and besides, if Grandmother should hear me—"

George chuckled. "A lady never argues with a guest or discusses politics with gentlemen," he told her with a severe face and twinkling eyes. "All right, let's talk about your eyes, which are the prettiest ones in the whole of Virginia."

"Why George!" exclaimed Carilla, delighted. And the huffy atmosphere vanished as if it had never existed.

The same could not be said for Williamsburg in general. By the first of August and the special convention, the atmosphere was very huffy indeed. Governor Dunmore was still forbidding the meeting, and the burgesses were still defying him, still meeting at the Raleigh instead of the closed Capitol. They not only endorsed their own idea of a Continental Congress, but they elected seven delegates to it, including Mr. Lee, Mr. Henry, Colonel Washington, and Peyton Randolph, who was chosen President of the Congress.

"Just wait until Cousin Matthew is getting *this* report," rejoiced Ronald, once more at perfect unity with his sister. "They've ordered all trade between Britain and Virginia stopped, and pledged supplies and help for Boston until that blockade is lifted, and Colonel Washington has promised to raise and feed a thousand troops to help break it, if Boston is needing them!"

Lauchlin, panting a little in the relative coolness of the summerhouse, looked up with a chuckle. "Och, won't Himself Dunmore be livid, just?"

He was even more livid when he heard about Mr. Jefferson's paper. So were a great many Virginians, including George. It was a great shock to be told that the English Parliament had no right to exercise *any* authority over the Colonies, and that if the rights of man were denied, then men had a right to act according to the Laws of Nature.

"Whatever *they* are," murmured Andrew with an impish glance at the others. Lauchlin stuck out her tongue at him, and Cousin Lavinia instantly rapped her on the head with a gold thimble.

"Mind your manners, my dear, or I'll put you on your backboard. I really do think Mr. Jefferson has gone too far. It's the influence of Mr. Henry, I dare say; I really must have a talk with him. One simply can't advocate anarchy."

But the Jefferson Paper was reprinted and read and hotly argued all over the Colonies. The simmering pot bubbled, particularly here, where the very air was charged as if for a thunderstorm. As if in the spirit of things, Williamsburg *did* have a series of thunderstorms, such as only Virginia can have. Even the fearless Lauchlin was awed, and Carilla frankly hid between featherbeds, however stifling, until it was over.

Governor Dunmore sulked in his palace and made life miserable for all who served him. Patrick Henry made more inflammatory speeches, and a truculent group of boys followed John Randolph down Gloucester Street one day shouting "Tory! Tory! Get a rope!"

Fat packets went from Woodlea to London with redoubled precautions and by all manner of route, via Deleware and Maryland ports, and even by New York. It was to be hoped, said Cousin Lavinia acidly, that they found the trip less contentious and warlike than the atmosphere right here on England Street.

Carilla and Ronald glared at each other, and Lauchlin impartially at both of them. Andrew looked as saintly as if he hadn't been deliberately provoking all three of them at every opportunity.

"Well, *I* put that drawing of Lord Dunmore right in the portfolio with the others," stormed Lauchlin. "And 'twas my best copy I'd worked on for an age, just, and I'm wanting to know what happened to it."

"Well, so am I!" Carilla sputtered, both hands to her aching head, which seemed likely to fall off in a minute—which might be just as well, at that. "It had my verses on it, too, and I can't even find the other copy of them, and I can *never* write them again!" She fixed an accusing eye on Ronald. "I'll bet you took them yourself, and sent them on to Great-Uncle Matthew without even waiting to ask if I had a copy."

Ronald at once flew into his own form of Highland rage, which was something like an arctic flame. He stood like ice, staring at her with burning eyes until Carilla was almost frightened. Lauchlin at once ranged herself by his side, fairly spitting.

"Ronald was telling you he never did so! How dare you put the lie on him? You— You *Sassenach!*"

"You tell 'em, Firetop!" murmured Andrew.

They all turned on him. "You shut your mouth, Andrew Dare!" they commanded with admirable unanimity.

"Reckon that's the first time all three of you have ever agreed in your lives," observed Andrew mildly, quite unabashed.

Ronald ignored him and turned to Cousin Nathaniel and Cousin Lavinia, who were watching in patient disapproval. "Do you believe I was sending it without asking did Carilla wish it?" he challenged them. "Do you believe, even, that I *could* have done so?"

"No," said Cousin Nathaniel instantly.

Cousin Lavinia lifted arched white eyebrows and went on embroidering scarlet poppies on a damask cloth. "Don't be silly, my dear," she said calmly. "If you said you didn't, you didn't. Carilla, I am quite shocked at you."

Carilla lowered her eyes because they were filled with tears, and she would *not* cry in front of Ronald. She saw clearly that she had made a quite unforgivable accusation —and it was all because her head ached so abominably, and the heat was so unrelenting, and probably fixing to have yet another thunderstorm—and oh, how she hated to have to apologize!

But Father and Grandmother were waiting, and so was her own sense of honor. She turned, bright head high and her round chin very firm indeed.

"I'm sorry," she said with great dignity. "I—" She paused, then looked right at Ronald with brave, honest eyes. "Well, of course I knew you wouldn't lie about it, and I didn't mean to suggest it—"

"Och," said Ronald, deeply embarrassed.

"—but you *do* make me so furious, Ronald MacLeod, I just don't know what I'm saying!"

They glared at each other.

"And that," drawled Andrew, "was the shortest truce on record."

Seventeen

CARILLA'S CONQUEST

On a velvet evening in August, Aunt Harriet's party took place, in the splendid huge Apollo Room of the Raleigh.

"Oooh, Mr. Stanton!" cooed Carilla, with a melting upward look from behind her fan. Her dress was of hyacinth-blue sarcenet over an amber and violet embroidered petticoat, an amethyst brooch held her delicate lace fichu, and a deep froth of the same filmy lace fell in ruffles from her elbow to wrist. The color and the candlelight made her eyes look like enormous pansies and her hair like old gold, and she knew it. After all, there *was* a high mirror just behind her brand new admirer. . . .

She smiled. "You're just the cleverest man I ever did meet!" she sighed. Melicent couldn't have done it a bit better!

Young Lieutenant Stanton, resplendent in the red coat and white breeches of His Majesty's Army, was entranced. Who said these Colonials weren't friendly? And this girl was clearly intelligent as well as pretty, too.

He simpered. "Oh, one does pick up a bit of wit and sophistication and all that, being on duty in different places, you know."

Carilla heroically resisted an extremely tart reply. This was her first conquest, and she intended to get from him every possible tidbit of inside news for Great-Uncle Matthew—preferably something reasonably earth-shattering, that would make one Ronald MacLeod simply sick with envy. She glanced virtuously across the floor, where a kilted Ronald led one Amy Ludwell, smiling, through a lively reel; while Lauchlin in a cloud of pale aqua was wasting golden opportunities, squabbling enjoyably with Andrew.

Concealing a yawn with that useful object the fan, Carilla once more peered upward through her lashes. "I reckon the governor is mighty proud to have you as an aide, isn't he, Mr. Stanton?"

Coming from the lovely lips of Mistress Carilla Treanor, this astonishing notion did not sound altogether ridiculous, after all. "Do you—I mean— That is, would you consider calling me Clarence?" he suggested hopefully to her.

Carilla's golden lashes dropped in a confusion not altogether feigned. Having conquered, how was she to make him produce information instead of awkward suggestions? "I— I don't think my Grandmother would consider that at all proper," she murmured truthfully. "After all, you know, we have only just met."

"Oh, I do beg your pardon!" He was all contrition. "Will you permit me to meet your family, and perhaps call one day soon?" he begged, clearly intending to correct this obstacle as soon as possible.

Carilla wondered why she wasn't more elated. After all, he was very tall and handsome, and he was at her feet, and that was just what she had wanted, wasn't it?

"Well— Perhaps you can meet Father tonight and ask," she conceded, and saw with some relief that George was coming to claim his minuet.

"I notice," said George not altogether approvingly as they took their places, "that you've got that English officer at your feet."

Carilla flickered a roguish smile at him. "I thought you liked the English officers, George," she said artlessly.

He laughed, turned her expertly under his raised arm, and matched her deep curtsy with a low bow. "Not when they take too much of your time," he said firmly, and Carilla sighed with pleasure. What a lovely ball! And she really was sort of the belle of it, too. And Ronald had just favored her with a most satisfying glance of deep annoyance. . . .

"Did you see Carilla playing up to yon gangling Lobsterback?" he grumbled to Lauchlin, as they met in the dance. "Doesn't care *who* she flirts with, does she?"

He had moved on before Lauchlin could answer, but she looked at his straight, angry back with considerable interest, wondering what he'd say if *she* danced with a Redcoat.

The Apollo Room was quite crowded with young people and their chaperones, who sat against the handsomely wainscoted walls. The tall windows were open to the balmy night, with a warm breeze coming through, and glimpses—if one looked hard—of fireflies outside. Cherry-red damask curtains hung from ceiling to floor on each side of the windows, and the fireplace was filled with red roses.

Mistress Treanor looked more like Dresden porcelain than ever in her gown of gentian-blue taffetas over silvery-grey, and when the dance ended and Lauchlin and Andrew reached her chair, she was talking graciously to Carilla's conquest.

"We shall all enjoy your company at tea one day, Mr. Stanton, but it is understood of course that Carilla is still too young to receive gentlemen callers."

Carilla arrived on George's arm. The two girls exchanged glances brimming with challenge and mischief. Melicent, all rosy laughter and pink taffeta, came up with Edwin.

Mr. Stanton bowed deeply, very much impressed by the girls these wild Colonials managed to produce. Mistress Carilla was like moonbeams, he decided with more romance than imagination, and this brown-haired one as pretty as a tea-rose, and the red-head like—well, like—Mr. Stanton's store of comparisons ran out. Andrew could have suggested to him things like wood-elves, wildflowers, fawns, and saucy-faced kittens. Since he didn't, Mr. Stanton bowed again and noticed how admiringly those dark eyes were fixed upon the splendor of his scarlet uniform. He preened himself a little, tried to think of a brilliant remark, and noticed—of all things!—a kilted fellow right there in the ballroom.

"My word!" he said lightly. "You Virginians *are* tolerant, aren't you? Fancy receiving one of those bare-legged savages socially!"

Oddly, this remark failed to have quite the effect he'd planned. Old Mistress Treanor frosted suddenly, and the three girls regarded him with what certainly seemed like a loss of warmth. Then the red-headed one spoke to him in a strange musical tongue.

"*Spruillse-ort, droch-inntinneach Sassenach*!" she lilted sweetly, and it was a mercy Carilla's grandmother could not understand Gaelic, particularly since Lauchlin detested the taste of soap.

"That is my cousin in the kilt," said Carilla coldly. After all, she might loathe Ronald herself, but no conceited pup of a Redcoat need think he could run down her family! Her fan indicated icy anger. "And this is Mistress Lauchlin MacLeod, who is his sister."

The young officer blushed furiously and fairly groveled in humble apologies. Carilla let him. Lauchlin received her share of apology with deep satisfaction and great amusement. Their eyes danced at each other. Then both of them caught a stern blue eye and hastily minded their manners. And the governor's aide, sweetly forgiven at last, went home that night and composed very bad sentimental poems about golden hair.

He appeared promptly on the appointed day for tea, and failed to conceal his surprise at not receiving any. He might have any number of cold fruit juices, or coffee, but—

"We don't drink tea," his hostess explained with crystal graciousness.

It seemed a bit odd. What about their guests, who might like it? Still, they *were* only Colonials, and one—*Was* that minx of a redhead laughing at him from behind her fruit juice?

She was, and at Carilla equally, who shot her a look of mingled threat and reproach. After all, she was doing this largely for the *Gadfly* wasn't she? And if she had to suffer the inane vanity of this fellow, whose ignorance of Colonial matters was as great as his conceit, why the least Lauchlin could do was refrain from laughing!

But Lauchlin was in one of her moods of wicked perversity, and even Cousin Lavinia's wrath to come couldn't quench her now. The things this *amadan* was saying! She couldn't resist. . . .

"Tell me, Lieutenant," she cooed, permitting a ruddy curl to swing over her embroidered green shoulder, "Is it often you lower yourself to associate with us poor Colonials and Barbarians?"

"Oh, no," said Mr. Stanton. "I mean yes— I mean—"

"Do have some more juice, Mr. Stanton," said Mistress Treanor with a forbidding glance at Lauchlin.

But Lauchlin now had the bit in her teeth. "How very nice it must be for you to serve under such a sonsie polite man as Lord Dunmore! Aren't you lucky, just?"

It wasn't at all the word Clarence Stanton would have chosen. Quite the contrary. He looked at her rather oddly, swallowed something, and indicated that he was indeed lucky, but would be far luckier if permitted to visit Woodlea again soon. After which he left without dropping so much as the faintest hint of any interesting bits of news.

"I don't believe he knows any," grumbled Carilla later from the discomfort of her backboard. (Grandmother's punishments usually had the dubious virtue of combining the unpleasantness with some desirable end like good posture.) "And you didn't help a bit, you wretch!"

Lauchlin turned her head on her own instrument of torture. "Never mind," she said with an impenitent chuckle. "We can be doing even better another time, and it worth the consequences. Besides, he could be letting slip something important any time at all. You'll just have to keep him dangling, 'Rilla, forever and ever."

Carilla groaned. Then she cheered up. After all, it did give one a pleasant sense of power to have an English officer in a state of helpless adoration, and it was undeniably flattering, too, to have him gazing at her as if she had just flown in from heaven, and writing poems. . . . Oh dear, *what* poems!

"Anyway," observed Lauchlin callously, " 'twill be good for yon Geordie to have a wee bit of competition. He's thinking too much of himself, is that lad."

"Just because he called you an immigrant, you've never forgotten it," Carilla retorted, not very heatedly. "And you'll have to help me with Lieutenant Stanton, and stop scaring him to death and confusing him like that, or I'll let you get your own news for Great-Uncle Matthew, so there!"

"Och, all right," agreed Lauchlin. "But 'tis you he likes. You could perhaps be waiting for the next thunderstorm and see would he spread his bonnie red coat over a puddle for you to step on."

Carilla giggled. "Or fall in the river and see if he'd jump in to save me."

They both giggled.

Mistress Treanor, who was clearly part witch and could read minds, made it a point that evening to give both girls a little lecture on character. When a female became a calculating little flirt, she told Carilla, or gave way to petty vindictiveness, she added to Lauchlin, it inevitably showed up in the face and eyes.

Alarmed, both girls fled to the mirror.

Eighteen

THE SKETCH

On a September afternoon Lieutenant Stanton appeared at the gate with a long face and a distressed pucker on his smooth forehead. He walked unhearing through a loud verbal battle between Haggis and the mockingbird, he was distracted all through tea, and at last he stammered pinkly that he wouldn't have the pleasure of visiting them any more.

Carilla stiffened indignantly. It was true she had been wondering what to do about him, since he was a deadly bore and hadn't produced one single item of interest to the *Gadfly*—but this was something altogether different.

Moreover, his series of excuses were so lame as to be a further insult. When he rose to leave, she gave her grandmother a pleading look, received a nod, and a moment later overtook the young officer on the veranda. Her small round face was flushed, her huge eyes not at all pansylike.

"I never heard such feeble excuses in all my life!" she told him trenchantly. "You'd have done better to say outright you're just bored."

"Oh no, please, Mistress Carilla!" he bleated. "It isn't that at all, truly! I— It isn't my fault, I assure you! I mean—" He trailed off in an embarrassed silence. On the lawn, the mockingbird made a diving attack on Haggis, who fled, yowling, for cover. Carilla waited, her face not very helpful or encouraging.

"It's orders," he confessed miserably. "I didn't— I mean, I was trying to be tactful. It's really awfully embarrassing. . . ."

Carilla thawed just a trifle. "I reckon you'd better tell me, then, instead of yammering on about working so hard, and that other nonsense."

He obeyed, his normal complacence quite demolished for the moment. "It's Lord Dunmore," he sighed. "He— He found out I was visiting you, and threw a fit. I ought to warn you, he thinks you're all revolutionaries at Woodlea. I tried to tell him you're as loyal as I am," he assured her, "but he wouldn't listen. He's a very—well, forceful—man, Miss Carilla. Even threatened to have me court-martialed if I ever came here again." And he glanced rather nervously over his shoulder at the emptiness of England Street, where nothing stirred except the spot in the hedge where Haggis had taken cover, and another spot in the magnolia tree where his enemy dared him to come out.

Carilla stared unseeing for an instant, reflecting on the thanklessness of trying to be reasonable and moderate in a quarrel. One side called you radical and revolutionary and democrat, while the other insisted you were a die-hard Tory. Carilla wasn't quite sure what she was, except that she was for English rights and against the governor.

"That horrid old fool!'" she said scornfully, shoving the lieutenant behind one of the white pillars, safe from prying eyes, and meeting his shocked look squarely. "You *know* he is, Mr. Stanton; you needn't try to deny it. Anyway, we already know he thinks we're a subversive lot here. He asked us to dinner last June and accused us of all sorts of dreadful things." She permitted her eyes to become wide and hurt and outraged, and inviting of confidences.

"Well, he does seem to have some grievance against your family," Mr. Stanton confided in what was surely a massive understatement. Carilla bit a twitching lip as she remembered Grandmother's last words at that ill-fated dinner party. But the young officer's next words pulled her to sharp and startled attention.

"I oughtn't tell you this, perhaps, but— Well, I was there last week when he received some sort of message: a sheet of paper and a note, I think. I didn't see what was on them, but the governor nearly had an apoplexy. He was shouting a lot of things like not needing any—uh—blasted note to recognize *that* artist, and it was more of that—uh—ruddy sedition from Woodlea, and he'd known it all along, and just wait until he got proof." He looked at her, worried but heroic. "But I never said a thing against you, and what's more, I don't even believe it. Although—" He looked judicious now, and a little superior. "One does wonder at times if your cousins go just a trifle too far in their joking. . . ." A delicate and tactful warning, surely? "And then, only today he found out I'd been visiting you, and— Well, you know the rest."

Carilla's mind was spinning. Artist! Merciful heavens, had he, after all, got hold of the *Virginia Gadfly*? But surely Andrew had retrieved both copies? Or had he? Or was it one of the sketches Lauchlin did in the Raleigh? Or—

He was staring down at her curiously, and she pulled herself together. "I'm trying to think what it could all be about," she told him truthfully. "But I do see it wasn't your fault, Mr. Stanton, and I'm sorry I was cross."

He looked pleased. "You do see that, then? And perhaps I can see you from time to time, anyway. I wouldn't even mind taking a bit of a risk," he ended gallantly, "to give you pleasure."

Carilla bit her lip suddenly, lowered her eyes, and gave him her hand to kiss. And Lieutenant Stanton, after carefully looking up and down the sleepy street, made a rather furtive departure just as Haggis slunk—equally furtive—out from under the hedge. They looked at each other in passing with rather absent-minded hostility.

Carilla didn't stop to notice. She hurried back into the house to give Grandmother the dismaying report.

"A lady," said Grandmother, "*never* shows herself to be flustered or upset about anything. Sit down and calm yourself, my dear. Lauchlin, send one of the slaves round to ask Andrew over for dinner. We can all talk about it quietly then."

Not that they really waited, of course. The quiet talk was only a continuation of the one the young people had been having all along. What sketch *was* it, and who had sent it to Dunmore?

Andrew denied that it could be the *Virginia Gadfly*, both copies being safe in his possession. And surely the caricatures of Virginia burgesses wouldn't particularly annoy the governor? But there were others. There was one of a pompous strutting turkey cock with the unmistakable face of Lord Dunmore, and there was the one drawn just after that dinner party . . . the one with Carilla's scurrilous verses underneath . . . the one that was mysteriously missing. . . .

They all looked at one another. The conclusion seemed inescapable. The means was another matter, and quite shocking in its implications. By what magic had it vanished from the portfolio—and who was the magician? There simply was no possible answer.

"It's quite useless to try to solve that, my dears," said Mistress Treanor crisply. "The point is, what damage has been done? Nathaniel?"

Cousin Nathaniel reflected for a moment, his lawyer's mind busy. "I don't think there are any legal steps Dunmore could take," he decided. "There were no signatures or labels; and there were no names mentioned at all in the verses, were there?"

"No, but he *must* know 'tis referring to that dinner party," Ronald pointed out, glancing darkly at Carilla. "Those verses—"

"Hold your tongue, dear," said Cousin Lavinia placidly.

"Oh, he knows, all right," Cousin Nathaniel nodded. "Proof is a trickier matter, and I doubt he'll try it. He does have the authority to arrest us out of hand, of course, or to ship Ronald and Lauchlin back to Britian—but as he hasn't done it yet, I fancy he doesn't plan to. Especially with the Continental Congress going on, and tempers at the explosion point as it is. No, I think it far more likely that he'll hang on and nurse his grudge and wait for an opportunity to get even. I rather think, you know, that dispatches to Uncle Matthew from now on had best be straight fact, without opinion."

Ronald scowled and Lauchlin stuck out her lip.

"It will be very good for you," said Cousin Lavinia. "Training in objective reporting is just what you need, to develop a sense of perspective."

And so the subject was officially dropped, but everyone was haunted by the thought of how the sketch—if it was the missing one—reached the Governor's Palace.

The Continental Congress went on meeting until well into October, and news trickled back tantalizingly about what they were doing. On a day of torrential autumn rain a courier from Philadelphia brought news of proceedings a great deal more extreme than anyone had expected. The Massachusetts radicals, led by Samuel Adams, had clearly taken over. They didn't stop at sending addresses to the king and people of England protesting that they were loyal citizens but would not put up with such unfair treatment. They didn't even stop at passing a Declaration of Rights and Grievances. They went on to ban all trade with Britain and vote a complete boycott of all British goods; and they set up local committees to enforce it. And, just in case England should go on being unreasonable, they arranged for another Congress in May.

"Just wait," predicted Andrew with a kind of ghoulish glee. "England will now undertake to make us loyal and affectionate subjects by more force. Remind me when we get married, Firetop, if our children don't love us, we'll whip 'em 'til they do."

Lauchlin considered this. "But I can't marry you," she objected. "Your front teeth stick out."

The rest of them ignored this silliness, which was going on all the time, and got tiresome. They sat somberly around the morning room, which was warmed and lightened by a small fire against the November rain, and the tacit ban on politics had been dropped. One breathed it, these days, and all other subjects invariably led there.

"If they do—" began Edwin. "Try to whip us into loyalty, I mean, with harsh, repressive laws—"

Lauchlin had a blinding revelation. "They do their own people too!" she cried. "There's the poor ordinary Sassenach is nearly as oppressed as the Highlander, and much more than we are here!"

George stopped looking at Carilla's hair and looked at Lauchlin. The wet-pebble opaqueness was back in his eyes, and the thought "common rabble" trembled almost audibly in the air. Then he looked through her.

"England has a right to demand our loyalty, and if we won't give it freely, then I reckon it's got to be enforced," he said.

"Just what I said," murmured Andrew, satiric. But Edwin and Carilla were both mulling this over. It sounded reasonable—but—

"Bah!" said Lauchlin insultingly in George's direction.

George reddened but went on looking through her. Edwin came out of his thoughts. "What if it really came to violence? Would anyone here really want us to take up arms against our own country?"

"Fine I would!" cried Ronald, enthusiastic.

"You don't count," Andrew told him. "England isn't your country."

"Aye but there are others, and not Scots, either!"

Lauchlin stared around triumphantly. "Were you thinking all those militia being raised and trained over the Colonies are for exercise, just?"

Crossed glares met: Ronald and Carilla, Lauchlin and George.

"Hear hear!" drawled Andrew, drooping an eyelid. "Hail the revolution! Up, girl, and at 'em! To arms!"

"Very funny," said Carilla sourly.

"I wasn't being funny, actually," he retorted.

There was a moment of depressed silence, none of them liking each other very well. Lady Seraphina jumped into Carilla's lap and arranged herself, purring gently. Then Lauchlin sputtered into laughter.

"Och!" she gurgled. " 'Tis Geordie is looking exactly like Lord Dunmore this minute!"

It was true. By a trick of light and mood, his usually pleasant ruddy face had turned to the surly one of the governor. Carilla gave a yelp of laughter, the boys chortled, and George scowled in real annoyance, rare with him.

"I swear these no-count immigrants have corrupted all of you!" he cried hotly. "You all get more and more sympathetic with un-English ideas and activities all the time, and someone ought to report the subversive things those two are doing, to the governor or someone!"

"George!" cried Carilla, shocked.

Lauchlin sat suddenly upright, not even noticing Ronald's sudden icy black rage beside her. "Geordie," she murmured into the dismayed silence as he stood up to leave. "Geordie!" she repeated more loudly as he ignored her and started to stalk out of the room. "Och, wee Geordie, you wouldn't have been sending just a wee bittie hint to him, yourself, now, would you?"

Andrew gave her a sudden sharp glance. George flamed bright red and tried to push past Carilla. His eyes were those of a dog caught still chewing the remains of a slipper. Carilla stared at him with round, incredulous eyes.

"George!" she whispered, grabbing the skirt of his fine cardinal coat and clutching it. "George, you didn't! George, those sketches you were looking at that day. . . ."

George turned, answered too quickly. "I haven't got it!"

"Oh *George*!" Carilla's voice was a heartbroken wail. "How could you do such a sneaky thing!"

"I told you I haven't got it!" George shouted into the thick grey silence. Lauchlin and the boys just looked at him. Carilla winced.

"What are you talking about?" demanded the mystified Edwin. "What is going on? Got what?"

A tear dropped from Carilla's eye onto Lady Seraphina, who removed herself in a huff. "It was one of Lauchlin's sketches and my verses, that we did after Lord Dunmore's dinner that time," she told Edwin, sounding almost extinguished in her disillusionment. "He— I know George took it and sent it to Lord Dunmore. And with a note, too! And now he's trying to deceive me by saying he hasn't got it. Oh, George, and I always thought you were a gentleman!"

Humiliated quite beyond endurance, George lost his head. "I didn't know you had anything to do with it, Carilla! I don't believe you could have written those insulting rhymes. And it was time someone got these filthy rebels put away somewhere, where they belong."

He had now damned himself completely. The silence swirled around the room and was shattered by the squeal of Edwin's chair as he shoved it back. "Why, you odious little toad!" said Edwin disbelievingly.

Andrew rose and drifted between George and the door, suggesting in a soft voice that he'd be glad to see George outside. "Not," he added fastidiously, "that I'd soil my hands on you, mind. But I reckon I can afford to buy a clean riding whip when I've finished."

Ronald's rage had turned into a feeling of sickness. Clean anger, even honest hatred, was one thing. But this two-faced malevolence that wore a mask of jovial friendship. . . . It was the more vile and sickening because Ronald had, against his will, come to like George.

Lauchlin was making a more horrifying discovery. George didn't in the least consider himself vile or treacherous, but an honorable gentleman, terribly misjudged. Carilla's last words had cut deeply: he was protesting. Gentlemanly behavior was reserved for one's own class, to which the MacLeods did not belong. "If I'd known those were your verses, Carilla, I'd have cut that part off! You should know that without my telling you!"

Carilla stared at him. She looked remarkably like her grandmother. "I don't suppose you'll understand that that makes it all the worse," she said, her voice small and cool and remote. "Please don't come here any more, George. I don't reckon we have anything to say to each other."

In angry and wronged silence, George left. An air of deep gloom remained behind, filling the morning room. Carilla began to cry and Edwin put an arm around her, and Lauchlin had a sudden glimmer of how deep this hurt went. These others had all laughed and played and squabbled together since babyhood, and now something that had been alive and warm was shattered and ugly.

"Och, and 'twas myself the cause!" she mourned, her chin drooping.

Ronald had gone into seclusion behind his eyes. But

Andrew patted her hand and shook his brown head. "Not really, Firetop honey. It was bound to happen one way or another, the way things are going."

Carilla looked up, wiped the backs of her hands fiercely across her eyes. "Oh, a *pox* on England!" she cried. "It's all their fault! I just think maybe Mr. Henry's right, after all, and we oughtn't to have anything to do with them ever!"

And Andrew grinned wryly.

Nineteen

BY THE RIVER

"I can't *think* why yon fat Dunmore hasn't pounced yet," mused Lauchlin, fingering the soft cocoa-brown velvet of her new riding dress and then raising puzzled eyes to Carilla, who was a dream in blue.

Carilla just shook her fair head, an amused eye on the spectacle of Haggis absent-mindedly swaggering across the lawn in some brand new role. "You'll be sorry," she murmured.

The mockingbird dived. Haggis, bawling for help, bolted under the hedge, from where he peered out reproachfully at the giggling girls on the sunny veranda.

Ronald, also dressed for riding, came out, raised a dark eyebrow at the hedge, grinned. A most welcome peace had reigned between him and Carilla since that awful business with George three weeks ago. Their feud, thought Lauchlin shrewdly, had been wearing a bit thin anyway. It would be quite impossible to continue now, in the teeth of real conflict.

Melicent and Andrew and Edwin arrived all at once, buoyant in the crisp gold of the November morning. Haggis, encouraged, ventured out of hiding. The mockingbird prepared to strike again.

"Get him, Haggis!" shrilled Lauchlin, and gave the MacLeod war rant. The mockingbird, shocked, tried to brake in mid-air. And Haggis in a sudden and novel burst of courage, made a spectacular leap upwards, shot out a black and white paw, and returned to earth triumphantly possessed of one long grey tail feather.

The mockingbird retreated in disorder. The six spectators cheered. And Haggis instantly turned into Alexander the Great with his trophies of victory. Look at him, he bawled, parading before them with his feather held triumphantly and rakishly between his teeth. He'd Won! All by himself, too, he added, daring Lauchlin to contradict him.

Lauchlin cheerfully declined. "We were wondering why Himself has not yet arrested us or anything," she told the others, starting down the steps, tripping over her skirt, and getting neatly caught at the bottom by Andrew.

"Hello, Firetop," grinned Andrew, setting her upright. "Your hair's falling down."

"Aye; let's hurry before Rhoda sees," she agreed, somehow managing to trip Carilla. Edwin steadied her. The boys had learned to be alert for such slight contretemps when Lauchlin was around.

"It isn't that Dunmore's not vindictive, either," Edwin mused, carrying on with the conversation. "Because he is. You'd think—"

"Och, he's set spies, just!" Lauchlin announced suddenly and loudly. Her small face alight with mischief, she pointed at the only other person to be seen at this end of England Street, a tallow-faced man just walking past. "Yon's a spy!" she announced.

The tallow-faced man looked horrified. Haggis, carried away by the excitement of the occasion, rushed up and bit Andrew on the ankle. Andrew yelled, everyone else shouted, and the tallow-faced man hurried off in great alarm to tell Lord Dunmore that the red-haired girl had somehow found out he was watching them, though he couldn't think how. Moreover, he added, aggrieved, she'd gathered a howling mob of young hoodlums there, and they were clearly preparing to attack him when he escaped. Presently he regretted that he hadn't stayed to face the attack, after all, for the governor was indeed vindictive, and bad-tempered, too.

But none of the young folk suspected for an instant that this was Lauchlin's day to display a touch of what Highlanders called the "Second Sight." They were mounted at last, and off, laughing and talking, for a ride up Jamestown way. They had to go clear up to Gloucester Street before turning west, to avoid the steep ravine that severed Francis Street and caused it to turn into France Street on the other side. Then left again, around William and Mary College to the Jamestown road. Edwin and Carilla led the way, their horses dancing slightly with the joy of movement. Andrew and Lauchlin followed, leaving Ronald to escort Melicent.

This greatly pleased that young lady, who was showing a growing tendency to flutter her eyelashes at Ronald and hang adoringly on every word. Ronald found this disconcerting. He could be as gallant in manners as anyone, but Virginia girls were *too* sweet and coquettish and worshipful for his taste. He smiled at Melicent—and decided that he liked females that were straightforward and spunky, like Lauchlin, and Cousin Lavinia, and—and Carilla! *Mo thruigh*!

It seemed odd to be paired up this way, not to have four boys and three girls. George left a large gap, a stout, red-cheeked good-natured gap, painful to think about. Even Lauchlin, though she kept telling herself that she had never really trusted him, felt wounded. No one really wanted to talk about it—and yet it was like a festering sore that could not be ignored.

"To be so dishonorable!" brooded Edwin, reining in his horse for a moment to stare at the autumnal splendor about them. "It's the sort of thing one might expect from the lower classes, but—"

"But we got it from our own patrician selves," murmured Andrew with an ironic one-sided smile. "Do you reckon it could be that we're not quite as superior as we think we are?"

"Andrew!" spluttered Melicent, scandalized.

"You Sassenach are all snobs," explained Ronald kindly. "You divide yourselves into classes—" He sliced the air horizontally. "—and assume yourselves are better than everybody below, and never think to see is it true or not."

There was a slightly embarrassed silence while they all remembered the Yorktown dock—and George. But Edwin shook his blond head.

"Oh, come now, Ronald, don't try to tell me you don't consider yourself better than the peasants on your father's land!"

"There *are* no peasants in the Highlands, whatever!" Lauchlin turned an indignant bronze head to him. "They are all clansmen—and *clann* is meaning family—and it is only that Ronald is next chieftain, and so he is having more education and responsibility."

"Precisely," said Edwin.

Lauchlin scowled, and Ronald fought back a sudden wave of homesickness for the clan brotherhood that no outsider could understand. "Och, but I'd never be setting myself up as a superior breed!" he protested, curling his lip at the notion. "What daftness! There's a dozen with more skill at stalking deer or guddling salmon or skulking in the heather; there's the MacCrimmons, the best pipers in the world; and Fergus, a feather-footed giant over crossed swords; and Seumas, with the canny common sense has kept me out of trouble this many a time—" He paused, lifted his head with unconscious arrogance. "There's all of them Highlanders and MacLeods, with more courage and honor and—"

Andrew began to chuckle. Ronald stopped and glared at him, but Andrew just twinkled back, unperturbed.

"Reckon your snobbery's just a mite different from ours, is all, Ronald," he pointed out. "Not class, but clan and country."

Ronald looked at him with reproach. Andrew was deliberately missing the point. " 'Tis the notion of class is all wrong!" he insisted. "Since you've no clan system here, you should be abolishing the aristocracy altogether, and starting a government run by everybody."

"Oh, Ronald!" giggled Melicent, sure he was joking. Carilla put her nose in the air and Edwin looked disapproving, but Lauchlin had an odd idea that Andrew might not altogether disagree.

"You've been reading John Locke and his notions on rule by Common Man," was all he said.

"Oh, aye," Ronald agreed shamelessly, and they started on.

Having curved past the college, the narrow dirt road now tunneled into the thick pine woods outside the town. While other trees were flaunting russet and tawny and golden leaves, these still arched dark green overhead, almost black in the gloom of their own shade. The young voices chattered and sang light-heartedly until at last they came out into the Black River swamp and paused. There was the ford crossing to the island where Jamestown had been built, and there was part of the now deserted church, looking lonely. Now that the weather was too chilly for picnics, no one came to enliven the place.

Or did they? A movement on the island turned into the figure of a frontiersman in deerskin shirt, who stood at the edge of the ford and stared across the river at them. He did not look, thought Lauchlin, particularly friendly. But on the other hand, she decided fair-mindedly, neither did they. In fact, they probably looked quite infuriatingly superior and arrogant.

"Might as well ride on," murmured Edwin, somehow managing to convey the impression that the woodsman simply wasn't there at all.

Carilla hesitated. "But what do you reckon he's doing there?" she wondered aloud. "Just camping on his way to join some of the militia?" She frowned a little. This seemed an awfully out-of-the-way place . . .

And then things happened too quickly to sort out. They never could decide afterwards whether it was sheer chance, or whether their singing and horse hoofs had been heard and planned for. In any case, suddenly the road was blocked and the wood seemed full of backwoodsmen. They were not a prepossessing sight. Great hulking men or lean wiry ones, all of them seemed unnecessarily hairy and dirty and sweaty and uncouth, and they all waved muskets about, and they had no look at all of knowing their place in society. Melicent nervously pressed her horse closer to Ronald's.

Edwin reined his restless horse to avoid the men who blocked the way. "If you'll kindly move aside and let us past?" he asked, courteously enough, but with an air of expecting to be obeyed at once by his inferiors.

A couple of men started to shuffle to one side, but the rest stood their ground, looking over the little group of aristocrats with narrowed eyes. Ronald, in turn, was studying them with an interest which was slowly pierced by faint uneasiness. He had been insisting that the common people should have equal rights and help run the government. Well, here were some of the common people. They didn't look very promising. But then, he remembered, they hadn't been educated yet. That, doubtless, would make all the difference.

"Waal waal," said a short man with hot intense eyes. "Look at the fine little Tory ladies and gentlemen out for a ride."

Lauchlin at once opened her mouth to deny this, but then closed it again. After all, some of them *were* Tories, so she could hardly explain that she wasn't. It was Andrew who grinned down at them easily.

"Reckon that depends on who you're talking to," he observed. "Some of our friends call us wild-eyed radicals and worse."

The backwoodsmen ignored this, considering it altogether unlikely. They scowled at the fine clothing, the velvet riding dresses and glossy boots and rich coats. They eyed the horses with angry and covetous eyes.

"Think yourselves better'n us'ns," growled a bulky, dark-bearded fellow. "Think you got a right to have fancy clothes and big houses and slaves to wait on you. Might be we'll learn you different some day. All men are equal, that's what we say, and we're fixin' to run this land, and have fancy slaves for ourselves, too."

Andrew raised a mocking eyebrow, and Lauchlin realized that he was thoroughly enjoying this. "Dear me," he drawled, ignoring Edwin's warning glance. "If all men are equal, how can you possibly figure on having slaves? They must be equal, too, you know." They frowned, not quite grasping this. Andrew made sure they did. "You're saying slaves and Indians are as good as you or me."

This was a great diplomatic error. The men turned ugly at once, pressed closer threateningly, shouted vile things. "Call a dirty black as good as us?" they snarled. "We'll fix you!"

Melicent let out one squeak of alarm and then held her tongue, white-faced. The boys glanced at one another in dismay, wondering how best to protect the girls. Lauchlin was still more interested than alarmed, but red flags of anger began to show on Carilla's dimpled cheeks.

"We'll start by having them horses," decided the short, hot-eyed man. "That'll likely get six of us in the cavalry. Reckon hit'll be a good joke," he went on meanly, "to have their own horses fight agin 'em."

Carilla boiled over. It was not entirely the idea of losing Swallow, although that was certainly part of it. But Carilla was not quite as passionately fond of horses as a good

Virginian should be, and right now she was hot with outrage, and injustice, and the humiliation of being at the mercy of these beasts.

"I suppose you think you'll make yourselves our equals by stealing our horses?" she blazed. "You want to pull everybody down to your level if they're higher, but let the ones under you stay there! You can't even think straight, you no-count rabble! If we say we're better than you, it isn't because of fine clothes, it's because we have a long tradition of self-discipline and manners and breeding and culture and education, and we work all our lives to maintain that tradition, too. You'd never think of that, would you? No, you want power and wealth and no discipline! You want everybody just as dirty and ignorant and ill-mannered as you! If your kind ever does run the country, it will turn into one big stupid mob, with no values except being like everybody else, and hating anyone who dares to be a little different or better or more educated; and—"

Carilla had a good deal more on her mind, but she never said it, because the bearded burly man reached up at that point and dragged her bodily off Swallow. At once the boys erupted into action—but they had hardly moved six inches before the whole score or so of rough men had closed in. Within about thirty seconds all six young people were off their horses and held fast by dirty and untender hands.

"Look here," Edwin began urgently. "The girls—" A horny palm silenced him.

The burly man placed Carilla's shoulders in the firm grip of another, and stood back to survey her, arms akimbo. She faced him, pale but unflinching—at least on the surface. His face held a kind of hatred that would be altogether terrifying if she allowed herself to think about it.

"Uppity little snit!" he grated. "Reckon you better take it back—and down on your knees to do it!"

"Shan't!" said Carilla briefly.

The man slapped her. It was a crashing blow across her cheek, so sudden and painful and unexpected that Carilla was simply too stunned for an instant to react at all. She didn't cry out, because it was not in her nature or training to do so. She simply gasped slightly, staggered a little, blinked, and then stared at him with no expression whatever. It gave the impression of quite astounding stoicism—and these men had never dreamed of the steel that could hide within a small, fragile little lady. They gaped, and Carilla had an instant to recover her wits and to fortify herself with a blaze of pride and anger.

She was only vaguely aware that behind her there were sounds of furious struggle as the boys and Lauchlin tried to help her. Her attention was wholly on the burly man, who recovered from his surprise and raised a hamlike hand again, slowly and menacingly. Carilla forced herself to look at it with an air of disinterest. She wanted to say something disdainful and cutting, but she couldn't seem to think of anything—and besides, her face was so stiff and numb that she wasn't sure if she could speak clearly. She concentrated instead on *looking* disdainful.

Crash! It seemed as if her whole head exploded in a roar of black and red. Everything tried to fade out for an instant; then she felt the hardness of hands holding her up, and instinctively she concentrated on standing upright. She would *not* fall down. She would keep her head high—if she could find her head. The murkiness before her eyes began to clear slowly. She took a deep breath and blinked things back into focus. And there were those slatey eyes again, still angry and merciless.

Carilla remembered Father once saying that the mark of a bully is that courage simply infuriates him and makes him even more of a bully. Good! She wanted to infuriate him! On a rising flood of angry pride, she knew herself to be the victor, stared back at him with level, unyielding eyes, reckless now of the outcome. The hand raised again.

Behind her, another man had come to help hold Ronald, who was in the grip of that fearful thing called Highland battle-madness. It distracted some awed attention from Carilla, but it didn't help her at all. Edwin and Andrew were struggling as well, Melicent was deathly pale, and Lauchlin . . .

Lauchlin disgraced herself and her country by crying. She couldn't help it; she couldn't bear to watch anyone being hurt; she would far rather be hurt herself. This was not saintliness, but merely that it was easier to bear the pain oneself than to imagine it for someone else. She made no sound. Tears simply crowded against her eyelids until they finally spilled over in a warm salt torrent down her cheeks.

By now some of the other men were beginning to stir uncomfortably, knocking a little girl around not being altogether to their liking. Andrew at once took advantage of this. He twisted his mouth free from the hand across it (which really had a most unpleasant assortment of flavors) and spoke in a low derisive voice which somehow captured the attention even of the chief bully.

"You-all reckon to win *independence*?" he asked in astonished tones. "Tut tut!" He sounded regretful. "You'll never make it, I'm afraid! Look here! It's taking two great big men to whip one slip of a girl, and another twenty to hold the rest of us—including two more girls! Why, there just downright aren't enough of you in the whole of the Colonies to lick a hundred Redcoats, much less an army!"

His manner was strangely indolent, his voice razor-sharp with scorn. Lauchlin fancied she could almost see it cut a bright swath through the air to lash against the backwoodsmen. They winced, stared, growled. And Andrew grinned in their faces, his white teeth an insult in themselves.

It had the effect he wanted. The burly man forgot Carilla for the moment and turned his wrath on Andrew, simply and forcefully. One blow in the face and another in the ribs doubled him, limp and winded, in the hands that held him.

Lauchlin began cursing in Gaelic, earnestly and steadily, the tears still flowing but not in the least interfering with her vocabulary. Attention shifted to her now—except for another man who moved over to take a turn holding Ronald. But even Ronald paused for a moment, awed. He hadn't dreamed his sister could curse so inventively. It was lucky no one else could understand what she said. Somehow Ronald didn't think these men would relish being called six kinds of evil monster, all descended from devils and three-headed serpents, whose sons would be cross-eyed and feebleminded, whose grandsons would have worms and be hounded by bad luck, and whose great-grandsons would kill one another in a war between brothers. Lauchlin's voice dropped an eerie two notes at these last words, and Ronald's skin prickled. She *did* sometimes have The Sight.

The thread of violence had been broken. Lauchlin ran out of breath and there was a pause. The burly man hit Andrew again in the ribs, but half-heartedly. He looked with vague perplexity at Carilla, a slight, still figure, standing erect by an extremely great effort. Her face was blank with the need not to show any weakness whatever.

He looked around at the rest of them. Since Ronald was still struggling like a pack of wildcats, he hit him with a musket butt. Ronald lost interest in everything for the moment. The burly man paused, as if wondering what to do next.

"Might as well kill 'em," suggested the hot-eyed man callously. "Corpses can't tell no tales."

But there was another stir at this, and mutters of protest.

"We ain't killers," objected a voice. "Leastways not of young'uns," added another. "Spunky little devils," admitted a third with reluctant admiration. "Leave 'em go. We'll be far enough away they can't no Lobsterbacks come nigh us."

There was a long argument, rumbling on and on while the young people lost track of time. Things had become a sort of gray humming vacuum for Carilla, and a dark void for Ronald. Andrew found events extremely blurred, and for Lauchlin everything had a sharp clarity that put them all out of time altogether. Did it really matter much?

And then, gradually, they realized that they were alone, between forest and swamp, alone in a thick silence, with horses and men gone and out of hearing.

Twenty

SHAKEN OPINIONS

Carilla found herself standing alone, which was surprising, because she had been wishing those men would go away so that she could lie down—only now they were gone, she didn't seem to be doing it. She looked around dazedly. Then Edwin's arm was around her, making her sit down, and Lauchlin was weeping over her, and Ronald and Andrew— What was wrong with them? They looked dreadful! Ronald was grey-white, and Andrew a sickly green! Carilla tried to mention this, but her stiff face and swollen lips did not seem to obey very well.

Melicent seemed to have half swooned, but no one paid her any attention at first. Then Edwin, passing with river water to bathe wounded faces and heads, spared her a glance.

"No time for megrims, Melly," he said with a total lack of chivalry. "There's only three of us not hurt, and we've got to help the others."

Andrew and Ronald both protested that they weren't in the least hurt, but this was patently a lie. Andrew winced when he moved, and Ronald had an ugly welt on his head and a peculiar look about the eyes. Lauchlin was suffering for all of them, silently, not allowing her tears to impair her efficiency.

"What will we *do*?" wailed Melicent, dabbing at Ronald's head with cold water. "They've stolen our horses! How can we get home?"

"Walk," Ronald said succinctly, enduring the cold water. His head seemed in great danger of shattering into a thousand pieces and flying away, but he dared not try to hold it together for fear of making an unnecessary fuss. If only things would stop blurring and shifting around that way! He blinked angrily, and even *that* hurt. "Can you walk, Andrew?" he asked. "We can the three of us be carrying Carilla, and—"

"I c'n walk perf'ly well," Carilla mumbled with spirit. She was sure by now that both Andrew and Ronald were hurt a great deal worse than she, and she was *not* going to let herself be babied more than they.

They set off with a minimum of fuss, considering everything, back through the gloom of the pine woods. It was slow and miserable. None of the Virginians was used to walking, even at best. The cold began to seep into their bones there in that deep shade, untouched by the mild November sun, and the girls were having trouble with the dragging trains of their riding skirts.

"Indeed, and one of us must be going ahead for help, just!" Lauchlin announced at last, wretchedly. Three of the people she loved best in the world were all in pain before her eyes, and she powerless to help. Someone must do something! "It is myself will go," she decided realistically. "Edwin will be needed here, being a lad; and Melicent could never be doing it; and everyone else is hurt. Besides, a Highlander is best for walking."

"No!" Andrew's voice had never sounded so commanding. "You're not going one step alone, Firetop! I'll go myself."

That was clearly nonsense, said Lauchlin, and he in pain at every step, and with his eye swollen shut, and doubtless all his ribs broken. Couldn't she and Melicent go together, then?

No, said the boys, they couldn't.

There was a despairing silence which Ronald ended by being masterful. "There's myself had best go," he observed casually, managing to look as if the bump on his head was already out of his memory. And he strode on ahead down the road quickly, before his sharp-eyed sister could notice how extraordinarily dizzy he seemed to be.

It was a very long and peculiar trip back through those pine woods. Ronald found himself more than once leaning affectionately against a tree, explaining why he had to hurry. Another time, he dimly remembered much later, he seemed to be pleading with a bush to take care of Carilla —unless the bush actually *was* Carilla? And even in his clearer moments, the road had a mischievous habit of moving out from under his feet while he wasn't looking.

He had no notion at all of time. But at last he passed the college and was in Williamsburg, staggering so drunkenly that the first people he saw stared disapprovingly and said it was only to be expected of those wild whiskey-drinking Scots. Mercifully, the next person he saw was Peyton Randolph—several of him, in fact. Ronald had the greatest difficulty deciding which of him to talk to, but since they were all extremely attentive, perhaps it didn't matter.

It didn't take much explaining. In minutes men, horses, and litters were racing back toward Jamestown, someone was fetching Doctor Gilmer, and Ronald was being borne gently back to Woodlea, protesting feebly that he had to get back to the others.

Williamsburg was deeply outraged. To think that common trash from log cabins in the back mountains could attack and rob decent young folk in broad daylight! It was a scandal and a shame, and even Patrick Henry and other supporters of the Common Man had nothing to say in their defense. A good many townsmen and plantation owners joined in the futile hunt for the culprits—one which had a better chance of finding them, observed the bandaged Andrew from his bed, than the army troops, who insisted on marching out in bright red columns that warned everything for miles around.

"If it should ever come to fighting," he predicted with unimpaired flippancy, "those sharpshooters from the mountains will pick them off like sleeping turkeys."

"There's six of yon sharpshooters will be too busy handling our horses," Lauchlin pointed out ruefully. But Carilla hadn't even a wan smile. For one thing, it still hurt her bruised face, and for another, she saw nothing even mildly humorous. Those awful men! If they were the sort of folk Ronald wanted to give equal rights— Well, she reckoned he'd have changed his mind by now, lying in bed this last five days with a concussion.

"Do you think they might find our horses?" she asked wistfully.

"No," said Andrew, and there was a raw note of grief in his voice. He had raised Baron from a colt, and loved him.

Ronald did indeed—once his head had decided to stay in one piece—have a lot of thinking to do. The whole incident had been a very great shock to him, for it had very nearly shattered his ideal of rule by the Common Man. Common Man, he felt, had let him down, and badly. Carilla's comments, however ill-timed and tactless, had been quite accurate, he decided bitterly, trying to find a cool place on the pillow. The beasts really weren't civilized at all, but uncouth, filthy, unprincipled, brutish— The question was, were they born or made that way? Could they ever learn the self-discipline that went with self-respect and any moral right to rule others? Ronald didn't know at all. He had always said that all Common Man needed was education. It was, he now feared, asking a great deal of education.

No one makes a better cynic than an idealist who has been dreadfully disillusioned. Ronald was on his way to becoming a splendid cynic when Lauchlin came in with more cold cloths for his head. She took one look at his expression and wrinkled her forehead.

"Och, I'm knowing you well, laddie," she observed. "What black beastie is gnawing at your mind now?"

Ronald, remembering that she, too, championed the Common Man, told her. Lauchlin bore up remarkably well —almost as if she had been doing some thinking herself.

"Folk are always wanting to fit neat wee tags on people and put them in neat wee pigeonholes," she told him sensibly. "Then they get angry if the people won't fit their labels. Remember the Yorktown dock?"

Ronald grinned ruefully and got the idea. Lauchlin was still serenely free from disillusion because she hadn't built up any rigid pigeonholes. She expected people to be unpredictable and different from one another. And as for Andrew, Ronald decided sleepily under the cold cloth, he went out and smashed every pigeonhole he could find, just.

Williamsburg forgot the outrage rather soon, for there were other important matters going on during that winter of 1774–5. Boston was still under the blockade, and the news was that there was hunger there, and sickness. A revolutionary government had been set up outside the city, and more troops arrived from England; and the latter and a group of patriots who called themselves Minutemen kept stealing ammunition back and forth from one another in a way that struck Lauchlin as almost comical. She drew a splendid cartoon of it for Cousin Matthew.

Boston was not the only place feeling the deadly impasse. Williamsburg and the rest of the colonies were suffering the effects of the boycott of English goods, now rigidly enforced. It was only to be hoped, said Andrew wryly, that England was feeling it as badly.

Melicent, after an unsuccessful day trying to buy Christmas gifts from nearly empty shops, glowered at him. She felt very strongly that nothing should be allowed to interfere with the niceties of living, and this whole silly argument was going much too far.

"Tempest in a teapot," she said crossly.

"Tempest *over* a teapot, you mean," drawled Andrew, and Lauchlin laughed appreciatively.

Melicent didn't. She didn't get the joke, and it merely reminded her that she'd give anything for a nice cup of tea. Also, that good-looking John Mason had suddenly stopped visiting her because their families disagreed politically. She ran home for a good cry, feeling that the world was probably coming to an end.

She was right, in a way, more than any of them fully realized, even though they saw bits of it falling almost every day. All those nice young English officers, once socially acceptable, gradually took on the aspect of enemies—an aspect familiar and almost comfortable to Lauchlin and Ronald. Soldiers stopped mail more and more frequently; a matter which simply infuriated the Colonists, and which also made the sending of Cousin Matthew's dispatches more and more risky, calling for fearful ingenuity. Moreover, there were fewer ships sailing back and forth from England.

Peyton Randolph's brother John, despairing of avoiding war, went back to England on one of those few ships, followed by others of like mind. Determined rebels were drilling everywhere they could find someone to drill them —even under Lord Dunmore's permanently apoplectic nose. Backwoodsmen poured over the western mountains to join them—and Ronald in particular found himself wincing every time he saw a buckskin shirt, and wondering afresh if democracy was really such a good idea, after all.

Melicent did more than wince; she turned pale. But if Carilla had any such emotions, she concealed them admirably, not even turning a hair at the sight of a bushy black beard. Ronald had to admire her mettle, though he wouldn't have said so for worlds. He hated to admit he'd ever been wrong—and he was in a beastly humor most of the winter, not fit to live with, said Cousin Lavinia severely.

Carilla excused him (but not to his face) by saying it was his concussion still bothering him. Lauchlin added wistfully that 'twas a very long time since they'd had a letter from home, and Ronald far more homesick even than she. Ronald said very little. Breathing black clouds of ill temper, he was struggling with what threatened to be an upheaval of his entire pattern of ideas. Not even Lauchlin knew what was going on in his mind until he threw his bombshell on a stormy January afternoon when they all sat around a pleasant fire, the girls sewing under Mistress Treanor's gimlet eye.

"I am wondering, now, if a rising is altogether a good idea," he remarked, diffidently for him.

"Ronald!" bleated Lauchlin, shocked.

He shrugged, looked defensive and stubborn. " 'Tis all very fine when a nation stands together against a foreign invader," he pointed out. " 'Tis different here, with neighbor set against neighbor, and no unity like in the Highlands. It is in my heart that perhaps Mr. Jefferson has the right notion, and the best thing a kind of political brotherhood."

Lauchlin gaped in wonder. "Never the day!" she breathed, almost doubting that it could be Ronald talking.

"Oh, hush up, Lauchlin," said Carilla, to her own surprise. "Go on, Ronald."

"I am not much liking the thing that is growing here," admitted Ronald, feeling for his own thoughts. "It has an ugly feel. I cannot abide venom."

"Oh, nor can I!" exclaimed Carilla, and they looked at each other with sudden appreciation. Did they both have the same sick lurching inside when a good honest argument turned malignant? Each of them wondered.

"Just a couple of angels of peace, that's what they are," murmured Andrew. "I'm surprised none of the rest of you ever noticed."

"Och, I had!" Lauchlin retorted solemnly. "Did I never tell ye how Ronald behaved on Skye, always so humble and meek, and forever trying to avoid any trouble—"

"Whose side are you on, just?" Ronald demanded crushingly in the midst of the laughter.

She wrinkled an uncrushed nose at him. "I've not decided yet," she announced sweetly. "I'm still thinking."

Cousin Lavinia had been serenely sewing, letting the conversation take its course. Now she entered it. "Does that mean, my dear, that when you do decide, you'll stop thinking?" she inquired with rather tart interest.

Her eyebrows were raised challengingly. Lauchlin met the challenge with a face gravely ingenuous—and dancing eyes.

"Doesn't everybody?"

Twenty-One

CONVERSATION IN A DRAWING ROOM

Carilla sat down to her sewing with a sigh, alone in the pale light of February that came in at the morning room window. She had just spent an extra half-hour on her backboard because of Grandmother seeing her with slumped shoulders. As a consequence, she felt more like slumping than ever. She smothered a sigh—but her back was like an arrow.

Still, she was just in the mood for a brisk battle when Ronald came in and stood looking at her. He had been abominably cross lately. So had Grandmother, due to trying to maintain two contradictory loyalities at once. Carilla couldn't get back at Grandmother, but Ronald should do nicely. She took a few demure stitches, pretending not to see him. Either kind of battle would do, she decided: a nice loud argument or something more subtle —just as long as it was clearly understood that they no longer hated each other.

Ronald shifted his weight uncomfortably. He surveyed her with a highly critical air. "You know," he told her judiciously, "I was not liking you a whit at first."

Carilla blinked, this not being exactly what she had expected. But she kept her self-possession admirably.

"Well, I reckon everybody knows that," she agreed. "And I didn't like you, either."

Ronald looked faintly disconcerted. His black brows crowded together over a nose that Carilla noticed for the first time was fine and straight as well as more than a little arrogant. "Whisht!" he told her with severity. "Do not be interrupting, for 'tis myself has a thing to tell you."

Carilla held her tongue from sheer curiosity, and Ronald went on with an air of someone reciting a speech quickly before he forgot it.

"You are very proud," he told her, not altogether approvingly. "And you must always be thinking yourself right," he added with no approval at all.

"So do you!" she retorted at once.

Ronald stopped and considered this. "Aye," he acknowledged fairly. "But 'tis yourself is vain, as well." He frowned.

Carilla looked him squarely in the eye. "So are you," she said with great clarity and deliberation.

"Me? *Vain?*" Ronald looked stunned. "You're daft!" he decided.

"You're just as vain as you can be!" Carilla pointed a derisive finger at him. "And the airs you give yourself in a kilt! You just ought to see yourself when you're wearing it, Ronald MacLeod! You *swagger*! And don't you tell *me* it swings all that much without you doing something to help!"

Ronald gaped and recovered himself. "Och, well, 'tis the kilt has a swagger sewed into it, just," he announced shamelessly and with some truth. "No matter. That's never what I was wanting to talk about, and do not keep changing the subject, lass, or I'll never be saying it."

He looked quite of a mind to forget the whole thing, and Carilla found that she wanted very much to hear what he had to say. "I'm sorry," she told him with a quite unnatural meekness. "Go on."

"I have it in my mind," Ronald continued with an air of great profundity, "that 'tis either yourself or myself has changed altogether these last months. I'm liking you fine now."

He stopped. Carilla smiled up at him through her lashes, but he didn't go on. Either he was quite bowled over by her smile, or—far more likely—he hadn't noticed at all, and was thinking of something else. After a moment he changed the subject completely.

"Is it yourself is fond of hot weather?"

Carilla blinked, gave an exasperated sigh, and gamely stayed with it. "You *know* I'm not. It always gives me a headache."

Ronald looked vaguely pleased. "You'd like Skye," he observed. Pause. " 'Tis in my mind you could be learning the Gaelic quickly, you having a sharp mind and tongue," he added, and turned to go, the conversation apparently finished.

Carilla found her breath just as he reached the door handle. "Now you just wait a minute, Ronald MacLeod!" she whipped, her voice stabbing him from behind and sounding so much like her grandmother that he jumped.

"Aye?" he said cautiously, turning to look at her. She had been looking adorable and friendly a moment ago. Now her eyes were violet storms and her round chin dangerous.

"Just by any chance," she asked him carefully, "was that supposed to mean anything?" Ronald looked baffled. She pointed a threatening needle at him. "You know, you could get into trouble that way. A girl who didn't know you better might think all that was leading up to a proposal of marriage, and then where would you be? It's just a good thing I know it wasn't, that's all."

Ronald looked alarmed. "Och, no!" he agreed hastily, and shuffled his feet slightly. "I was away off to think about it," he added vaguely, making things considerably worse.

"I see." Carilla nodded brightly, her toe tapping the floor under her quilted taffeta petticoat, and her sewing forgotten on her lap. "All by yourself, I suppose?"

Ronald nodded at her tolerantly. Certainly, all by himself. How else? And why was she looking so annoyed? "I'd be telling you, after," he offered generously.

"Ooh!" she cried furiously. "You are the most *conceited* boy! And you'd make a terrible husband, too. I shouldn't think any girl in her senses would ever marry you."

He looked so surprised that Carilla nearly laughed—but so crestfallen that she didn't. "What's wrong with me, then?" he inquired with deep interest and what might have been the start of a twinkle in those deep-set grey eyes.

Carilla sat straighter. "To begin with, you're extremely stubborn and opinionated, you know."

"Fine I know," he agreed cheerfully. "But usually I am right." He deposited himself on a low hassock and regarded her with great affability.

"You're not!" she contradicted, beginning thoroughly to enjoy this little scene. "That's just what I mean! Now, Edwin is much pleasanter to have around, and not nearly as fond of arguing, either. I don't reckon you'll ever get tired of arguing, Ronald."

"No," admitted Ronald at once, not at all abashed.

"And when you're upset or annoyed, you sulk inside a huge, thick, invisible black cloud, and refuse to say what's wrong, so that everyone near you is depressed as well."

Ronald conceded this, looking only slightly sheepish.

"And I suppose you'll always strut and swagger in your kilt, and insist that Highlanders are superior to anyone else in the world."

"Aye so!" He looked astounded that she could question it. "And will that be all, then?"

Carilla eyed him with severity. "Isn't it enough to start with?"

He considered this. He developed an expression of distinct smugness. "I'm none so bad a fellow, after all," he decided, pleased. "Shall I be asking Melicent will she have me?"

He looked bland as butter. Carilla, not to be caught out, looked back at him with a face like cream.

"Oh, yes, I should," she told him with enthusiasm. "I'm sure Melly would just love Scotland!"

They smiled at each other sweetly. The smiles turned reluctantly to grins. They began to laugh.

Twenty-Two

WORLD TURNED UPSIDE DOWN

Ronald walked home in the hyacinth twilight, his emotions pulling two ways at once while his mind repeated the words he had just heard repeated at the Raleigh. He must get them down just right for the *Gadfly*, and then he could try to decide what he thought about them.

But that was more easily determined than done. The process of remembering caused the short hairs at the back of Ronald's neck, under his queue, to prickle. Patrick Henry had made another speech, in Richmond, and it was of white fire!

Is life so dear or peace so sweet, as to be purchased at the price of chains and slavery? Forbid it, Almighty God! I know not what course others may take, but as for me, give me liberty, or give me death!

Every instinct in Ronald roused to that challenge. His hand itched to hold a claymore, or even the less thrilling but more efficient musket. But the new misgivings that had haunted him all winter rose again, vague but stubborn, muttering darkly that war now would be a mistake, war here would sever something best left together. Surely, said the feeling with an echo of Cousin Lavinia, such disputes should be settled by peaceful negotiation?

But Mr. Henry had answered that, too. "Gentlemen may cry peace, peace," he had shouted. "But there is no peace!"

Ronald felt as if he himself were the battle-ground, with Lauchlin and clan and country pulling one way, and his Treanor cousins tugging the other—and Andrew, of course, nipping around to help whichever side might be weakening. Ronald grinned at the fancy, but without much amusement.

And then he stopped, as swiftly alert as if he were back on Skye, and a Redcoat behind every gorse bush.

"Hsst!" It was a deeper shadow in the shadow of the magnolia tree by the coach road. Ronald regarded it warily, feeling rather like Haggis trying to decide who was going to pounce on whom.

"*Dhia dhuit, avic.* It is yourself is Ronald MacLeod?"

Ronald untensed a trifle, for in this land another Highlander was not likely to be an enemy.

"*La math leibh,*" he replied softly. "Myself it is, surely. What is it you are wanting?"

He ventured closer, still cautious. A short, dark figure stepped out so that Ronald could see him well enough in the fading daylight. Pure dark Pict he was, clearly; one of those in whose blood ran none of the tall red and blond Celtic strain.

"There's myself is Sean MacLeod of Stornaway," he said in the Gaelic. "And with a letter from Kildornie and another message perhaps urgent. Is there a place where we can be talking unseen and unheard?"

Ronald, his fingers itching for the letters from home, controlled himself, nodded, and led the way down the coach road and into a quiet corner of the garden. They sat down on a stone bench, and Sean looked around in a faintly hunted way before he began to talk again in a low voice.

"There's myself was seized for owning a wee bit of a black dirk," he said, "and made a sailor on the *Magdalene* instead of being sold as bond slave, because," he went on with modesty, "there will be no sailors anywhere like the men of the Hebrides. 'Twas my cousin Callum in Portree saw me when we were docking there, and smuggled me letters to you from Kildornie, for it was said the ship was bound for Virginia. He was telling me where to find you and what you are looking like. But there's Mr. Collins was never letting me off the schooner the whole time we've been around."

He paused. Ronald nodded and let Sean continue his own way.

"I was in two minds should I jump ship or try to go back home, and then I was hearing a conversation and your name in it." He cocked his black head at Ronald. "Is it yourself has been angering the fine Sassenach governor here? And is there something about London and a fly?"

Ronald gripped the small man's arm, leaning forward tensely. "Tell me what you were hearing!" he commanded.

Sean rubbed his arm and obeyed. " 'Twas making little enough sense to me," he said. "But he was talking to the captain and saying yourself and some others are not so very clever after all, and he has been confiscating a packet from a courier and found a London address, and once it reaches London there will soon be a black day for you and some others."

Ronald sat very still in the darkening garden, sorting this out, and paling a little as he did so. Lord Dunmore was on the track, then. Thank goodness for the false name and complex system of delivery! Even so, it was a bad business indeed! At any moment Cousin Matthew might be arrested and hanged, and perhaps Cousin Sarah and Mr. Fisher with him—and a letter of warning would take weeks to arrive at best! He put his head in his hands.

Sean plucked his sleeve. "There's bad it is, then?"

"I don't know," Ronald gloomed. "It could be sore bad, *avic*. And much worse it could have been without your warning," he added, remembering his obligation. "My thanks to you, for you may have saved the life of a grand fine old man. What can I be doing in turn?"

"You can be pointing a direction," said the small man promptly. "For it is myself has jumped ship at last. And since they could be hanging me only the once, I just was leaving the bos'n a wee bittie unconscious as I went. A bonnie blow it was, and myself longing to deliver it all these weeks."

Ronald grinned appreciatively. It occurred to him that if war should come, there would indeed be a third generation of Highlanders fighting against a third Hanoverian king, though they had to cross the sea to do it. "I've some silver on me, and little enough to help a kinsman. And I can be pointing the way inland, where you will soon find either free wild country or a militia, training men to fight the Sassenach."

He had guessed shrewdly. "That is the thing I am wanting!" exclaimed Sean. "The Redcoats could not be getting at me there. Och, 'tis myself could do fine with a bonnie battle or two against the Sassenach!"

Ronald at once began to empty his pockets of silver. "Mind," he warned, "you'll find few enough fighting for independence from England, Sean, but only for civil rights and the lifting of taxes and such. They are the most of them content to remain English."

Sean cackled with a rusty laugh. "Wait until the blood is flowing, and then see do they not change their minds. Na, na, laddie, let the first shot be fired and the first man fall, and there's a road with only the one ending. Wait and see. And now, kinsman, I'm away off, for who knows will they be coming to find you or me or the both of us, and it doing the neither of us any good to be found together."

He rose, and Ronald set him on the road to Richmond with an appropriate "*Tapadh leat*" meaning both "thank you" and "may you be a hero." And then he raced back to Woodlea.

It was a tranquil scene in the drawing room, with the adults reading, the girls playing backgammon, and Lady Seraphina primly arranging herself for a nap on top of Lauchlin's carelessly dropped embroidery. Ronald shattered the tranquility with a brief and pithy account of Sean's story, and four dismayed faces turned to his.

"*Ochone*!" cried Lauchlin, paling, "What can we do?"

There was a long pause. "Nothing, but to send a warning at once, and hope it reaches him in time," said Cousin Nathaniel.

"And hope it reaches him at all," Carilla corrected him, her face pink with emotion. "To intercept private letters like that, it's— It's—"

"Altogether dishonorable," finished her grandmother in a tone that made this the worst thing that could possibly be said about it.

"We'll just have to send a number of warnings, and hope for the best," decided Mr. Treanor. "I'll personally deliver one to the next trustworthy ship's captain out of Yorktown—and just minutes before he lifts anchor. And George Wythe will take one to Baltimore when he goes next week. And you did tell me, didn't you, Ronald, that Uncle Matthew had protected himself reasonably well in London?"

"Aye so," Ronald remembered with a slight sense of reprieve. "It should be taking the Sassenach a bit of time to be tracing him even when the message arrives in London; but they could be stopping all our warnings at that end, just." He scowled, brooded over it for a moment, and then sighed. "Och, well, and it the best we can do. And I might as well be writing him that speech Mr. Henry just made, whatever."

Lauchlin, whose dark tilted eyes kept returning to the packet forgotten in his hand, could keep still no longer. "What's yon?" she demanded, pointing.

He stared. "Och, the letter from home! How could I be forgetting?" And he tore it open at once, there in the candle-lit room, for all to hear.

It was a short letter, not filled this time with the usual warmth and humor that made Mother's letters such a delight. It was to the point. "Bairns of our hearts," it began, "at last you can be coming home again, for Captain Green is replaced now by a new man with a fair mind and a soft heart in him for the Highlander, and who says perhaps the Act of Proscription may be raised before many more years are up."

Ronald stopped reading. There was a simply thundering silence.

"Oh, no!" cried Carilla, who had somehow convinced herself that they would stay always in Williamsburg.

"Och!" began Lauchlin, and stopped. A blaze of joy at the thought of home immediately became tangled with stricken bewilderment. She felt as if she had suddenly become two Lauchlins in one body, pulling it in opposite directions. She wanted passionately to go home! The sound of whaup and curlew, the scent of whin and heather and salt wind from over the Minch were in her ears and nostrils. But she didn't want to leave Virginia!

Without any warning, Lauchlin faced the penalty of allowing oneself to love more than one spot on earth—and the people there. She was no longer heart-whole. No matter where she was, for the rest of her life, part of her would always and always be homesick for the other place. It was not fair! Why had no one warned her?

She looked at Ronald, but he had retreated far behind his own eyes. In any case, he would never truly love any spot but Skye. Nor could any of the others understand, surely. Feeling utterly alone, Lauchlin sat still, drenched with misery and the salt tears that poured silently down her face.

"My very dear!" Grandmother's voice was no longer silver, but the color of a cello note. Lauchlin found herself enveloped in the scent of violets and a sense of comfort that was surprising. Delicate old hands took hers, and she found herself being led firmly from the room.

Ronald hardly knew she was gone, for he was wrestling with his own problem, and feeling rather like Haggis tangled in several balls of wool.

"But I can't go yet!" he bleated, beginning to stride about the room in a way that seemed to turn his apple-green breeches to a swinging kilt. "Not yet," he repeated, coming to a halt by the window and staring out unseeingly.

The locked vault of his need for Scotland had broken wide open, and he was blind and dizzy with longing for the clean sweep of heathered hills, for austere mountains, and the tang of northern air, and the music of the Gaelic speech and song. A storm of homesickness raged in him, deeper and more passionate than Lauchlin would ever know, and the wilder for having been ruthlessly buried for so many months.

Before him was the dusky warmth of a late March evening in Virginia, sweet with birdsong and flowers: a fair land indeed. Just now it had for Ronald all the appeal of sugared rose petals set before a starving warrior.

"Have to *think*!" he muttered distractedly, and proceeded to do so. Could he leave now, with the Colonies teetering on the verge of a rising which he himself had—however slightly—helped stir up? It was true, he was no longer sure a rising was altogether a good thing, but did not that, perhaps, make his obligation the greater? If one helped sow dragon's teeth, was it one's duty to stay and help cope with the crop? Even though one had already begun wondering if oats might not have been a better idea?

Ronald didn't at all know. He made a sound like a strangled groan and turned to Cousin Nathaniel. "Can I be walking out on things here?" he demanded, ignoring Carilla as if she didn't exist.

But Carilla was feeling too quenched herself to be

resentful. She lifted Seraphina on to her lap for comfort, blinked wistfully at the crushed pile of Lauchlin's embroidery, and stared in silence at Ronald and her father.

Mr. Treanor crossed to the window and placed an affectionate hand on Ronald's shoulder. "Don't rush at problems headlong, son," he suggested. "Like Uncle Matthew's possible danger, this isn't an instant emergency. It doesn't have to be decided this minute or even this month. And if you should feel it your duty to stay here longer, your parents will surely understand. But there's a common notion that you might examine very carefully before you decide, Ronald."

He paused. Ronald, already feeling slightly better, regarded him inquiringly. "What is it, then?"

"It is the belief that a man proves his courage and responsibility by fighting. It's easy enough to fight—especially if everyone else is doing likewise. But might a man's duty not sometimes lie in refusing to fight? Or might it not be the lonely and difficult path of resisting mass emotions, and label-thinking, and even non-thinking; and finding your own ethics, and following wherever they lead?"

Ronald was silent, thinking about this, trying to apply it to himself, or even to see if it applied at all. Some of it went against the whole weight of his life on Skye—but it had a logic, and a challenge, and a strong appeal for an individualist like Ronald. He looked at Cousin Nathaniel, wondering what hard task his own conscience might demand of him should fighting come.

"Dinner," said Cousin Nathaniel as a musical tinkle sounded from the back of the house. "Come, Carilla dear." But he had one last remark for Ronald as they waited for his mother and Lauchlin to appear. "If your father is much like you, Ronald, I have the greatest admiration for him. The last twenty-five years have taken far more courage than either of us can easily imagine."

Ronald glanced at him, startled, and was very thoughtful all evening.

He had company. They were all subdued, and all went to bed early. Carilla wept into her pillow, at the thought of parting with her cousins. Lauchlin lay awake with a wet face and wished desolately that a person could be twins and in two places at once, for her heart must surely break in half otherwise.

Ronald tossed inside the canopy of his four-poster and longed to be on a hillside in Skye; or in a small boat, wrapped only in a plaidie and the trenchent wind. Perhaps there he could think clearly. For how— Oh, dear God, *how* was a body to know what was right and brave and wise?

But God, as Ronald had learned by now, was not in the habit of handing out the answers in a nice, clear-cut vision or two. Not to ordinary beings. No, if He answered at all, it was by subtler means. And Ronald had for some time nourished a strong suspicion that God frequently made people work out their own answers—and then put them to the test.

He scowled and punched his pillow, which had turned unaccountably hard. So far, his heart gave him very little indication of which way his answers might lead.

Twenty-Three

ANOTHER HORNET

Carilla sat in the sunny entry hall and rubbed under Seraphina's soft complacent chin while she waited for Rhoda to finish Lauchlin's hair and release her. Shafts of light checkered the green-and-white wallpaper, reminding her that the hot season would soon be here, and the perpetual headache . . . and perhaps Ronald and Lauchlin would soon be back in the rigorous climate of Skye, leaving her unbelievably lonely. How odd that it was only a year since they came! And how unfair that they should create places for themselves in her heart, and then go away and leave empty holes. But if Ronald once decided that he wasn't, after all, morally obligated to see this disagreement through here in the Colonies, then he'd be on the next ship back, and Lauchlin with him!

Carilla sighed.

And then someone walked in at the front door. He didn't ring or knock; he didn't present his calling card; he simply appeared, rather like an energetic wave at high tide, tossing a mane of white hair and shouting for Lavinia.

Carilla leaped to her feet in great astonishment, dumping the affronted Lady Seraphina on the floor. For three seconds she stared with a perfectly blank mind, and then memory functioned. "Great-Uncle Matthew!"

He blinked, looking considerably more shaken than the

occasion seemed to demand. "Bless my boots!" he croaked. "You're *not* Carilla! You can't be! She couldn't have grown *that* much!" His hand wavered about three feet off the ground, as if measuring the height of a small child, then moved reluctantly upward. He looked again at the young lady who confronted him. "You're not Carilla, are you?" he pleaded.

Carilla sternly subdued a giggle, and merely nodded, grave-faced.

"But I brought you a doll," he protested reasonably, clearly hoping that this might cause her to change her mind.

The giggle won. "Oh, Great-Uncle Matthew!" she chortled. "You always forget! I was already much too old for dolls when you left, and now I'm sixteen."

It had been a long time since anyone saw Matthew Lennox at a loss. "Bless my buttons!" he said simply, and clutched at his hair. "Lavinia!" he shouted again, urgency in his voice.

Upstairs a door opened and slammed. There was a scurry of feet, a bump, a slither, and Lauchlin appeared sprawled on the stair landing, her hair half down her back. "Cousin Matthew!" she squawked, picking herself up and falling down the lower flight. And then, just about to launch herself helter-skelter at the old man, she stopped quite suddenly. The drawing-room door had quietly opened, and a tiny ivory-and-lilac figure with silver hair stood there. She wasn't frowning. She didn't need to.

Lauchlin hastily straightened her twisted panniers and made a demure curtsy, her face radiant. Cousin Matthew —who had watched her descent with frozen fascination— now looked from her to Carilla with an air of great reproach. She had grown up, too! A bewildering habit of the young, it seemed. One never got used to it.

Something in the quality of the moment caused him to turn toward the drawing-room door, in no doubt at all about who stood there. Some people never changed.

"Lavinia, dear sister!" he said, and kissed her on both cheeks.

Grandmother managed very successfully not to look pleased. "You're a terrible nuisance, Matthew," she told him severely. "I had just got Lauchlin trained to the point where she managed to behave more or less like a lady quite a good deal of the time—and now look!"

"Good for her!" Matthew retorted incorrigibly. "The only reason you act like a lady yourself, Vinnie, is because it's easiest for you to rule the roost that way, and because you know it's becoming to you. If it weren't—" He didn't finish, but winked outrageously at the girls, and scooped an arm around each of them. "Where's Nathaniel? And that young scamp Ronald? Hasn't he started a revolution yet? Cousin Sarah sent her love and some gifts. . . . Why, Lauchlin, honey, what are you crying for?"

She smiled at him wetly. "You're no taken and hanged," she explained with great relief. "And us thinking maybe you were!"

"Ladies control their emotions, my dear," said Cousin Lavinia so mildly that it wasn't a reproof at all. "Come into the drawing room; and we'll have coffee I think, Micah; and send Jason around to see if Mr. Treanor and Master Ronald can be spared from whatever they're doing."

They all sat there a little later, Cousin Matthew luxuriating with hot coffee and a breathless audience. He was enjoying himself tremendously.

"Reckon that stolen packet of Dunmore's is still on the high seas somewhere," he decided, relishing the idea. "The birds have all flown. We decided to quit while we were still ahead. Made quite a splash in London, the *Gadfly* did. Raised a hornet's nest, you might say. They buzzed all over the place, trying to find out who published it. You can't imagine—"

"Can't we!" interrupted his sister tartly. "Never mind; go on, Matthew. What do you plan to do now?"

He cocked his head happily. "Don't reckon to find things dull around here," he predicted cheerfully. "I didn't want to miss any of the fun, and I didn't want to get stuck on that side, either, so when the *Jennifer* showed up—and maybe her last trip, too—I just shipped aboard, and here I am." He beamed around the room, an elderly snow-haired imp. "Fixin' to make trouble, of course. Maybe I'll just have a little chat with Mr. Purdie about the *Gazette*, and pay a visit or two to the Raleigh. Lots of scope for gadflying around here!" He winked at Carilla.

He was as good as his word.

He held forth at the Raleigh about English belief and opinion to a group of fascinated men. And every time they concluded definitely that he was on one side, he switched deftly to the other, stepping on as many toes as possible in the process.

He told the aristocracy that they were a dying race, and that they would be forced sooner or later to turn government over to the common people—and even to free their slaves and give *them* the vote as well. Not to mention women. "Though not, I daresay, for a good few years yet," he conceded generously.

With the Tidewater Aristocrats seething at him and the backwoodsmen cheering, he turned his guns on the latter. "You think the Red Indians exist just to be robbed and cheated by you, eh?" he demanded. "Even the English have more decency that that! England is trying to protect those poor Redskins over the mountains, and let them have some rights to their own land. So don't preach to me about all your holy and righteous ideals of freedom. I know as well as you do that what you're really after is to get rid of the English restrictions on helping yourselves to all the Indian land you want. Freedom to steal, eh? Freedom from law and ethics, eh?"

And having successfully infuriated everyone within hearing (except perhaps a few like Mr. Jefferson and Mr. Wythe) he strutted off, looking outrageously pleased with himself, to raise havoc at the *Gazette* office.

Lord Dunmore's informers, of course (including the tallow-faced man, who had been demoted to the Raleigh) reported everything. So did everyone else. But for a while, the governor did nothing. He had problems more important than one more troublemaker in a colony filled with them. Treason was in the very air these days!

To be sure, the governor's troops and the two armed British ships standing by in the James river were an adequate force for keeping order so long as Virginians were divided among themselves. But lately they tended to unite and make common ground against him—their lawful appointed governor!—at the slightest provocation. And Lord Dunmore was uneasily aware of that filled Powder Magazine right in the center of town. For Indian attacks or slave risings, ostensibly . . .

Lord Dunmore brooded. Ridiculous to have ammunition loose in the hands of common civilians. They should depend on troops for protection. And in these days of widespread sedition, that Powder Magazine was no less than an invitation to revolutionaries and a threat to law and order. It was even, he realized with annoyance, a deterrent to the arrest of well-known subversives like those inhabiting Woodlea! Outrageous! He wished the Powder Magazine in the river!

This gave the governor an idea. He sent for Acting-Captain Collins of the British schooner *Magdalene*, and then for the captain of his troops, and then for Lieutenant Stanton. When they had finished discussing certain plans, he felt a good deal better.

Twenty-Four

POWDER MAGAZINE

Spring gathered momentum, but with an air of uneasy expectancy, as if afraid to say "boo" for fear it might start something.

She wished it would, muttered Lauchlin, who was in a perfectly vile mood ever since that letter from home.

"Lauchlin!" reproved Mistress Treanor.

"Anything you say, Firetop," murmured Andrew, who practically lived at Woodlea these days. "When we're married—"

"Oh, hold your tongue!" Lauchlin snapped, and stalked

off to find Haggis, the only person whose company she appreciated any more—probably because he was the only one as unreasonable as she.

Not that she would admit to being disagreeable. It was the fault of everyone else, she told Haggis, scratching him all around his ears. Nobody understood how she felt. Ronald's heart was entirely in Skye, and the others were all whole-hearted Virginians, and only she was caught in the middle. She rubbed Haggis along his jaw and on down his chest, and he rolled over on his back and stretched out delightedly.

Lauchlin went on scratching, her eyes fixed on the sky, which was turning golden-green in the west. April the twentieth—and a year ago they were still alien here, and she about to start Mrs. Hallam's school, and Carilla still an enemy. Now Williamsburg was doubtfully preparing for The Season again—mostly with last year's gowns and a feeling that perhaps it was tempting fate. Lauchlin wouldn't be a bit surprised. In fact, she wondered whether it was altogether business matters that had taken Cousin Nathaniel to Richmond this week.

Haggis, for sheer deviltry, scratched her. Lauchlin smacked him and stamped back into the house, where the others were now gathered in that tranquil few minutes before candle-lighting, while the sky deepened and then paled to lemon and oyster and smoky amethyst. Peace was in the very air, and a little of it began to creep along the edges of Lauchlin's stormy mind when from the center of town there came a sudden roll of drums, sharp in urgency.

"What is it?" she cried as they all jerked to attention.

"It's the alarm!" Carilla looked astonished even in the dusk. "But that's just for Indian attacks and slave risings and things—isn't it? Great-Uncle Matthew—?"

But he already had the window open, and his snowy head poking out to peer down England Street.

"Calling the Independent Companies and militia to arms!" he announced gleefully. "They've been practicing it lately, just in case. It's coming from Market Square—and I don't reckon it's slaves or Indians, either, Carilla m'dear. Sounds more like Red*coats* than Red*skins* if you ask me. Well, m'lads?" He turned expectantly to Andrew and Ronald, eager as a boy. "Shall we answer the call?"

There was only one answer to that, of course. In a moment they were headed swiftly down the street.

An angry crowd muttered around a gaping Powder Magazine and another was forming down at the end of Palace Green, in front of the Governor's Palace. The air was charged with violence ready to be unleashed. It was at once clear that the ammunition had been stolen from the town, and it wasn't at all difficult to guess who was responsible. The details were a little vague because of everyone growling and shouting at once, but Ronald gathered presently that the marines from the *Magdalene* had overcome the guards, taken the powder, and headed back for the ship.

"Didn't make it, though," someone cackled over the din. "We raised the alarm, blocked the way. They're holed up in the palace!"

At once Cousin Matthew and the boys moved to join the larger crowd on Palace Green. Cousin Matthew was in his element, quite ready to start the revolution then and there. Andrew—who really was *very* much like his great-uncle—had that same unholy smile Ronald had seen once or twice before. But Ronald himself, after a very few moments packed in the midst of the crowd, began feeling as he had in London, wanting to knock down everyone who touched him, or even came near at all. Sweating a little, fists clenched, he fought his way to the outskirts where he could breathe again, and stood panting, quite ready to slay anyone who crowded him. He felt a sudden and complete sympathy with Cousin Nathaniel's horror of mobs.

They were shouting at the palace now, threatening to storm it, deterred only by the muskets aimed at them from every window. Andrew and Cousin Matthew were in the thick of it, and Ronald smiled sourly at the irony. He, the fire-breathing rebel, was standing back and wishing Mr. Jefferson or someone were here to bring order; while that pair of would-be philosophers were quite carried away by the spirit of things.

A clatter of hoofs raced up the street then, and Peyton Randolph's powerful figure threw himself off his horse and strode up to the mob. "Hold on!" he shouted, tall and stern and commanding. "What goes on?"

"We're just getting our gunpowder back, Mr. Randolph," a man yelled back. "You just stay there and leave it to us."

But half the crowd began to turn, everyone telling what happened, so that it was some minutes before Mr. Randolph got things clear, and even longer before he could make himself heard.

"You think this is the way to get it back?" he demanded. "Don't be stupid, friends! Go back to your homes, and I'll present a formal demand tomorrow for the return of the powder."

It wasn't at all a popular suggestion. "Turned Tory, Mr. Randolph, like your brother? That ain't no way to deal with swine like Dunmore! Whose side are you on, anyway?"

Mr. Randolph's big frame looked bigger than ever. "I'm surprised you can ask that!" he returned forcefully. "Who is President of the Continental Congress? Tell me that."

The crowd deflated a trifle. "You are," a few voices admitted without much enthusiasm. Ronald, from his vantage point to one side, felt as if he were watching a wild animal and a trainer who might or might not get it under control.

"Very well, then!" The trainer's voice rang authoritative. "Do you think we're going to win anything at all if we turn into a leaderless, lawless rabble? That's sure defeat! You've elected leaders; now in the name of heaven trust them! And if it comes to fighting," he added grimly, "you'll be a lot more use alive and in the militia than dead in some petty fracas like this. We'll get the powder back—if we have to lay siege to the palace; I promise you that. But we'll have no more mob actions. Now most of you go home. Just leave enough men here to make sure no one can leave the palace."

There was a tense pause. Violence hovered in the air like a cresting wave, pausing in awful balance while no one knew whether it would crash into a breaker or slide back harmlessly. And then tension eased. Men shrugged, grumbled, and obeyed. And Ronald breathed more easily.

And then—it was Andrew, not Ronald, who felt the sudden urgent sense of misgiving. "The girls!" he said, appearing at Ronald's shoulder. His voice was strained. "Ronald, we came off without leaving them and Grandmother any protection except the slaves!"

Ronald started to demand why they should need protection, but then Andrew's alarm touched him, as well. They turned.

"Ronald!" The voice was faint but familiar. "Andrew!

Ronald! Cousin Matthew!" Down Palace Green came a flying shadow, full skirts lifted, panniers bounding.

"Firetop!" Andrew swept to meet her, held her tightly for an instant, shook her a little. "What is it?"

"Help!" said Lauchlin, coming straight to the point. "The Sassenach are arresting us all, at home. Cousin Lavinia—"

As far as Ronald was concerned, she was talking to the air, for he was already on his way. Andrew, more practical, grabbed Lauchlin by the wrist and turned to find Mr. Randolph.

Mr. Stanton had not been very happy about this evening's assignment from the beginning. For one thing, he didn't at all like the idea of arresting Mistress Carilla and her family, and he knew Lord Dunmore had put him in charge of the task for spite. And then, for another thing, he hadn't quite liked the way it was arranged, with him taking a dozen soldiers and going to arrest the Treanor household *en masse* precisely twenty minutes after Mr. Collins' marines made off with the ammunition. As a plan of attack, he felt it lacked flexibility.

He was perfectly sure of this when he heard the drums beat the alarm. That was *not* part of the plan. He even hesitated briefly before carrying out his orders. But Mr. Stanton was a young man with not much initiative, and what little he had was quite squelched by now. So he sighed and marched his men up England Street, expecting the worst.

Nor was he disappointed. The whole affair didn't in the least turn out to be the swift, silent, efficient arrest Lord

Dunmore had in mind. By the time Ronald raced up the street, Lieutenant Stanton was a very much wilted man, at bay in the drawing room caught between the crossfires of Carilla and her grandmother.

"Don't be silly, young man," the latter had told him with tart sweetness when he arrived. "Will you have a glass of sherry?"

"Are you fixing to put us in irons?" inquired Carilla. No one would have guessed how frightened she was. Somehow the memory of those backwoodsmen by the river was very much alive now she was confronted by another group of enemies, so that every time Mr. Stanton moved his hand suddenly, Carilla had great difficulty not flinching. That was one reason she had nodded to Lauchlin to be the one to slip out and go for help, because in an odd way she felt that she had to do the hardest thing.

"We've already told you the men aren't here," she added sweetly.

This reminded Mr. Stanton of something. "Where's Mistress MacLeod gone?" he demanded, looking around.

The two ladies just smiled at him. "Who?" they asked.

It was a great relief when a sudden clamor among the soldiers left outside announced the arrival of Ronald. The Lieutenant rushed out to see whom they had caught, and with a distinct sense of relief. This didn't last long.

By the time Andrew appeared on the scene (well ahead of Lauchlin, Matthew Lennox and the hastily organized remains of the mob, in that order) a certain amount of mayhem had already been accomplished. Ronald was being held by several soldiers, all of whom were needed. Carilla, also firmly held, was on the porch earnestly telling them what she would do if they injured a hair of

Ronald's head. And Lieutenant Stanton wasn't saying or doing much of anything. He was, in fact, lying on his back on the front walk.

"Splendid start, Ronald old fellow," drawled Andrew, inspecting him with approval. "Shall I hit him again, or pick on someone else?"

"Get that one helping him up," called Carilla, closing her ears to any comments Grandmother might make from the doorway. "He called Ronald a dirty barbarian."

Andrew just managed to comply before the soldiers found their wits again and arrested him, as well. At this rate, thought Carilla ruefully, they'd have the whole lot of them in no time.

Mr. Stanton, on his feet again, nursed a bloody nose and reflected bitterly that this was *not* his fault. He had followed orders. Was he to blame if the marines bungled their task, if the townsmen behaved like a lot of hotheads, if these folks declined to be arrested in anything like a decent civilized manner? He achieved something very near a snarl as Matthew Lennox and Lauchlin raced up neck-and-neck and hurled themselves into the midst of his already demoralized troop.

The unfortunate man's ordeal didn't last much longer. England Street was suddenly filled with Colonials who moved with a most ominous silence, much more alarming than the yells of a mob. It was a purposeful silence, the silence of men who had been already cheated out of one good fight this evening, and who asked nothing more than the excuse to crack a few Redcoat heads.

They were armed, too, Mr. Stanton noticed at once. So much for Lord Dunmore's clever plans to disarm all civilians. Things would simply have to wait, he realized. He and his men were considerably outnumbered at the moment, and he had no orders to start shooting.

Torn between anger and mortification, he turned to Mistress Treanor, a tiny monument of self-possession in all the tumult. "It won't do you any good," he told her with some bitterness. "His Lordship will just wait until the mob has gone home, and then send enough troops to arrest you all. . . . and now young Master Dare will be included as well." He looked at Andrew with dislike.

"Quite," drawled Andrew offensively. No one else said anything, except for the crowd in front, which shuffled its feet, and muttered dark threats, and waited hopefully for the slightest excuse to start something.

Lieutenant Stanton decided not to give them the excuse. With what dignity he could muster, he marched his depressed soldiers back to face Lord Dunmore.

If it was any consolation, he left equal depression behind. His last remarks had been perfectly true. The governor had a legal right to arrest anyone he wanted, and there was not a great deal they could do about it, since he also had the troops to enforce his right. Tonight had been luck. Next time there would be no crowd already united against England. Next time there would be more Redcoats, and with orders to fire, quite likely. Next time the arrest would be carried out—and who knew what might happen before their friends were able to get them released or even brought to fair trial? Mr. Treanor had been saying for a long time that more laws were needed to protect people from that sort of thing.

With such a frightening prospect facing them—and in the near future, too—it would not have been surprising if Mistress Treanor had for once in her life become flustered. She did not. Instead, she graciously thanked the swarm of men for their friendship and aid, and sent them home with such sweet compulsion that they went without another word. Then she swept the rest of them into the house.

"I think we had all best put a few clothes and essentials together at once," she suggested in a voice that made it a command. "If His Lordship sends more troops back to arrest us tonight, we shall certainly need them."

"Don't reckon he will, Grandmother," put in Andrew laconically. "He's bottled up in his palace with the ammunition from the Powder Magazine, and we've got guards to see that nobody gets out without a sight of trouble."

"Good," said Grandmother, looking pleased. "Nathaniel will be back tomorrow. Ronald, will you ask Jason to pack some things for him, too? Andrew, you run home and do the same thing. Matthew, did you tell me the other day that the *Jennifer* is up the river somewhere?"

Twenty-Five

THE LAST WORD

"Nonsense!" said Mistress Treanor. "Of course we're not running away!" She looked around the crowded cabin, which at once became a fit setting for her. "We're merely paying a return visit to our Scottish kin."

Lauchlin looked around at the seven of them in there,

still looking a bit dazed from the suddenness of it all. Captain Duff had been a bit dazed, too, she remembered with amusement—although he had risen to the occasion splendidly. And of course she and Ronald and Cousin Matthew were getting to be old hands at hustling themselves aboard ships and out to sea one leap ahead of the Redcoats. Her eyes met Cousin Matthew's, and they twinkled at each other comfortably.

Cousin Nathaniel couldn't resist teasing his mother a trifle. "And such visits are usually carried out at a moment's notice?" he suggested a trifle wryly. He had not been particularly happy at being torn away from his law practice with no warning whatever.

"Quite," agreed Mistress Treanor blandly. "When the occasion demands it. After all, Matthew does so quite often. And we have plenty of kinfolk and neighbors to look after things while we're gone. There's no reason at all not to take this trip, and strong reasons why we should."

They all thought of the strong reasons why they should. Pressing reasons, one might say.

Andrew chuckled suddenly. "Besides, running away would be undignified. And can anyone imagine *Grandmother* being undignified?"

No one could, of course. The notion was clearly preposterous. The subject was dropped. But there was another thoughtful silence while they all remembered Mr. Randolph's words.

"I don't think it will be very long," he said. "Things are reaching a crisis, and I think Dunmore will soon resign—for the sake of his health, perhaps. He's going to have to give that ammunition back, and he isn't going to like it a bit. Still, I think we can win our point peacefully—if we can avoid any incident that will touch off bloodshed. On the whole, Nathaniel, the most helpful thing you can do just now is to remove the whole lot of you from the area until Lord Dunmore either calms down or goes back to England. I'll keep you informed, and Wythe can take over your clients."

Looked at in that light, Lauchlin decided, it certainly was not running away in any cowardly sense. Even Ronald was convinced at last that now his responsibility was to avoid being the cause of an eruption of violence. Och, how he had changed!

She looked around the familiar tiny cabin, now crowded with cloaks and boxes and baskets in addition to people. She arranged her full skirts neatly around a large basket near her feet, and shifted her weight. It was easy to see who were experienced sailors. Every time the *Jennifer* heeled to port or starboard, the others were caught napping. Lauchlin grinned derisively as Andrew staggered and caught himself. Then she stopped grinning and said "Oof!" as Carilla sat suddenly and heavily in her lap.

"Landlubber!" she jeered.

"Fishface!" returned Carilla with spirit.

"I am not going to listen to that sort of nonsense all the way to Scotland," said Mistress Treanor firmly. "Behave yourselves."

The big basket at Lauchlin's feet slid forward, and Ronald gently shoved it back, because Lauchlin was sitting there like a daft loon, gathering everyone in with loving and happy eyes. Her terrible dilemma of divided love had been partly postponed, for if she could not take Williamsburg and its warmth to Skye, at least she could take the people whom she loved there. For a few blissful weeks—even months, perhaps—she would have them all together,

her two families, and not have to face any heart-tearing separations . . . yet . . .

She looked up, because she could feel Andrew's eyes upon her. "I have a good idea, Firetop," he announced with the expression of Columbus discovering America. "Let's us get married!"

Ronald grinned. " 'Tis yourself had best be careful, Andrew," he warned. "Who knows when she'll be taking you seriously, whatever?" He flickered a glance at Carilla, who looked back very sternly indeed.

"*Am* serious!" Andrew protested, looking indignant. "How many times do I have to say so? I aim to marry her, and I told her so the first day we met, didn't I, Firetop?"

"Never the day!" squawked Ronald, jerking to startled attention and staring at Andrew doubtfully. "You're never *meaning* it!"

"Of course he means it," said Cousin Lavinia serenely. "Didn't you know, my dear?"

Andrew grinned at her appreciatively. "Thank you, Grandmother," he said and cocked a quizzical eye at his uncertain audience. "Stands to reason I wouldn't propose for a solid year if I didn't mean it," he pointed out gravely. "Said so all along, you know."

They began to believe him, especially when they noticed that Lauchlin was showing no particular signs of astonishment. This could not be said for her brother. "You're daft!" he told Andrew. "She's— You're— It— She's too young," he finished lamely.

Andrew looked unmoved. "Then I'll just go on proposing until she's older," he said. "Even if I have to interrupt your precious rising to do it, Ronald."

"Och, would you stop in the middle of a war, just, and

tell it to wait until you've got married?" Lauchlin demanded, bright-eyed.

"I sure-nuff would, honey," he assured her solemnly.

Ronald looked at them, and no longer thought it a joke. He looked at the grown-ups, who were all pretending to be deaf, and not making a very good job of it. They looked perfectly delighted at the thought of taking Lauchlin back to Williamsburg some day, for good.

But this was precisely what Ronald couldn't swallow. All very well if some day he should decide to marry Carilla and take her to live on Skye, which was merely another word for Paradise—or would be, if only the Redcoats would go home—but it was a different matter altogether for Lauchlin to think of *leaving* Scotland.

"She'd never do it!" he snorted.

"You just be minding your own business, Ronald MacLeod," she flashed, turning on him. "I'm no saying a thing," she added cautiously, "except that I'll be making up my own mind . . . some day." She gave Andrew a glance half mischievous and half apologetic.

Andrew smiled affably. "Mind you don't make me miss the rising," he murmured, and it occurred to Lauchlin that this was the second time he had mentioned it as if it were a certainty—and his grandmother had not said a word!

She looked at Cousin Lavinia, who was now busily being blind as well as deaf—no easy task in such cramped quarters. She looked back at Andrew. Fine she liked him, with his humor and courage and passionate *caring* about people hidden behind all those freckles and eyelashes and teeth. And fine she liked a certain tender teasing quality reserved just for her. Och, he was a bonnie lad indeed!

But how could she possibly be deciding anything now, with home ahead and the thought of it stirring through her veins? She would not even try, for that meant being torn in two again. No, she must wait. She must back to Kildornie, and wait until things got back in perspective, and then see. Would her roots hold her fast there in the land of her bones and blood—or would she find that the most of her heart, after all, was with a certain white smile?

Lauchlin sighed, for whatever the choice, it was certain to be painful. Still, it was a fine way to test her heart, she decided ruefully, for a love that could pull her halfway across the world again was a love that nothing could shake or dim.

Her dark eyes wandered back to Andrew, and she found that he had been watching her. Listening to her thoughts, she suspected at once, in that certain way he had. But it would never do for the two of them to fall out of character, whatever!

"You see," she explained, "I could *never* be deciding such an important thing before I've seen you in the kilt. You might have knobbly knees, or something."

The basket at her feet came to life.

"Yaaah!" said Haggis derisively.

At the top of the hill, the courier allowed his lathered horse to stop and rest for a minute, for he had ridden hard. Around him stretched the hills and forests of Virginia, and to the east the blue slab of Chesapeake Bay lay warm in the April sunlight. It all looked so peaceful . . . and was its peace to be shattered by his news?

He had started south with nothing more nerve-shattering than the rumor that King George had asked his Hanoverian cousins for German troops to send over here to put down any possible revolt in the Colonies—an act certain to turn many loyal Englishmen into firm rebels. But he had been overtaken by news which quite overshadowed this.

Blood had been shed! There had been a small but bitter skirmish in some small town up north that no one had ever heard of—Lexingham, or some such name, though someone else said it was at a place called Concord. . . .

Might this be the Beginning? And of what? The courier had the eerie notion that the whole future of the Colonies might already have been changed. Perhaps even the world, he decided, carried away by excitement. Just wait until the Virginia Assembly heard *this*!

Far out in the bay, a ship lifted its sails to a light western wind. An American ship, to judge from its lines and rigging. They wouldn't have heard the news yet, would not hear for weeks, perhaps. . . .

Never mind. The courier flicked the reins and started down the hill. They'd be back.

Author's Comments:

I wrote *Hornet's Nest* not too long after the MacCarthy years, which is ancient history–or terra incognita–to most people now. Then, it was very real and very scary. People hardly dared open their mouths for fear of being reported to the Un-American Activities Committee (which if nothing else was *certainly* un-American). We seemed to be falling straight into a dictatorship where there was no longer a Bill of Rights, and everyone whose opinions were even slightly to the left of Genghis Khan was suspected of Betraying our Forefathers and Advocating the Overthrow of Established Government by Force and violence.

So I took a wicked pleasure here in presenting both leftists and rightist viewpoints of the 1770's ("Liberal" was not an insult, then: on the contrary. It meant and still means open-minded and free from bigotry.) I tried to show, accurately even though in fiction form, that on the whole our revered revolutionary forefathers were devout practicing Left-Wingers. They did not merely *Advocate* the violent overthrow of an established government: they *did* it.

My DAR relatives quite hated me for a while.

Some of my dearest ailurophile fan-friends much enjoyed the cats, especially Haggis. I'm so glad! Particularly after one review, which took (as the Scots would say) "a scunner" to him. In fact, they disliked him so much that nearly half the review was spent in objecting to "a repeated note of slight coyness about a cat," and the other half in quoting examples. Aside from that they said, they really liked the book.

Oh well, you can't win them all. And I'd rather have the approval of Carla, Donna, Darice, Caryn, Michele and the rest of you than the unknown and unlamented reviewer, anyway.

About the Author

Sally Watson: Born January 1924 in Seattle, Washington. Picked up phonics from Mother's kindergarten before I was two; the next thing anyone knew I was reading independently–which I went on doing for 12 years of public school–under my desk instead of arithmetic or geography. Rotten grades, didn't know how to study–I just read and wrote. Mum said I wrote my first book when I was four. Four pages, lavishly illustrated, begun with total phonic accuracy: "The sun roze up." From that, she decided that I should grow up to write books for children. Well, it was true I loved words and had a collection–just for fun–of synonyms for "said" and adverbs to accompany it. But when Mum suggested that I might write books for children, I sneered. For one thing, I'd read a book that convinced me one had to be a total genius and collect rejections for ten years. For another, I was going to travel all over Europe and study Highland Dancing and Judo and be a Prima Ballerina, I was.

At 16 or so, I discovered that I wasn't. Not a Prima Ballerina anyhow, and darned if I was going to settle for the corps de ballet. Disgruntled, I further realized that alone among my peers I hadn't the least interest in marriage and families. Nor in office work–the only thing going for women in the '30's.

Joined the Navy in 1944 and after *that* mess was over, I decided to go to college–and applied to Reed without knowing enough not to. They took me, it turned out, on "possible potential," and I waltzed innocently in...and by the time I realized that I would have to commit several *major* and sustained miracles to stay there, it was too late to do anything else. I was hooked by the intellectual excitement. (An astrologer once told me I had "a jack-ass determination that never knew when it was beaten–and consequently seldom was." True, I guess. A useful–albeit sometimes uncomfortable–quality.) At any rate, it was there I learned the discipline to write–but still had no idea of *doing* it. That childhood conviction was still with me.

But what to do? I still wanted neither marriage nor the office work I was temporarily stuck with. Moved to San Francisco, and then L.A., where (on Hollywood and Vine, true to cliché) I ran into an old high school friend who had *just had a children's story published in a real magazine!* Mental barriers collapsed all around me with almost audible crashes. I rushed home and started *Highland Rebel* that night.

I must have had a lot of writing dammed up in me. The first draft wrote itself in three weeks, the final in another three. It was accepted by the first place I submitted it–Henry Holt–*without revision!* And I was such a novice I didn't even know this was remarkable luck. (Needless to say, it never happened again.)

After three books, I had enough money to go to Europe for five months. Three more books, and I went back to England for a year and studied Highland dancing and wrote some more books. Passport and money ran out, so back to California for five years, helping Mother put out the first-ever audio-visual phonics course (which I now see duplicated virtually everywhere I turn. Never mind, Mother had good material, and the more who use it, the better.) Once it was accepted for publication, I realized I could now *live* in England on royalties, whereas I couldn't begin to in the U.S. So I went there and did that, and joined in Mensa, and went on writing books, and took up Judo at age 45, and I reckon I'm the only woman ever to do that and make Black Belt. Third Dan, at that.

Then, in a bout 1972, the bottom fell out. Up until then, my books were selling slowly but steadily, mostly to schools and libraries; and every time stocks got low, they just printed up a new edition. Now tax laws, it seems, were changed so that it was now uneconomical for publishers to keep books in stock over the turn of the year. So all twelve of my books went out of print almost simultaneously. And I was engrossed in Judo and also in copper enameling, and gardening my English country garden, and raising cats. So I stopped writing. And old fans kept writing and asking for copies of my books–and there weren't any.

After 24 years in England, I came back to America–the Sonoma County (*not* Napa) wine country, and joined a cat-rescue-and-adoption group and helped form another; and old fans kept on pleading for copies, and I discovered that feisty heroines are more needed now than in the '50s and '60s...so...